TO LOVE ANOTHER DAY

A NOVEL

ELIZABETH ROSENBERG

ISBN 9789493418127 (ebook)

ISBN 9789493418103 (paperback)

ISBN 9789493418110 (hardcover)

Publisher: Amsterdam Publishers, The Netherlands

info@amsterdampublishers.com

To Love Another Day is part of the series New Jewish Fiction

Copyright © Elizabeth Rosenberg, 2025

All Rights Reserved. No part of this publication may be reproduced or transmitted in any form or by any means, electronic or mechanical, including photocopy, recording or any other information storage and retrieval system, without prior permission in writing from the publisher.

PROLOGUE

What did it feel like to grow up in a family where there were no old people? To be inundated with images in movies, magazines and books of what appeared to be happy families gathering around a groaning dining room table, laden with food and lit candles, the wise elders sitting at the head of the table, the place of honor. What did it feel like, when many of your classmates referred to their Omi and Opa, Bobby and Zaidy, Grandma and Grandpa taking them on special trips and you could never join in that conversation? What did it feel like to never have the luxury of packing your overnight pink Barbie luggage and having sleepovers in your Bobby's house, being allowed to stay up late, spoiled and indulged, having your every wish fulfilled merely because your grandmother adored you? What did it feel like to never be able to go to a cemetery and pay respect to grandparents or great-grandparents, because no graves existed? What did it feel like not to have grandparents from either your mother or father's side, not a trace of their existence to remind you of where you came from? Not one old sepia photograph taken in years gone by, a bracelet, an antique dish or painting that once belonged to a revered grandparent? It meant these girls felt less special, subconsciously yearning for the comfort and powerful unconditional love and support they surely would have enjoyed had their grandparents survived WWII and been an intricate part of their lives.

Not having grandparents was quite simply a loss of epic proportions for Magda, Suzi and Judy Rosenbaum, Jewish sisters growing up in the 1960s in Brooklyn, New York; born to Hungarian parents who were survivors of the Holocaust. The gaping hole where grandparents belonged, defined them for a very great part of their lives. It left them feeling disconnected from their roots, unanchored and untethered, similar to how adopted children described their feelings.

As they got older, the sisters slowly came to terms with the myriad ramifications of being born to Holocaust survivors who were also immigrants. They felt conflicted because they were comfortable in their homeland while their parents made it abundantly clear to them that they felt like strangers in America. They often felt guilty for being ashamed of their parents who spoke English with a very heavy accent and were extremely uncomfortable caught between the world they knew and the world their parents were from. In school, while reciting the "Pledge of Allegiance" and learning about America's illustrious history they felt proud to be citizens, while at home where they were exposed to a very different European standard of conduct, subjected to what felt like old-fashioned, overprotective and overbearing parents who were almost always on edge, waiting for a disaster to happen, they were reminded yet again that they were "different" than many of their peers.

Inadvertently, their loving parents while valiantly trying to adapt, adjust and cope with the aftermath of surviving the Holocaust and emigrating to America, often sent mixed messages to their naive, young innocent children who were devoid of any understanding of the catastrophic circumstances that befell their parents before their birth. Looking at their vulnerable misplaced parents who certainly didn't identify with American values or traditions, invoked in these children a strong sense of responsibility that they, merely because they were privileged to be American born, regardless of their age, developmental, social or emotional needs, felt responsible to shield and protect their hurt, sad and often overwhelmed parents.

Later in life, as mothers to their own daughters, occasionally, the three sisters were somewhat envious of their daughters, for the indulgences and extravagances that their own mother bestowed on her grandchildren, something they themselves had never experienced. They were mesmerized with how naturally their own mother took on the role of *Bobby*, grandmother to her nine granddaughters who adored their endlessly generous loving always available grandmother who never seemed to be plagued with the chronic health issues they vividly recalled from their childhood.

As married women, Magda, Suzi and Judy talked incessantly about their mother Ava in this new role of grandmother. They, who did not have grandparents, observed their mother hawkishly as she taught them how to be grandmothers when their own daughters got married and had children. Exactly like their mother, they struggled with mixed emotions, albeit different ones. On the one hand they admired their mother's utter delight in everything their own daughters did, even when they themselves were not so enchanted with their daughters. On the other hand, they resented bitterly when their mother would inform them of her implacable opinion on how to dress their daughters, how to maximize their potential, failing to acknowledge that maybe just maybe, these mothers themselves had sufficient intelligence on how to raise their own second-generation American daughters who had very strong opinions that did not coincide whatsoever with their grandmother's European standards. Even as mothers and wives, these children of Holocaust survivors knew that regardless of how much time had passed, they still felt compelled and obligated to emotionally buttress and support their parents. They made themselves available to their mother in whatever capacity she needed them, exactly as they had done as children, even if it interfered with their responsibilities to their own families. Mostly what they absorbed from their own childhood was that their main job in life was to make their Holocaust survivor parents happy, to invest all of their energy into making up for the overwhelming grief their parents still carried decades after liberation from Auschwitz.

It was a formidable task, that not one of them was equipped for and it affected each of them in profound ways. Magda anesthetized her feelings of resentment as the first-born child, with food, Suzi fantasized about becoming rich and famous and Judy became a selective mute. The girls lived their lives determined to make their tormented mother happier, regardless of the personal sacrifices they would be forced to make; from choosing whom they would marry to where they would live and how they would raise their children. It was the least they could do to somehow make up for their mother's horrific suffering.

1

"That which does not kill us makes us stronger."
—Friedrich Nietzsche

1961

    Magda Rosenbaum was having yet another nightmare in which she was defenseless and utterly terrified. The nightmares were a constant, for as long as she could remember. She was in a huge field, surrounded by masses of hysterical people of all ages. People around her were being tortured, shot point blank, running, trying desperately to escape. And in her dream Magda anxiously sought her mother and sisters, terrified that she would witness them being murdered and she would be left alone.

    Magda woke up bathed in sweat, breathing heavily. She opened her eyes and even in the dark could clearly see her younger sister Suzi sleeping peacefully. She envied her. Why, she agonized, did she have these horrible dreams? As a child she often wondered what in her life could possibly account for the horrific images that met her in her sleep? It seemed as if in her dreams she was someone else, reliving events she had never experienced, thought about or knew about, memories that by day were suppressed and involuntarily erupted at night. For Magda, sleep was the enemy. Often, she would read until she could no longer keep her eyes open and hope, as she drifted to sleep, that she too would have a pleasant night's sleep. But invariably when the nightmares came, she was on her own to figure out how to calm herself.

Sitting upright waiting for her racing pulse to subside, Magda sought comfort. It never occurred to her to seek out either of her parents. She was well aware of their nocturnal habits that made them unavailable to her. Her father typically came home most nights at 2 a.m. and her mother who when she finally fell asleep after taking valium, a muscle relaxant, was out cold. As she got older and became more aware of what the tattooed numbers on her mother's arm represented or why her relatively young father who appeared healthy had false teeth, Magda knew not to tell her parents that she had an issue. It was absolutely wrong to burden them with anything as trivial as her nightmares or fears. By the time Magda was nine years old, she instinctively understood from the oblique references to starvation, pain and fear, that her parents needed their children to be perfect; they simply did not have the fortitude to deal with more than their own nightmares and sad memories of the life they once knew.

For Magda, the only thing that consoled her was the sweet Mounds coconut candy bar she had carefully hidden in her book bag. As she tore the wrapper, she felt enveloped by the allure of the chocolate bar. It tasted so good and in an instant the fear roiling inside of her soon dissipated. But invariably as she ate the forbidden candy bar, Magda cried. She hated being fat, it singled her out and not in a good way. While her sisters Suzi and Judy were naturally *nagyon csinos,* slim and trim the way their impossibly thin and chic Hungarian-born mother Ava wanted them to be, Magda was, to her own utter dismay, shorter, rounder and predisposed to being chubby. Her younger sisters never had to hold their breath to struggle into their A-line skirts or worry that their dreaded back fat nauseated their mother, who could not hide her revulsion seeing pillows of fat bulging out of her bra straps. As hard as Magda tried, she knew she was fighting an uphill battle. Not only was her father quite overweight, which meant she resembled him genetically, but also, she simply loved to eat. But what was she to do? She too, like her parents, had few resources to help her.

Once, in desperation Magda considered approaching her favorite English teacher Mrs. Fishman but discarded the idea soon enough knowing that might mean her parents would be called to school to deal with this issue. Similarly, asking her aunts for help would be the equivalent of telling her mother, because much as she loved her aunts, their loyalty was to their sister above all else. And so, it was food that Magda turned to; truly there was something about food that soothed her emotional self. Even anticipating a meal raised her spirits. As luck would have it, she was in her happy place often enough, in the kitchen by herself, in charge, free to cook and bake whatever she pleased, while Mamuka rested yet again from another one of her frequently debilitating headaches.

On days when Mamuka was incapacitated with her chronic migraine headaches that required total bed rest in the dark, it was Magda who was unanimously elected and expected to prepare dinner for the family. And Magda rose to the occasion. She instinctively understood that her own needs were trivial compared to Mamuka's headaches and sadness. What did it matter if her friends were getting together? What did it matter if she had Regents exams practice? Could her own studies or enjoyment be more important than doing something for poor Mamuka? And in her heart Magda also knew that the lure of the kitchen was very powerful for her. There was a feeling of satisfaction that enveloped her when she was surrounded by food.

In Ava's small but meticulously well-organized kitchen, Magda was in heaven. Food made her very happy and in turn she wanted her family to experience the same sense of euphoria. She knew she made her sisters and her father happy with her expansive repertoire of delicious food. While no one ever dared complain about Ava's healthy suppers, the nights when Magda prepared dinner were huge crowd pleasers. Everyone seemed more relaxed without Ava's watchful eye, observing who ate what, particularly their father and Magda. Although no one ever commented, Magda knew that she was not alone in feeling free when she prepared the meals while dear

Mamuka lay on her pristine white sheets, wearing her pale pink long-sleeved nightgown and silk *teichel* kerchief on her head. Mamuka, even when not feeling well, was always immaculately groomed, conscious of her appearance especially as a religious woman, which meant she was modestly but fashionably dressed at all times. Mamuka set the bar very high, and Magda lived in a constant state of fear, dread and anxiety, obsessing that she couldn't live up to Mamuka's impossibly high European standards. And so, food became the solace she sought when she was plagued with feelings of resentment and inferiority. She was never going to command the automatic and unwanted attention her glamorous Mamuka naturally got when they walked on Eastern Parkway or when they walked into *shul* on Rosh Hashanah; it seemed as if everyone in the small synagogue was in awe of her mother's rare beauty. Even in the fish store, people noticed her beautiful mother. For Magda, the kitchen was the one place where she could garner attention and admiration.

Although the main courses were something Magda copied from her mother, she always took it a step further. Whether it was broiled chicken or salmon, Magda used oil liberally frying the food, not roasting or baking the food the way Ava did. The sound of the oil sizzling in the large round Farberware stainless steel skillet always fascinated Magda from the time she stood on a step stool in her aunt Kati's house. In her *nene's* huge kitchen, she was allowed to help, carefully adding the chunks of potatoes to the thinly sliced onions already sautéing in a pool of oil; while at home, Mamuka made it implicitly clear that there was only one cook in her kitchen.

But there was a heavy price to be paid for all those marvelous moments in the kitchen. While food seemed to mollify her, especially in the middle of the night when she felt so alone and was a trusty dependable companion she could turn to ever since she was a child; in school, it was her enemy. At age 13, Magda was 5'2" tall and extremely self-conscious about how developed she was. She presented as a curvy girl, with a round face, full breasts, a protruding stomach and rounded hips. She had dark-brown hair which she wore long and slightly wavy, like all her friends, trying to look exactly like

Annette Funicello, Sandra Dee and Sally Fields, movie stars who were gorgeous icons of beauty.

Magda was by anyone's estimation a very pretty girl, except that she herself didn't think so. It was becoming more and more obvious to her, with each passing day that she needed to lose weight if she wanted to fit in with her friends, most of whom were naturally petite, slim and trim, constantly talking about boys and wearing clothes that accentuated their slim figures. If the dynamics in school weren't enough stress, overhearing her mother speaking to her aunts and making it sound like Magda's weight problem was "killing" her mother, made Magda burn with shame and guilt. How humiliating to hear her mother practically mocking her, and then in the same breath practically crying because her first-born daughter was overweight? Often Magda wondered why her mother was so fixated on her weight and why her mother had to share everything that happened with her sisters.

2

> "Fall seven times and stand up eight."
> —Japanese Proverb

Magda couldn't come to terms with being such a huge disappointment to her mother because she was not a size six or eight. What was it that made size so critically important to her mother and her aunts? Why was how big you were more important than your character? Magda was plagued with thoughts of disloyalty. On the one hand, she loved and admired her mother very much, but simply couldn't make sense of her mother's shallowness in judging her so harshly. She also knew objectively that she was smarter, kinder, and prettier than both of her younger sisters, and far more mindful of their mother's vulnerabilities; but apparently none of that mattered. And there was also the incessant gossip that her being overweight engendered and Magda bitterly resented being talked about. She understood that so long as she was fat, nothing she did would ever matter to her mother. At every family party or holiday gathering, she and she alone seemed to be the collective "problem" of her mother Ava and her two aunts, Zita and Kati. The look on their faces when they saw her bordered on revulsion, mixed with pity. Was she that horrible? Were there no other problems in the family or in the universe to worry about?

Magda just couldn't come to terms with how this made her feel. On some days she ate herself into oblivion, sneaking into the kitchen after everyone was asleep, stealing money from her mother's purse so she could buy herself potato chips and milkshakes at the luncheonette near school. And always, after consuming these forbidden foods, she physically and emotionally felt sick and disgusted with herself. It was not easy being the daughter of a very demanding, highly critical, extremely attractive mother, who also happened to be a Holocaust survivor.

From as far back as she could remember in her childhood, Magda Rosenbaum was aware of the fact that her mother was very different from other moms. While for the most part, nearly everyone Magda came in contact with came from a similar background, over time, as her world expanded, Magda began to recognize that not everyone's mom was sad without reason or explanation. Magda became keenly aware of the fact that she had classmates and summer friends, and friends of friends who were not all descendants of Holocaust survivors. Jenny's mom for example did not speak with an accent, Molly's mom always volunteered to go on class trips and Kara had two sets of grandparents who actively participated in their grandchildren's lives. To Magda, all these differences mattered a great deal; it made her feel different from many of her peers and consequently, she felt most comfortable with her sisters and much younger cousins because they and they alone could relate to her.

It was the concept of grandparents that was most disturbing to her. Having what she thought of as an older set of parents, who weren't chronically stressed, nervous or plagued with headaches or fears, was alien and foreign to her. Not only didn't she or her sisters have grandparents, neither did her cousins, or any of the other girls from her neighborhood whom she only saw when they attended *shul*. Those girls did not attend the same yeshiva as she did. They were being raised far more religiously than she, her sisters and her cousins, and would most likely marry rabbis or men who would learn Torah day and night.

Magda knew these girls were never exposed to the lifestyle her mother encouraged, where she was free to indulge in endless romance novels, go to the movies, ice skate at Prospect Park or watch television shows. Often, she felt sorry for those girls who were so sheltered, but since she only saw them on the holidays when they all attended the synagogue in Roszi *nene's* house, she didn't give much thought to them. Technically, Roszi was not their biological aunt, rather a cousin, but Ava insisted that properly raised young ladies would always address every grown-up they encountered as either *nene* [aunt], or *baci* [uncle], to show respect. It was what European parents demanded of their children, even if those children were not born in Europe and were bonafide American girls who enjoyed dancing the twist and watching Dick Clark's American Bandstand while answering their mother in Hungarian.

While Magda bitterly resented the way her life was organized and planned by her mother and aunts, there was one major benefit in that her aunts had ideas that Mamuka didn't. Magda was grateful for the many conversations she overheard between Kati and her mother strategizing on how best to provide her, her sisters and her cousins access to the broader culture of the arts, music and theater, a world that the mothers themselves didn't experience firsthand in Baia Mare, but were eager for their precious American-born princesses to experience. It seemed as if Mamuka and her sisters were on a sacred mission to give their daughters everything that America had to offer. Ostensibly, all their own personal dreams had died in Auschwitz; it was only their daughters who mattered. Beyond the miracle of survival, that was all that they ever seemed to focus on.

Very often, in the middle of the night when Magda couldn't sleep, she ruminated on the fact that her mother and two aunts all evolved in different ways as survivors of the Holocaust. Kati *nene* was far more open and confided in Magda that she was definitely less mindful of all the interconnected and intertwined stringent laws surrounding Orthodox Judaism that stemmed from the Torah. She explained to Magda that the Hasidic way of life that she was born into in Baia Mare, a little town in Hungary, essentially ceased to exist the day she and her sisters were cruelly separated from their family. On that terrifying day when they were transported to Auschwitz, one of the two largest killing camps erected by the Nazis in a Polish town that was now occupied by the Germans, Kati lost her fierce devotion to Yiddishkeit. Never considering that perhaps she was sharing too much with her curious niece, Kati explained in detail that she would have happily assimilated and submerged herself fully into the popular American culture, including removing her *paruka*, the wig religious married women traditionally wore, but couldn't because she was deathly afraid of Ava and Zita's reaction. Magda understood that Mamuka clearly was the most spiritual and religious of the three sisters and that Zita *nene* didn't care about anything besides having children and passively went along with whatever her sisters decided. "You see, Magduska, we sisters who survived together can't live without each other." And while Magda wanted to say that she didn't understand what her beloved aunt meant, she simply nodded her head. Nothing mattered more to Kati than what her sisters thought. Not her husband, not her children, only her two surviving sisters. Somehow, Ava became the de facto symbol to Kati of what their revered mother would have wanted and expected of her.

It was very important to her mother, Magda came to realize that all three sisters were in lockstep. Without a mother of their own to guide them, they made decisions on whatever happened, together. None of their husbands ever were part of this caucus. It was Ava, Kati, and Zita who decided collectively in whose home they would celebrate Pesach, where in the Rockaways they would rent bungalows in the summertime to escape the oppressive heat, and when exactly they would vacation at the kosher Crown or Algiers hotels in Miami Beach in the wintertime, to escape the brutal cold. In fact, from what Magda could glean, the husbands had very little function beyond going to work and supporting their families. On more than one occasion when Magda awoke from her nightmares, she thought about the future and hoped that one day her husband would be far more American, not at all like her European father or uncles, and would want to be involved in every aspect of their lives together.

The thought of a marriage based on love and commitment rather than a European post- Holocaust marriage based on necessity, pleased Magda, especially because she obsessively read romance novels where falling in love was the singular pathway to happiness. It was from these novels that Magda formed her own worldview. She was determined that she was not going to turn into her mother. She was after all an American girl even if technically she was born in Germany in a displaced person's camp after the war. Often, when she couldn't sleep, Magda thought about her childhood. Maybe, she mused, that as an infant she was deprived of food there in Bergen-Belsen and then on the ship to America as well and that fear of not having enough food to sustain her lingered in her subconscious to cause her to always seek out food. Decades later in therapy with her mother and sisters, Magda was astounded to hear her mother say that she was incapable of nurturing her first-born baby. Ava, crying uncontrollably in that therapy session, informed her daughters that she remembered mechanically attending to her baby's needs, but never really connecting with her infant daughter. The words Ava uttered were a revelation to Magda.

Magda remembered the day that she finally had the will, motivation and impetus to lose weight for good. It was in the sixth grade, a year that was challenging enough because junior high school represented having numerous interdepartmental subjects with a variety of teachers instead of one homeroom teacher for Hebrew subjects and one homeroom teacher for English subjects in the yeshiva she attended. But when her mother had to have emergency surgery to have her appendix removed, Magda knew in her heart that if she lost weight, it would help her mother's recovery. In fact, her aunt Zita delicately suggested and encouraged it. She remembered the conversation as if it happened yesterday, when in fact it was three years ago.

"Magda *dragam* [dear]," said her aunt Zita hesitantly, "don't worry about anything. I am coming to help run the household while Mommy is in the hospital. Don't worry, she will be fine."

With that, Zita *nene* sighed and looked at Magda as if she had the most novel idea. "But you know vat," she said excitedly, "I have an idea that would really make Mommy feel very good."

Magda looked at her aunt, whom she saw as a pseudo-grandmother figure, someone she could talk to, someone who was never too busy to give her a hug or offer advice, someone who almost never had headaches and loved making wonderful meals like Hungarian goulash without obsessively worrying about the dreaded calories stemming from the delectable scrumptious dish simmering in sauteed onions. Zita was different from Ava. Although the two were very close and had endured the Holocaust together, Zita was in fact calmer and more introspective. She was never hysterical, sad or talked about her personal losses. Where she put those feelings, Magda certainly didn't know, but to her, Zita *nene* was the person she trusted most in the world.

"Tell me, Zita *nene*, what can I do to make Mommy happy and recover faster?" she asked breathlessly, hoping against hope that it would not be to get all A's. Much as she tried, Magda was finding junior high school challenging. It was a lot harder than she anticipated and suddenly her classmates seemed more driven, more focused, and just smarter. Or maybe it was her? The teachers also piled on the homework and Magda didn't always have enough time to do her assignments when she was obligated to make dinner, clean up and help her younger sisters with their homework. She herself wasn't especially driven to get straight A's, it was what her father Lajos expected of her, his first-born child.

Her father was always working, and when he wasn't working, he was either at the synagogue for prayers or visiting his beloved *Rebba* [rabbi] to see how he could help him. If it was before Sukkot, the wonderful holiday that came after the somber holy fast day of Yom Kippur, when they ate meals in a *sukkah* booth, her father was the one who personally built his Rebba's sukkah, minutes after the fast ended. If it was before Pesach, then it was her father who was baking *matzahs*, the special Passover "bread", around the clock for a month before the holiday started. It seemed as if Lajos Rosenbaum had far more important things to do than to be at home with his family. Often, Magda could not fall asleep, tossing and turning in her bed, waiting in the dark until she finally heard her father, in his melodious voice softly call out and announce to his wife that he was home, by lovingly saying, "Avala, *ein vadyag*." Then Magda felt safe and could fall asleep. She wished that just once, it was her name her father called out to announce his "I am here," but that never happened. The only person Lajos cared about was his beloved wife Ava whom he adored. To Lajos, the sun rose and set on "Avala."

Unfortunately, more often than not it was 2:00 a.m. when her father got back from Williamsburg, a neighborhood in Brooklyn that became an enclave for Hasidic survivors who had emigrated to America after the war. This was where Lajos's beloved and revered *Rebba* lived, recreating in Brooklyn the very town Baia Mare where he lived before the war. Often, when her mother was annoyed at her father's obsessive devotion, both with his time and hard-earned money, Magda heard them fighting in their native tongue. Magda thought it was awful that they would argue. In her romance novels, couples in love did not argue. It made her very uncomfortable and she didn't know whom to side with, because she desperately wanted to please both of them. Her father was often terrifying when he got angry, and Magda tried hard to stay out of his way. She hated his temper, how red his face and neck got. He was just plain scary. And because he would never allow himself to get angry at Ava, he typically took out his anger on his oldest daughter. By default, Magda felt that being the first born made her an easy target for her father's explosive temper.

"Vell," said Zita *nene*, "I think that your mother would be delighted if you would lose 15 pounds. You know how she worries."

Magda looked at her aunt and was stunned. If Zita *nene* thought this was what was standing in the way of her mother's happiness, then she had to immediately do something. She looked at her aunt and responded: "Zita *nene*, there is no one I trust more than you and if you say that, then that's what I will do. Let's keep it a secret and I will start today."

Zita looked at her eldest niece and for a moment felt a tiny twinge of guilt. There was absolutely nothing wrong with her niece, who genetically resembled her brother-in-law Lajos's family. It was her ridiculous sister Ava who had these insane ideas about how her daughters had to look in order to attract a "fine" boy from a good home. Zita thought it was quite hypocritical that she was advising her niece to lose weight when in fact her own two daughters were truly overweight, and she never said a word to them for fear of hurting their feelings. Zita idolized her daughters, they could do no wrong, merely because they were born healthy and in America. She showered them with gifts, with exotic dinners, and catered to their every whim, expecting nothing in return except their love. Turning to Magda whom she loved as much as her own daughters, she asked, "Do you need help darling?" And Magda, conditioned to be independent because she always had to look out for herself, merely smiled valiantly and reassured her *nene* that at 11 years old, she knew what she had to do.

Magda went on a diet. A very calorically restricted diet that she forced herself to adhere to. She ate a small bowl of corn flakes with skimmed milk for breakfast, a large red apple for lunch and a small plate of chicken breast and salad for dinner. No one seemed to notice that she was not consuming enough calories for her nutritional needs. In a matter of three months, Magda lost nearly 20 pounds and was down to a glorious size eight which made her mother ecstatic. When Ava showed off her eldest daughter, she told everyone around her that Magda's transformation added years to her life. While Magda herself was thrilled to be slim and the apple of her mother's eye both physically and emotionally, she didn't feel well. She had less focus for her studies and less physical energy which meant she had to give up playing volleyball. Her hair lacked luster and her skin was not as clear as it used to be. But it was all worth it because it made her mother happy. The days when she was not receptive to her friends in school or was moody and grumpy, at home, especially to her sister Suzi, the nights when she dreamt about food or cried herself to sleep because she was hungry, were totally secondary. All she had to do was remind herself of what Ava had suffered during the war. If Ava was happy because of something she could do, it was worth denying herself. Once, when Magda almost broke her diet, she reminded herself that her mother and her aunts starved in Auschwitz under far worse conditions.

Who wouldn't want to make their mother happy, especially one who had lost her own mother and father, brothers and sisters, aunts and uncles, nieces and nephews, and was beaten, tortured, and starved for 11 long months in Auschwitz, all before her 20th birthday? For Magda, there was absolutely no choice between her own needs or those of her mother's, and she made sure to let her younger sisters know what sacrifices she personally made to make their mother happy, trying hard to convince them that this was also their job in life, their responsibility for being born to Holocaust survivors. It never dawned on Magda that maybe this level of demand was too much of a burden on her or her younger sisters; if anything, she trusted her aunt Zita and that was final.

For the duration of her teen years and up until her mid-forties, Magda was on a merry-go-round with her weight, up and down like a carousel ride. Knowing instinctively that her mother did not have the stamina to be involved in helping her become permanently svelte and just wanted her to take control of her weight, Magda found resources on her own. With the help of her best friend Karen's older sister, she went to the famous diet doctor in Queens, New York whose pills were guaranteed to take away the appetite. That worked and Magda was slim. However, as soon as she went off the pills, she gained back all the weight she lost and then some. Thus began the road to literally trying starvation, starting with the liquid diet with protein shakes, the grapefruit diet, laxatives and diuretics, the Beverly Hills diet and then the gold standard, the Atkins protein diet. Ava, by this time, was fully aware that her eldest daughter was on various diets but did not interfere. In fact, Magda had the distinct feeling that her mother was secretly proud of her for committing herself to this most important mission. But inside it made Magda sick to know that the only time she pleased her mother was when she was in her thin phase. Then Ava loved her, praised her, shopped with her, and hugged her.

Magda, in desperation, began to think of the future. She felt suffocated by the chokehold on her freedom that her mother's fears imposed on her. There had to be a way in which she could escape and be free to live her life. Nightly, she reviewed her options and concluded that the only way for her to ever move forward was to get married. Girls that were Orthodox did not go to out-of-state college. Girls who were children of Holocaust survivors did not entertain thoughts of moving out before marriage as many girls did after college, before marriage, because that would upset their highly anxious mothers who obsessively worried about their safety. And then it came to her, late one night, after she awoke from another nightmare. There was a way out. Marriage! It would certainly please her parents who often talked about the kind of young men they would seek for their daughters. Marriage would be the vehicle by which she would be allowed to find her own happiness. In fact, marriage would provide her with a new family of her own, a husband and children who would love her unconditionally. Certainly, it would be nice to get away from her mother who doled out love and affection only if she was slim, and from her father who, when he was home, always seemed to be yelling at her, not at his precious Avala or his darling little Judy or Suzika. For some reason that Magda couldn't quite figure out, she was everyone's target. Yes, she thought, a husband and a baby would almost certainly be her salvation. Her baby would adore her, her husband would idolize her, and she would be blissfully happy. Magda was satisfied and finally fell asleep.

3

"Perseverance, secret of all triumphs."
—Victor Hugo

Suzi Rosenbaum was a musical genius. She could hear a song and sing it perfectly. Whenever her mother Ava had a headache, she was the only one who could make Mamuka smile. All she had to do was sing, and Ava would look happy. She knew from mean fat Magda that Mamuka had been through the war, but she tried hard to put that out of her mind. In fact, Suzi, at age 11, already developed a pattern of behavior to protect herself. She simply avoided looking at Mamuka's delicate right arm and seeing the dreaded tattoo of numbers. She was thankful that they were religious observant Jews and therefore Mamuka almost always, in her desire to adhere to the modesty rules, wore long sleeves, winter, spring, summer and fall. Suzi remembered the first time she saw the tattoo and innocently asked her mother why she had used magic markers on her arm and to her surprise and shock, her mother began to cry.

"Don't ask me, *dragam*, Suzika," she tearfully said, while trying to catch her breath. "I can't talk about it. Ask Magda, she will tell you."

Suzi remembered feeling sick inside for making Mamuka so sad. She was sure Mamuka would get a headache and be in bed and it would all be her fault. And when she approached Magda, Magda's ferocity and anger scared her. Magda was like the prime minister in their home, the one who ran the household, appointed to this position by Ava, the figurehead president who simply could not keep up with all the emotional and physical demands of the job of being a mother.

"Are you *bolond* Suzi," screeched Magda, mixing Hungarian and English, "only a crazy stupid idiot like you would ask Mamuka about her numbers. You know I told you and Judy last year what happened to Mamuka and Tatuka and Kati and Zita."

Magda's words were filled with such derision that Suzi shrank.

"I forgot," she said in a low voice.

"You forgot?" screeched Magda. "Really Suzi? How could anyone forget that their parents were in the war? How dumb are you?" She left the room, shaking her head.

That night Suzi cried herself to sleep, sorry she was born, sorry that she had upset her mother, and sorry, most of all, that Magda was her big sister. She was jealous of Judy, who was the baby and could do no wrong. When Ava wasn't sick with her head or stomach, she played with Judy, dressed her in exquisite clothes and wheeled her in her brand new SilverCross carriage that Kati and Zita *nene* bought as a gift to console Ava for not having a baby boy after two girls. Ava and her sisters yearned to have just one boy child amongst them so that they could properly honor their sainted father's memory by giving his name to a grandchild. Once again Ava was conflicted. She was deliriously happy to have daughters, but also felt guilty.

Suzi hated being in the middle of Magda and Judy. Magda was a bully who often pinched her, and Judy was useless, except on *Shabbos* [Sabbath], when they were not allowed to watch television. Then she would play Barbie with her little sister, who smiled but didn't talk a lot.

True to her nature, Suzi simply cast aside her upset from the night before and was in a good mood when she woke up the next morning, excited because today she would get to sing in choir. She got dressed in her yeshiva school uniform, navy-blue skirt and white button-down blouse, brushed her hair, and went into the kitchen.

She was actually relieved to see Magda at the stove, not sure what she would have said to her mother had she been there. Magda glanced at her, and gave a small nod of approval, which made Suzi feel safe. Magda seemed to have forgotten the fight too and actually smiled when she asked Suzi what kind of cereal she wanted for breakfast.

Magda gave her a huge bowl and liberally sprinkled sugar on the cereal which Suzi appreciated. "Magda," she asked, "won't Mamuka get upset if she finds out we had sugar on our cereal?"

"Nope," said Magda confidently. "Mamuka took her medication and is sound asleep. By the time she gets up, I will clean up the kitchen and we will all be out of the house. Don't you worry Suzika, when I am in the kitchen, you will always have whatever you want."

Suzi impulsively went over to Magda and hugged her. On days when Magda was in a good mood, she felt so much better. The problem was that there was no rhyme or reason for when Magda would be happy or sad, mean or nice. For Suzi, these inconsistencies were simply how her family members were. Magda, the oldest, seemed to be the most like Mamuka and Tatuka, she and Judy seemed somehow to be more alike.

At school though, Suzi felt terrible. She couldn't keep up with her Hebrew subjects. *Dikduk* [Hebrew grammar] was incomprehensible to her—no matter how hard she tried—and *historia* [Jewish history], from the Spanish Inquisition to the Roman siege of Jerusalem was just plain boring. It was only during choir practice that she was animated. Then she was the star, the one that everyone acknowledged was special. She knew she was never going to be as smart as Magda or as cute as Judy, but she also knew that someday she was going to be on a stage, maybe at Radio City Music Hall or on The Ed Sullivan Show. She would sing in multiple languages, maybe even an aria from *Madame Butterfly*! As Miss Reager taught math, Suzi daydreamed about how she would appear on stage. She would be wearing the most gorgeous pale pink sparkly gown with a thick satin sash to accentuate her tiny waist. Her hair would be artfully arranged in an updo like Grace Kelly the famous Hollywood star who married the prince of Monaco. She would choose between her magnificent jewels to adorn her ears, fingers, neck and wrists, satin high-heeled shoes to give her height, and the final touch; professional makeup that made her look glamorous. And after her spectacular performance, the stage would be littered with bouquets of flowers thrown by an appreciative audience, who would shout "Encore! Encore! Brava! Brava!" Suzi almost cried from happiness. Suddenly, she felt a hard tug on her arm and snapped out of her idle reverie.

"Suzi," whispered her best friend Jennifer, "Miss Reager just asked you for the answer."

Suzi was in a daze; not even sure what Miss Reager was teaching. She looked at Jen who muttered under her breath "X=20." Suzi looked at her gratefully, cleared her throat, and offered the solution to a kind but slightly impatient teacher.

"Yes," said Miss Reager. "That is correct. Okay, girls do pages 12-16 for homework. See you all tomorrow."

As the girls all dutifully began to pack up their bookbags, Suzi paused long enough to thank Jennifer. "I won't ever ever forget this," she said humbly and earnestly. "When I am rich and famous, I will be sure to tell everyone how you helped me in school." And she added as an afterthought, "How about I do tonight's *navi* homework and give you all the answers?"

For some odd reason Suzi had a knack with Prophets, and she was able to sail through Hebrew subjects like *navi* and *chumash*. Jennifer Weisz looked at her best friend and almost felt sorry for her. She knew Suzi had a beautiful voice, but what were the odds that a Jewish girl from Brooklyn, New York with an unusual voice was ever going to be discovered? Barbra Streisand, who was discovered while attending public school at Erasmus High on Flatbush Avenue, a mere 15 minutes away from their yeshiva, but felt like 15 million miles away culturally, already held that honor. Jennifer was a smart girl. In fact, she was a whiz at math and hoped that one day she might help her husband if she married an accountant. She had no delusions like Suzi who she observed daydreaming in class all the time. She fervently hoped that her best friend would settle down and become a little more realistic. She could be head of production later on in high school and head of choir and maybe even a music teacher. That would be amazing if it were enough for Suzi Rosenbaum. But somehow, Jennifer doubted it. Though she loved her best friend, she was aware that Suzi Rosenbaum wanted the impossible.

"Suzi," she replied carefully not to offend her best friend's offer, "that is really very nice of you. I'm not that great in Hebrew and my brother would never help me, and as you know, my mom doesn't really know any Navi, so thanks, but you really don't have to repay me. You're my best friend."

Suzi looked at Jennifer and almost cried. Jennifer was so kind. Why, she wondered, couldn't they be sisters? Instead, she was stuck with Magda and Judy. Even Josh, Jennifer's brother, teasing them and throwing spitballs at them when they tried to study in the Weisz den, was always at least in the same mood every single time she saw him. Suzi wondered for the 100th time why Magda and her parents were so unpredictable. She knew she wasn't going to be stupid ever again and ask questions. She would keep her mouth shut. One day, when she was older, she would figure it all out or maybe find a book or a doctor to explain stuff to her. Her parents and Magda too, all seemed scary to her.

For now, she was glad Jen was her best friend. Every day she could count on her best friend. At night they often spoke on the phone when they each could gain access to the house phone and nearly every Shabbos, they hung out together. Suzi loved when Jen came to her house and Ava was in a good mood. Then Suzi would show off. She knew it wasn't fair or even nice, but Ava, when she was feeling well, looked like a film star. With her dark hair and blue-black eyes, everyone said she looked like the gorgeous film star, Elizabeth Taylor. And while Suzi didn't want to be unkind, it was a fact that Jen's mom was just not glamorous. For starters, the Weisz's were Polish. Ava and her aunts Kati and Zita were Hungarian, and often reminded their daughters adamantly that Hungarian women were the prettiest, chicest, most elegant of all women and not one Polish woman could come close to their instinct for glamor, fashion and beauty. And maybe it was true, Suzi thought. Jen's mom Branya was so nice, but she was so plain. She never wore makeup or even a pretty dress. Suzi doubted that Mrs. Weisz even polished her nails the way her mother and her aunts did.

According to Jen, she almost never saw her parents. Both of them worked very hard in the family bakery, six days and nights, only taking off on Shabbos. Jen would always bring her best friend silver pound cake and *rugelach*, goodies Suzi never brought home, but ate on the bus ride home. She knew Mamuka would be very upset if she saw the baked goods. That's how she was. So Suzi enjoyed the delicious treats at recess and on the bus and gave away the rest. She never stopped to wonder why her mother could not tolerate any baked goods in their home aside from what she baked for holidays and the loaf of rye bread or plain egg *kichel* biscuits that Tatuka brought home from a kosher bakery on Lee Avenue in Williamsburg. It seemed as if Mamuka always had to have things her way, in a certain order, nothing out of place, everything very clean and orderly. At a glance, Mamuka knew exactly what was on hand in her pantry. If anyone tried to change the way she set things up, Mamuka got upset. That's just the way she was.

So Suzi sang. She sang when she was scared, she sang when she was unhappy, she sang when she was lonely, and she sang when she was happy. Her voice had great range and depth, and more than one music teacher advised her to hone her potential by taking singing lessons. When Suzi told her father what her music teacher said, he scoffed. Instead of acknowledging her talent, her father, like many European parents who believed praising a child was akin to spoiling them, he simply reminded his middle daughter named for his beloved mother, that she came from a long line of very talented people. That was the end of the discussion. Suzi knew better than to ask again. Tatuka was hardly ever around, and when he was, the things he said did not always make Suzi feel good. He wasn't mean to her like he was to Magda, but he wasn't anywhere near as nice as he was to Judy. Suzi wondered if she talked less, like Judy, if Tatuka would be nicer to her? It seemed that the less Judy said, the more Tatuka tried to please her. He brought her gifts even if it wasn't her birthday or *yomtov*, a holiday like Chanukah when everyone routinely got some presents. Suzi wondered all the time, trying hard to figure out how to behave in order to get what she needed. In school her grades suffered because of her inability to focus. It was only when she sang that she was able to concentrate fully. The rest of the time she was vacant, thinking and pretending, looking to escape from her bleak thoughts about her family.

Suzi, though she didn't know it, was not so different from her own mother Ava, who for 11 long unbearable months in 1944, though much older, at the tender age of 19, did the exact same thing. When the daily physical and emotional torture at Auschwitz was more than she could bear, Ava simply tuned out. She worked for excruciatingly long hours, her only sustenance a crust of what looked like bread, with no break. Mechanically like a robot, she performed the work assigned to her, sorting through the clothing of the dead bodies, never once allowing herself to think of whose clothes she might find, terrified that she would, one dismal morning, come across her own mother's *tichel* [headscarf], apron or housedress. Ava and her sisters knew, from the minute they were ordered by the notorious Doctor Mengele to one side and their mother and older sister Surika, holding and refusing to let go of her babies to the other side, that they would never see them again. One cruel female Nazi guard told one of their *lager* bunkmate sisters to look at the smoke from the crematoria if she wanted to see her mother.

Ava learned how to control her dread, terror, revulsion, and thoughts of suicide, obsessively fantasizing instead on freedom and what she would do on that day, when the war was over. She thought about what she would eat, what she would wear, what books she would read, how long she would regrow her hair, what music she would listen to, what blanket she would cover herself with and what sheets she would sleep on and where she would go walking with her beloved sisters Zita and Kati. She would never ever be separated from them, she promised herself, because they were the reason she was alive. They, just as emaciated and weak as she was, nevertheless literally carried her when she couldn't walk anymore, and they fed her when she simply
stopped eating.

Suzi moved through the day in school, occasionally wondering what her future would actually be like. There were days when she thought she wanted nothing more in life than to be exactly like her mother, cooking and cleaning and shopping on Kingston Avenue, talking daily on the phone with her own two sisters. But then there were days when all she could think about was an opulent luxurious life, far away from her family, in a very different environment that made her happy all the time, without the veil of secrecy and sadness surrounding her.

4

"The only true wisdom is in knowing you know nothing."
—Socrates

Judy was the baby in the family. From as far back as she could remember, she knew she was a huge disappointment to both of her parents, simply because she was not born a boy, something she had no control over. She tried hard to please both but there was nothing she could do to make up for the fact that neither of her parents could give a name for their deceased fathers since she was a girl. To cover their disappointment, her parents treated her like a baby long after her childhood years were behind her, merely because she served no essential purpose like Magda and Suzi, named for their sainted mothers. Even when she was a teenager, Judy still felt like a baby. In many ways, her oldest sister Magda was more like a mother figure to her because Mamuka was often not well. But when Mamuka was ok, Judy was thrilled.

Judy, at the age of eight, intuitively knew that she was luckier than both of her sisters. She was everything they were not. She was pretty, she was slim, she was smart, and most of all, she was obedient. Most importantly, she never complained. She constantly thanked her parents for everything they did for her. She tried very hard to keep

Tatuka's temper at bay and Mamuka's migraines from happening. She spoke Hungarian when spoken to, she watched the exact same shows that made Mamuka laugh. She became quite adept at imitating Lucille Ball and loved seeing Mamuka laugh at Lucy's antics. Even Ricky's accent made Mamuka laugh. She thought of Fred and Ethel Mertz, the older couple who also were on *I Love Lucy*, as grandparents and loved them. She laughed with Mamuka at Benny Hill although she had no clue what British humor was, except that it pleased Mamuka. But on her own time, she was scared. She was not unaware of Tatuka's temper and occasionally of him losing his temper and hitting Magda. On those days she made sure to stay out of Magda's way. It was why she loved going to Kati *nene's* house. There, things were different. Not necessarily better than in her house or by Zita *nene's* house. She just loved being with her cousins and often talked more to them than to her own sisters. She especially hated her sister Suzi who teased her and made fun of her. Often, she would ask her mother if she could live in Kati's house and the answer was always the same.

"Is this why I survived Auschwitz?"

Then Mamuka would start sobbing. "That a child of mine wants to leave me? How can that be true?" Mamuka would ask out loud, as if someone would answer her. So, Judy did what she always did. She apologized to Mamuka for even mentioning wanting to move out. Then she apologized to Tatuka for upsetting and making Mamuka sad. And if that wasn't enough then she had to face Magda's wrath and Suzi's too. By the time she finished apologizing to everyone in the house, Judy started to believe she was as crazy as Magda told her she was. Her entire family thought she was adorable as long as she was sweet and compliant, but the minute she spoke and expressed her feelings, they all turned on her. So, Judy retreated inside herself. She kept quiet and kept the peace. If Mamuka had a headache or was sad when she lit her candles on Friday night, then at least it wasn't her fault. In fact, she stayed away from her aunt Kati, because she was worried it pained her mother that maybe she liked Kati more than her. The adorable dark haired little girl eventually stopped talking altogether.

When it came time for her to start first grade, her parents took her to a doctor. Finally, someone allowed her to speak and let her say what was on her mind. She played in the doctor's brightly lit office, with the dolls and blocks and drew pictures for the doctor. She took the medication she was given and while oftentimes it made her mouth dry and gave her weird dreams, she took it to please her parents. She talked in school, not more than she needed to, but just enough so that there were no issues. Only at home, in their small brownstone house on Empire Boulevard, was Judy quiet. She sat at the dinner table, night after night, eating her supper in silence. Over time, her two sisters made up for her silence by arguing and talking loudly, often to the point where Mamuka would mildly and politely ask them to lower their voices, reminding them that refined Hungarian girls did not shriek or howl, much less at the dinner table. Everyone got used to the fact that Judy didn't talk, she was Tatuka's little *lemala*, his sweet nonverbal lamb. As a *lemala* she wasn't expected to do anything except be respectful and have manners. It didn't make a difference to anyone when she excelled in school, eventually winning a full scholarship and an opportunity to attend an Ivy League school. Even then she could not advocate for herself. It was understood that the mere thought of Judy dorming at Yale, Princeton or Harvard in Connecticut, New Jersey or Boston was out of the question. Magda, and by then Suzi, who was starting to resemble Magda, looked at her in horror.

"Don't even mention it, *lemala*," said Suzi in a semi-threatening tone, "unless you want to put Mamuka in the hospital."

Judy knew in her heart that even after the school guidance counselor called her parents to ask them to reconsider, that nothing would ever change the fact that Ava was often both strong yet weak, passive yet aggressive, happy yet sad, and not able to ever let go of her daughters whom she often referred to as "my life."

Judy found that statement confusing. How could your children be your life? Didn't you have a life before you became a mother? And if they were their mother's life, she often wondered, then where did that leave them? Lifeless if she didn't let go of them? Perhaps what was even more confusing, was being called *lemala* by her immediate family. Her being docile and meek was a constant source of amusement for all of them.

Judy indeed felt powerless. Nothing would change, until maybe, when she was married. At least then, maybe she would have the right to speak up and even go to college. But that meant she had to be set up on a date with a very kind boy. Was that even possible, she wondered? And how would she even know? People could pretend to be nice and then, when it was too late, their true colors could come out. Judy Rosenbaum was not very optimistic or trustful. Her own family taught her not to be.

5

"To live is to suffer, to survive is to find some meaning in the suffering."
—Friedrich Nietzsche

1965

Magda was aware of the fact that her mother took pills to help keep her calm, as did her aunts Kati and Zita. Dr. Biffer, the kindly family doctor prescribed Valium to Ava, who in turn broke the pills into halves and doled them out to her sisters. Magda didn't think her mother, or her aunts were addicted to these pills, but often she wondered why they needed a medication that the Britannica encyclopedia described as a muscle relaxant? Wouldn't it have made more sense, she wondered, for them to see a doctor who was trained in helping people who were nervous, fearful, sad or depressed? Magda knew that psychiatrists and psychologists treated patients who had mental health issues. She also instinctively understood that there was never going to be a right time for her to give her mother advice. Even though in the past four years she had proven herself to be very smart, she knew without a doubt that her mother would not take kindly to a discussion about any kind of psychotherapy treatment. Magda could practically hear her mother.

"Magdushka, can a doctor bring back my mother or my baby sisters? Can a doctor undo what I suffered or witnessed with my own eyes? The screaming, the bright lights overhead, the Nazis who enjoyed torturing us?"

To which Magda knew she would have no answer. After all, as smart as she was, pulling all A's and poised to be English valedictorian when she graduated high school in three months, Magda knew that neither she nor anyone else could ever begin to understand what the survivors of the Holocaust went through. And if her beloved mother chose to take Valium or smoke cigarettes to calm her nerves, then so be it.

So, Magda simply swallowed her concern and her own anxiety for her mother's mental and physical health and continued to try to please her mother, to make up for all that she lost. No one had to tell her; she knew because she knew.

With graduation around the corner, Magda was excited. While on the one hand she was ready to move on, a part of her wondered if she wasn't a little bit in love with Yitzy Gross, whom she saw on Eastern Parkway every Shabbos afternoon when she and her friends went for a walk. Yitzy made her laugh and feel carefree. She almost always forgot about the things that worried her when she was with him. She dismissed him from her mind, because in one of their long nightly chats when Ava couldn't fall asleep and needed Magda to keep her company, Ava made it patently clear to her that marriage was not about love, it was about position, status, and rank, something only Europeans understood. Magda knew she could never fight for Yitzy; there was no point, her mother would win. She was after all the arbiter of wisdom, being European born.

Magda consoled herself with thoughts of what lay ahead for her. By September she would start dating, and with a little luck, be married by next June. Magda knew that over the summer she would need to lose more weight so that when Ava took her shopping for her special "dating" clothes designed to dazzle her dates, she would smile in delight at how thin and sophisticated Magda looked.

The thought of having her own life was intoxicating. For a moment Magda vowed to open her home to her younger sisters, so that they would have a place to escape to when Ava was sick and Tatuka was by the Rebba. But then she reminded herself that she would have a husband and if she wanted a happy home and a good marriage then she would need to focus on the marriage and not have her sisters underfoot. For the most part she ignored them both. On occasion she bonded with Suzi, who was closer in age than the *lemala*, who it turned out was actually quite smart but still acted like a baby and rarely talked at home.

6

"Man's knowledge cannot extend beyond his own experience."
—Locke

The whole family was abuzz right after Pesach when Magda was officially notified that she would be valedictorian of the class of 1965. As the first-born child among her mother and her aunts, this was a big deal. All the girls were scheduled to get new dresses for the graduation, their hair done at Tony's beauty salon on Albany Avenue, and then all the families would gather and have a formal sit-down celebration dinner which Ava was catering. It would be held in Zita's house, which was larger, and similar to the Pesach *seders*, could hold all of them far better than Ava's much smaller home. Ava had Lajos send an airmail invitation to his only surviving brother, Rummy, who lived in Israel in a town called Bnei Brak, where many survivors of the Holocaust migrated too, after liberation.

    She knew Lajos felt guilty that he could not afford to financially help his pious brother, who had eight children and wrote *sfarim* [religious holy books], which, while noble, was not enough to support a family. Lajos was in no position to do more than send his brother a small check twice a year, before Rosh Hashanah and

Pesach. Ava felt it was absolutely the right thing to do. Additionally, Ava sent her sister-in law Roszi assorted dresses and scarves when she got a great buy at her favorite clothing stores, Loehmanns and Shoppers Club. She genuinely liked Rummy's wife, who had made her and Lajos feel incredibly welcome on their first visit to Israel 15 years ago. Roszi was much younger than Ava, a child survivor, given away with her younger sister by her parents to trusted neighbors in 1939 before they were forced into the ghetto. That a surviving aunt found both children after the war was a miracle and the two made their way to Israel where in time, Roszi met Avram as she called him, but Rummy to everyone else, and married him.

Now, however, much as Ava would have liked to do more for her brother-in-law and sister-in-law, she and Lajos had a "big girl" on their hands and all their resources had to go towards assuring that Magda would make a very good *shidduch*. A marriage that, by virtue of being a match with a good family, would raise their own status and pave the way for the younger daughters too. It was exactly what Mamuka would have advised her to use her *sechel,* her innate smarts.

For Ava, Magda marrying a good boy meant everything. They would spare no expense. Starting with a new wardrobe, straightening Magda's unruly curly hair and a consultation with Dr. Edward Weissman, the pre-eminent plastic surgeon in New York City that Zita insisted could take Magda from pretty to gorgeous with a new nose. Naturally, Lajos was adamant that he did not have the money or desire to have his daughter undergo surgery. This led to many rounds of fighting with Ava eventually winning. First, she stopped talking to Lajos, communicating with him exclusively through Magda, who passionately hated being in this position but had no choice other than to please her mother who looked so unhappy. Then she had Zita, whom Lajos admired, call him. When that had no effect on her husband, Ava sweetly convinced her family doctor, the kind Dr. Biffer, to call Lajos at work and express his concern for Ava's nerves and fragility. Finally, Ava would sit at the Shabbos table crying, tears raining down her cheeks. It was uncomfortable for the girls to see their mother so unhappy, it made all of them feel helpless. As expected, it was more than Lajos could take. Her trump card was the money Lajos spent on his Rebba.

"Are you going to sit there, Lajos Rosenbaum," asked Ava between serving her chicken soup and main course, "and tell me to my face that you can afford to hire a contractor to remodel the Rebba's house, but you can't afford to insure your daughter's happiness for life?"

Lajos bit his tongue, he loved his Avala too much. He sighed and kept his temper in check. "*Igen dragam,*" he replied in Hungarian. "Yes darling, *megkeresem a pénzt drágám* [I will find the money]."

Once again, the three girls were left confused and uncomfortable. Granted, everyone's parents argued, but this was different. They never discussed it, but each daughter, in her own way, wished it never happened or if it did, that it would happen behind closed doors.

Before graduation on June 16th, Magda had her nose job. By September, when Ava officially took her to Mrs. Berger, a fellow Hungarian survivor who became the local *shadchanta*, matchmaker in Brooklyn, to register her, Magda looked unrecognizable. Magda was in love with her new nose and looked in the mirror all the time. For the first time in her life, Magda agreed with her mother; looks mattered a lot.

Ava felt validated for forcing Lajos to find the money for the nose job so that she could give her daughter the best possible chance at marrying a good boy. Doing right by your daughters was not a simple matter, but Ava was as fierce as a lioness when it came to her daughter's happiness. She had no doubt that Magda was going to have the best life and she as Magda's mother would glow with pride when Magda, once married, on the next holiday, walked into *shul*, wearing a human hair *sheitel* created especially for her by Malkala Fox, the wig maker everyone flocked to before the holidays. If the boy on Crown Street that Magda used to flirt with was a sacrifice, Ava didn't care. That family had nothing to offer her. Ava and her sisters knew their own saintly mother would be very disappointed if they married off Magda to the Grosses who originally came from Maramureş, a town in Romania that was beneath the Rosenbaums of Baia Mare. Ava recalled the abject horror by which her beloved

Mamuka considered the town and citizens of Maramureş. By breaking up this puppy love, by forcing Magda to keep slim, she was not only doing Magda a favor but also honoring the memory of her own beloved mother, Devorah. That was all that mattered.

7

"One word frees us of all the weight and pain in life. That word is Love."
—Socrates

As if on a schedule, Magda started dating. It didn't much matter who she was attracted to as long as her parents and aunts approved of the *shidduch*. They all reassured her that the final decision was hers. When Hershel Goldstein arrived in his red car to take her out, Magda had a feeling that he was the one. She told Suzi after their first date that when she looked at Hershel, everything was wonderful. Suzi was astounded, having never thought Magda could become so sweet and soft. In a matter of months, Hershel proposed.

Suzi was very excited about Magda's upcoming wedding. It was all she could think about. For once, everyone in the family was in a good mood, planning and preparing for the big day. The only hiccup was when they went gown shopping. Ava had a vision which she and her sisters thought was the height of elegance, a snowball wedding which meant everyone in the bridal party would wear white gowns. When Magda mildly protested saying she preferred to be the only one wearing white and thought pale pink as a secondary color for the wedding party would be beautiful, Ava immediately developed a headache. Right there in Kleinfelds, the well-known bridal house in Bay Ridge, Brooklyn, while Magda was being fitted in her snow-white gown. Seeing Ava turn pale and asking the sales associate for water was enough for Magda.

"Mamuka, please," she tearfully began. "I am so sorry for aggravating you. Of course, I want a snowball wedding! What do I even know?"

"Are you sure, Magdushka," asked Ava, "because I want this day to be one you will never forget."

"Yes, Mamuka," said Magda quickly, "it will be everything any bride could ever want. I just want you to be okay."

With that the color scheme for the wedding was set. Kati and Zita took their daughters to Manhattan to Lord & Taylor, one of the city's oldest and most well-known department stores, to shop for their gowns. All of them would be bridesmaids marching in groups while Suzi and Judy, the sisters of the bride, would march by themselves, with Suzi marching immediately before the bride, signifying her status as the next big girl.

Suzi didn't particularly care for her newly acquired brother-in-law, Magda's soon-to-be husband. In her eyes, he wasn't especially handsome, smart or rich. What Magda saw in him she could not fathom, but she hoped that deep down Magda loved Hershel as much as she said she did. Suzi was a voracious reader and her ideas of romance centered on the many Jane Austen novels she read. How wonderful it would be to see Magda as happy as Elizabeth Bennett!

From the time Magda started dating, the two sisters stopped fighting. Magda loved the attention she got and found that her younger sister had many good ideas and keen observations. Suzi understood Magda's hesitations and reservations, based on the fights their parents continued to have nightly. Now the topic of course was the wedding, the weekend *Sheva Brachos*, the lavish seven nights of post-nuptial parties that were expected to be as lavish as the actual wedding. Kati and Zita would of course each host one party, the groom's family would as well, and the bride's family would host the parties over the weekend. Lajos nearly exploded when Magda informed him of her idea to host the Shabbos in a hotel.

"Avala," tried Lajos, "are you aware of what this will cost?"

When Ava ignored his question, tensions escalated, with Ava crying and Lajos feeling dreadful that he had to deprive his beautiful Ava of her dream weekend.

"Lajos," asked Ava, "why did I survive if not to see my daughters to the *chuppah*?"

Once again, Lajos felt a pang in his heart for not being nearly as successful as his close friend Imre or his brother-in-law. "Don't worry, Avala," he reassured his wife. "I will get the money and you will have everything the way you know is best for our Magdushka."

Lajos left the house and drove to Williamsburg to seek counsel from his Rebba. He was already in debt to Yankel Shapiro for a lot of money. At this point, borrowing more wouldn't change anything except his overriding sense of shame and anxiety at how he was ever going to repay this money. There had to be something he could do to be able to afford the lavish wedding Ava wanted. He would gladly give up on sleep, take on extra work if necessary and sell the few stocks he bought, hoping that one day they would triple in their worth.

Lajos was a very astute man and followed the stock market, hoping that perhaps there he might find an opportunity to make money. In spite of his own Hasidic upbringing in Baia Mare, he read the New York Times every day, listened to 1010 WINS on the radio, and tried in general to speak English, rather than Hungarian or Yiddish. He was not the jealous type and was actually very accepting of God's hand in determining who would have wealth and who wouldn't. He just was not successful at earning enough money to satisfy Ava who was determined not only to dress fashionably, but to travel, go to the theater, send the girls to sleep away camp, and the aforementioned wedding. Lajos didn't care much about most things, least of all material things. If not for Ava, he would never buy new shoes, shirts or suits. The thought of pampering himself was almost obscene when he reflected on what happened to him, his parents, his sisters, and brothers.

He never talked about them or his four years as a slave in the Hungarian army. He tried hard to erase the pictures in his mind. The cruelty, the humiliation, the beatings and sadism that he and his best friend Zimmy endured together on a daily basis. By the time the war was over, and he was liberated, he weighed 75 pounds and had no front teeth. He didn't care if he lived or died. Yet, when he met Ava and her sisters in Cluj, a small town in Romania, he felt a tiny spark of life. He was well acquainted with Ava's family and secretly always had a crush on the beautiful Ava Reiss. When Ava agreed to marry him, he felt a sense of purpose. Now, these many years later, the only two people that mattered to him in life were Ava and his Rebba. They were the reason he got up every morning.

The Rebba, while a source of contention between him and Ava, was legendary in Belgium, California, England, and New Jersey where many of the Rebba's followers lived. Some were men who became extraordinarily wealthy as nursing home operators, real estate investors and diamond dealers and most were only too happy to help a fellow Jew. In the Rebba's neighborhood, in Williamsburg, from Lee to Havermayer and Marcy Avenue, people respected Lajos Rosenbaum as the Rebba's most ardent loyal Hasid. They stood when he walked into a room, eager to shake his hand, even though he was not dressed in the classic Hasidic garb and did not have a beard or long side curl payos. When Lajos arrived in America with Ava, her two single sisters and baby Magda, who was born in Bergen-Belsen, the displaced persons camps set up after the war for survivors, he was determined to become an American. Right there at Ellis Island, he chucked his black hat. It was Ava who reigned him in and insisted that they would not abandon the traditions they were taught. She was determined to honor her parents and recreate her mother's home in New York, but in her own style.

Rather than argue with her, Lajos was actually glad that Ava knew what was best for both of them. He had enough to contend with, by day, dealing with the many aspects of running a business. In his small factory that produced knit coats, sweaters and jackets, Lajos tried hard to become rich. But something always seemed to interrupt the flow of business.

Almost every day, the women he hired didn't come to work, and when they did, they failed to do their piecework and meet the quota that he needed them to fulfill so that he could make money. On top of that, suppliers failed to deliver yarn, thread or buttons, the heat didn't work, or the lighting was poor in the building he rented from one of the Rebba's wealthy real estate Hasidim who was happy to give Lajos a break and allow him to pay the rent when he was able to do so. At night, when he finally put his head down to rest his weary body, the nightmares came.

Lajos hated going to sleep and postponed doing so every single night until he was so tired that he fell asleep instantly. Though Ava offered him the same Valium that she and her sisters took to help them sleep at night, Lajos refused, afraid it might make him look weak. Instead, he sometimes drank a glass of schnapps to help him unwind. But invariably, almost every night, in the span of the three or four hours that he routinely slept, he would wake, his heart racing, his cheeks wet from the tears that coursed down his face, to find his beloved Ava holding him, talking to him in a low soothing voice reminding him over and over that he was safe. She never referenced what happened in the night, not even when they were fighting, though these night terrors went on for years and years. That was Ava, and Lajos was extremely grateful to her.

8

"Where there is love there is life."
—Mahatma Gandhi

Spring 1966

Judy was as excited as everyone else in the house that there was going to be a wedding. In fact, she adored her soon-to-be brother-in-law and the two of them often went outside on the porch together. Hershel encouraged her to talk, and Judy eventually did. He was so kind, and patient. He brought her Twizzlers licorice and pretzels and books, and they would discuss the books for hours. Hershel was enamored with Magda's baby sister as he himself was an only child.

For Judy, Hershel was the first male outside of her father and uncles that she ever had contact with, and he was a welcome change. Besides being young and good-looking, Hershel was just a nice person. He never called her *lemala*, did not tease her, criticize her, or make fun of her. Judy never forgot his kindness and later in life when Hershel needed a friend, she was the one who stood by his side. While others condemned Hershel for some of his alleged business practices, it was Judy and Judy alone who stood by his side. Not his wife Magda, not his own mother or mother-in-law, not Ava, Kati, Zita or Suzi, not even Hershel's own daughters. It was Judy, his youngest sister-in-law, who was by then, stable and off medication following her suicide attempt as a teenager, a wealthy woman in her own right, who found him an attorney and it was her money that paid for the attorney.

Judy fidgeted at her first fitting. She was scared to tell her mother that the gown made her itchy. She was scared to tell her mother that she was afraid she might spill soda on the gown. She was scared to tell her mother that the gown was too long, and she was afraid she would trip and fall. The gown felt so heavy and cumbersome to her. In fact, it seemed to Judy that she was just afraid all the time. She was afraid of her two big sisters, of her teachers and classmates, of thunder and loud noises, of people on the bus or train, of puddles and snow when she might fall and hurt herself, of riding her bike or skating or of her piano lessons. Fear was a constant in her life, but looking at Ava's face, Judy decided to once again be quiet. Magda had drilled it into her head ever since she was six years old, and she never forgot Magda's dire warnings about aggravating Mamuka. Looking at her youngest child, Ava thought Judy looked like a royal princess in her white silk satin gown, with the hand sewn applique flowers trailing down over the left side of the gown, from the waist to the bottom of the gown. In truth, Judy herself, while terrified, loved the gown too.

9

> "We are what we repeatedly do. Excellence, then, is not an act, but a habit."
> —Aristotle

With the bride's gown on order and Suzi and Judy's gowns arranged, Ava was now free to start looking for a gown that befit her status as mother of the bride. Zita and Kati, in the latter's brand-new light blue Cadillac, picked her up on a beautiful spring morning right after Pesach. Though Lajos incessantly made fun of Kati's driving, he was relieved that Ava did not involve him in getting her to the city. The wedding was set for October 23rd, a full week after all the high holidays, including Succos, were over. It was enough time to attend to all the details of the wedding. The three sisters marched into Bonwit Teller, the premiere department store on Fifth Avenue and E. 55th Street.

Ava, who never shopped at the very exclusive, very expensive Bonwit Teller, was extremely impressed with the elegance and beauty of the store; in her mind it was very European. When she tried on the first gown she began to cry, as did her sisters. Here they were, 23 years since the war ended, shopping in the chicest store in all of New York City. Who would ever have believed that life would lead them to New York City, that they, out of all their siblings and relatives and parents, survived the war? Ava started heaving and soon she could not catch her breath. On many occasions in her life, out of nowhere, she often felt like she was drowning or about to die. Not ever describing those symptoms to any doctor, she had no idea that what she was experiencing were panic attacks, commonly associated with post-traumatic stress disorder. And right there in the dressing room at Bonwit Teller, the guilt at having survived, to live long enough to see her first born married, juxtaposed with the image of her dead parents and baby sisters and brothers, all of whom deserved to live as much as she did, was simply too much to bear.

"I can't," she stammered.

Both her sisters understood what she meant. They crowded around her and simply held on to each other. Kati finally broke the tension and unbearable sadness by laughing. "What is the matter with us, standing here like fools, crying in Bonwit Teller? Are we not Mamuka's daughters? What did she teach us? She would die of shame if she saw us now. We have to live and be happy for her!"

Ava looked at Zita and then at Kati and smiled. "You are right. The only thing to cry about is the price tag on this gown. There is no way I can buy it. Lajos will kill me."

With that, the sad moment was over, and the business of husbands became the topic. All three sisters were hardly the picture of wedded bliss, but they accepted their husbands as a necessity of life and focused exclusively on their children. They certainly were not aware of their own foibles, idiosyncrasies, tendencies to shut down, symptoms of anxiety or depression that were part of the landscape of their lives. The conversation went on for a few more minutes and then Zita looked at Kati and began to speak.

"Ava *dragam*, listen carefully, because I am only going to say this once. Since Magdushka turned 16, Kati and I have been saving up for this day. Both of us have been sewing and doing tailoring and earning money. We are buying this gown for you. And you are not going to say one word! You know how we feel about Magdushka. We were right there when she was born. The miracle of her birth after what we went through. Your child is our child, our own girls are much younger, and we want to be part of this incredible day."

Ava stared at her sisters, not believing what she heard and unable to utter even a single word. She was filled with a range of emotions and only wished her beloved Mamuka could have been there to see what had become of her three daughters. "Thank you, my beautiful, beautiful sisters," said Ava softly and lovingly. "There are no words to thank you for once again giving me life."

All three knew exactly what Ava was referring to. The brutal inhumane Death March in January of 1945 that they were subjected to, when the SS officers forced them and all their fellow inmates at Auschwitz to evacuate the concentration camps. It was an attempt to prevent the survivors from falling into Allied hands and bearing testimony to the atrocities committed at Auschwitz. Ava simply lost every last hope of surviving the war while on the March and wanted to lay down and die. Both her sisters had seen women who stopped walking. They were shot on the spot. They knew that the risk of being seen lifting their sister who could no longer walk on her own in the freezing cold, would mean instant death for all three. But carry her they did until she signaled to them that she would walk.

Walking out of Bonwit Teller, holding hands, the Reiss sisters looked young and carefree, and as happy as any other shoppers in Manhattan. For one glorious blissful moment that's exactly what they were. Beautiful, happy, confident young women who were out shopping. Not Holocaust survivors who lived with excruciating memories they could not shut off, of pain, hunger, fear, bouts of depression, rage, terror and anxiety.

They crossed W. 56th street as they exited the store and leisurely walked arm in arm, exactly like they did as teenagers at home in Baia Mare when they had finished helping their mother and had time to stroll through the gardens near their home. They headed towards the famous diamond district on W. 47th Street for lunch at the kosher restaurant above the dealer's club. Kati got visibly excited oohing and ahhing over the gems in the showcases. Her luminous blue eyes opened wide as she lingered over the diamond bracelets, the ruby earrings, the sapphire necklaces and emerald bracelets.

"Someone please remind my husband that my birthday is coming up," she said cheerfully to her sisters.

Both Ava and Zita looked at their Katushka and laughed. For them, jewelry was lovely but so were the paintings in the museums, nice to look at but not necessarily to own. Neither cared as much as Kati, and they knew their brother-in-law would have to appease his wife's overwhelming desire to be surrounded by gems or there would be no peace.

Over lunch they talked incessantly about the wedding and Hershel's mother, a woman they conceded raised a good son but certainly was not in their class. Ava later came to openly despise all three of her *machatanestas*, the mothers of her sons-in-law. The only women she admired, liked and cared to be with were her two sisters, the ones who lifted her when she was down, who reminded her that she had to go on living.

10

"Happiness is the highest good."
—Aristotle

When Ava got home from the city, she immediately changed her clothes and began to prepare dinner. Miraculously, she did not have a headache and prepared a low-calorie, lovely meal for her family, ever mindful that now everyone, not just Magda, had to be on a diet, on high alert, to look their best for the wedding. Ava was humming in the kitchen as she quickly set the table and tossed the salad. She was in a happy mood, still overcome with emotion at what her sisters had done for her, flabbergasted that they had kept a secret from her for nearly two years simply to be able to buy her the gown of her dreams. Perhaps it was to make up for the fact that her wedding day was so vastly different than even Zita's or Kati's. Both of them got married in New York, while Ava and Lajos got married in Cluj.

Her wedding was composed of 10 people, with Zimmy and his wife walking Lajos to the *chuppah* and Kati and Zita escorting Ava. It was painful for Ava to think about her wedding. She was an orphan at age 20 on what should have been the happiest day of her life. There was a photographer. How Lajos found someone to take photos she didn't know, but the pictures were too hard to look at. Not one person was smiling.

Ava heard the phone ring and grabbed it. It was Lajos and for once she was happy to talk to him, knowing there would be no arguments about money. She was wrong. Instead of being thrilled at Kati and Zita's gracious gift, Lajos was utterly humiliated. "They think I can't buy my wife a dress for her own daughter's *chasana*," he yelled.

"Lajos, no, you misunderstand," pleaded Ava. "This has nothing to do with you. They wanted to do something special for me."

But Lajos wasn't buying Ava's explanation. On Shabbos when his two sisters-in-law came over to visit, he could barely look them in the eye. He felt as if they deliberately wanted to make him look bad in Ava's eyes. Secretly he knew that they abhorred his close relationship with his Rebba.

At precisely 5:45 p.m., Suzi and Judy walked into the house. Magda was scheduled to arrive at 6:10 p.m. from her new part-time job in the newly built Jewish Center on Ocean Parkway in Midwood. Ava was thrilled that Magda went to the gym first, every single day to exercise, attended a few classes at Brooklyn College twice a week until the wedding, and had this job. Ava greeted her younger daughters with hugs and kisses and both girls were effusive in their delight to find their mother up and about, with no headache in sight.

The girls vied for Ava's attention, telling her about their day. Even *lemala* was a little more talkative. Ava lavished praise over whatever they told her. When Magda walked in, the dynamic changed. Magda after all was the *Kallah*, the bride, and deserved her mother's full attention. The girls washed up and sat down at the table. They did not expect their father to walk in anytime soon and so they began to eat.

Suzi loved Ava's cooking, the tomato soup with string beans, the freshly made broiled salmon and even the huge green salad and small portion of rice with sauteed mushrooms, onions and french peas. As they ate, Ava described her gown in great detail and revealed what Kati and Zita had done for her. All three of her daughters validated her feelings of gratitude as they cried out of happiness for having aunts who made up for their mother not having a mother on this important milestone in her life. It seemed as if the wedding was far more about Ava than Magda.

In bed that night, Suzi wondered how life might have been had even one grandparent survived the war. Would Mamuka have been different in any way? Would they have gone to live in Israel instead of emigrating to America? As she fell asleep, Suzi Rosenbaum was sure of only one thing. One day she would be rich and famous, singing to sold out auditoriums and concert halls all around the world and she would buy her mother the most beautiful diamond necklace. Yes, she thought, she would make her mother happy, just like her beloved aunts had done today. There was no sacrifice too big to see her mother happy.

11

"Being deeply loved by someone gives you strength, while loving someone deeply gives you courage."
—Lao Tzu

Shortly after Magda and Hershel's elaborate *vort*, the party that was the official announcement of their engagement, it suddenly dawned on Judy that Magda was really going to be moving out of the house for good. Judy began to panic. Suddenly she understood her mother Ava better. It was really hard to go about your day when something else was on your mind. For Judy, Magda was like a mother-figure, the one she turned too. Magda had always been there for her, cooking her favorite foods, encouraging her to talk, and expressing her fears and even helping her with her homework when Suzi refused because she was practicing her solo for the Purim *chagiga* festival at school. What, wondered Judy, ever would she do without Magda who would now be busy with Hershel and then a baby of her own? Judy was terrified of losing Magda! There had to be a way to stop Magda from moving out.

Judy felt a range of emotions at the thought of just being in the house with her parents and Suzi, from panic to anger to betrayal. Mostly she felt confused, sad and lonely. Not once did it occur to her to share these feelings with her mother. It was hard to know when to talk to Mamuka, who was a wonderful mother when she could be.

Judy remembered that incredible day when Ava took her out of school for a Wednesday matinee performance of *Fiddler on the Roof*, playing on Broadway. Judy wore her white Shabbos coat and mink muff that Kati bought her for her birthday. She loved the show although it had its very sad moments. She remembered being astounded at Ava's total lack of emotion, while the many Asian families sitting near them openly sobbed when Tevye declared his daughter dead because she married a gentile. How was it she wondered that her mother didn't empathize with the poor milkman in Czarist Russia who just like her was singled out for being a Jew? And yet, an entire row of people of a different race were overcome with emotion? It was peculiar and it made Judy uneasy and nervous. Exactly how she felt on most days when Ava was emotionally distant. It was why she had to come up with a plan.

Judy knew that no one would actually listen to her, as if *lemala* could actually come up with an original thought, much less some sort of plan. As she tossed and turned in her bed, she finally thought of something that could work. The family could fix up the basement and turn it into an apartment for the young couple and it wouldn't cost them a penny. This way she could still have access to Magda and even Hershel. Yes, thought Judy, this would appeal to her father because it would save him money, and to her mother because she could keep a close watch on Magda. Judy tried hard to figure out who would be the best person to tell her idea to. As she drifted off to fall asleep, she had the answer. She would call Zita *nene*; everyone listened to her.

The next morning Judy got up early. Ava was still sleeping; her sisters were showering and blow-drying their hair and her father was of course in *shul* in Williamsburg. He never missed *davening* morning prayers, the *shacharis* with his Rebba, and by the same token was never present to see his girls off to school. Being in the Rebba's *shul* for prayers was crucial to Lajos. He was there for Rosh Hashanah and Yom Kippur and often went for Shabbos so that he could sit by the Rebba's *tish*, the elaborate table that held dozens of the Rebba's

Hasidim. Every Friday night, hundreds of devoted disciples sat transfixed as they listened to their Rebba's words of wisdom.

On those Shabbos*sim* when Lajos was away, Ava and the girls moved into Zita's house so that they would not be alone. For Ava, it was an inconvenience to have to pack for herself and her three daughters for 24 hours. For what? Just to have a man make *kiddush*? She would gladly have given up the *kiddush* and the blessing over the challah too, to avoid the packing. It just was extra work, if only Lajos would stay home where he belonged! Once, in a fit of rare rage, Ava threatened to call the Rebba to let him know what she thought of his devoted disciple Lajos deserting her and the children, causing her enormous stress. But when Ava discussed her plan with her sisters, both were horrified and warned her to never ever embarrass Lajos like that, no matter how wrong he was.

Judy tiptoed over to the telephone in the kitchen and dialed her aunt's number.

As soon as Zita Goldstein heard her nieces voice, she inhaled sharply and said, "What is it Judyka, who is sick?"

"Oh, Zita *nene*, I am so sorry," said Judy tearfully. "No one is sick, I just need to talk to you."

Zita's elevated blood pressure went back to normal, and she concentrated on what her niece was saying. As soon as she got the gist of what Judy said, she laughed heartily, a sound that infused Judy with joy and hope.

"This is a fantastic idea darling. Judy my angel, you are a genius. Your parents have had sleepless nights and so many arguments, looking for a suitable apartment, and here they will save the rent money and the young couple will be able to buy a house that much sooner," she concluded gleefully.

Zita never once stopped to think that this was too much information for her young niece to process. Although there were few boundaries observed when it came to talking about their husbands, some of their memories, thoughts about life and money, because the sisters had an inability to control their impulses, mostly it was their eldest daughters who were affected as they became the de facto therapists for their mothers when they needed to talk. All the children in all three homes observed and were often exposed to too much information and yet, as adults they mostly concluded that it was far better to hear from their mothers rather than be left with what their own imaginations could conjure up.

"Really, Zita *nene*? Do you think everyone will agree? I mean…" Judy couldn't continue.

"Yes darling," said Zita. "This is such a marvelous idea that I am hoping when my Bailu gets married, to do the exact same thing. Leave it to me. Your uncle Chaim will send the workers from his construction company. That will be our wedding present. It will be beautiful. Darling, I can't wait to call Mommy and Kati and tell them MY idea."

"Thank you so much," whispered Judy. "No one ever listens to me, but coming from you, it will be different and Magdushka won't have to move out, hooray."

Judy hung up the phone and patiently waited for someone to come into the kitchen to give her breakfast. She decided that she would *daven* and pray extra hard, that Zita *nene* would be convincing, and that her mother would love the plan. What Magda and Hershel thought was really not that important compared to what Ava thought.

Just like that, it was a go. Ava absolutely loved the idea and was extremely grateful that Zita would oversee the project, including the cost of the construction and renovation while she shopped and prepared for the wedding. She convinced Lajos that this was the most practical idea and that it would only be for two years, maybe three. Hershel and his parents were barely given a minute to digest the news when construction began in the basement. In a matter of weeks, the basement became a beautiful two-bedroom apartment with its own separate entrance. Magda was stunned at the idea of not moving into her own apartment but decided it wasn't worth fighting about. After all, it would only be for a few years.

Judy literally started talking after it was decided that Magda and Hershel would live in the basement. She daily thanked her mother and sisters and left notes by her father's bed thanking him too. She wondered why she cared so much and decided it didn't matter. The bottom line was that she felt safer and less nervous.

Magda wasn't leaving, just relocating, and that was good enough. Judy didn't care that no one ever found out it was her idea. Yet, months later when Magda had her first fight with Hershel, for the first time, she actually felt sorry that they all lived in the same house. Ava fell into her bed with a migraine headache and Suzi and Magda patently ignored her request to be allowed to hear what the fight was about. Magda treated Suzi as her confidant, exactly the way Ava used to treat her, giving her details about her marriage that were entirely too personal and certainly not for an innocent naive religious teenager. But Magda didn't care. She was mad at Hershel and needed an ally and Suzi was it. History was repeating itself.

From that day on, once Hershel broke the news to Magda that he might have given her a sexually transmitted disease over the summer and suggested she get checked out, Magda began to gain weight. She didn't care anymore about pleasing her husband or even her mother, because she had looked it up and found out that the only way to get an STD was by having sex. Since she was a virgin when they got married, there was no way she had given it to her husband first! Which meant that Hershel had had unprotected sex with someone else. The thought crushed Magda. Wasn't she good enough for Hershel? Should she divorce him? She thought long and hard, not wanting to involve her mother but finally felt she had too. When she told her mother, Ava's reaction knocked her out completely; the pain of her mother's accusations was worse than what her husband did to her.

"Well, Magdushka," said Ava shaking her head in disbelief, after hearing what Magda had to say and mortified at the mere thought of telling her sisters what had happened, "I can't believe that a daughter of mine, with all the advantages of growing up in America, couldn't figure out how to keep her husband happy. There will be no more talk about divorce. You will wipe your eyes, put on your best *sheitel* and makeup and don't ever mention the word divorce again."

Magda was stunned and crushed to the bone. Her mother was blaming her for Hershel's indiscretion in the summertime when he went with his friends to Atlantic City while she stayed home with baby Daniella. Was there no justice in this world, wondered Magda bitterly. How could her mother be so cruel?

And then Ava finished by saying, "There has never been a divorce in the history of our family. Do whatever it takes to make your husband happy. Time to grow up darling. Do you think living with Tatuka is a picnic every day? Do you think being divorced will be better? And what about your daughter? She will hold you responsible for taking her father away from her, because make no mistake Magdushka, he will get remarried and have more children in no time and where will that leave Daniella?"

Magda could no longer keep her tears back. All her life she did everything to please Ava and this time was going to be no different regardless of what it did to her. How could she look Hershel in the face and agree to continue being his wife when she no longer loved him or trusted him? She sat there crying without saying a word and was astounded at how Ava could be so harsh. Not once did her mother look sad for her. How was she going to live in a loveless marriage? How could she pretend in front of her sisters who looked to her for guidance and inspiration? How could she pretend everything was alright in front of her parents and aunts?

Magda tried to talk to Hershel, but it was useless. He was overcome with so much guilt that he turned into a different person. Where once he was a talkative, fun-loving man who had goals, now he smoked day and night and didn't care about his career. On top of that, his parents openly blamed Magda, accusing her blatantly of being a bad wife. It was a mess.

For Magda the only comfort was her darling baby girl Dani. She adored being a mother and vowed that she would always be emotionally stable and available when Dani got older. She was never going to turn Dani into her confidant, not ever saying one bad word about Hershel. The fact that she lived in her parents' basement was both a blessing and a curse. On the one hand, it was wonderful that Judy came often to play with Dani, giving Magda some free time, but by the same token, she felt like her mother was entirely too involved in her life, questioning her every move.

After many sleepless nights, Magda decided that she would go back to work and save money so that she and Hershel could buy a small house. Maybe the move into their own home would make a difference. Shockingly, Hershel was the one who wanted to stay in the basement. Magda couldn't figure out how Hershel could possibly feel comfortable surrounded by her family, but he was adamant that they were staying. Magda gave in, but only temporarily. Thereafter every month she brought up the topic until finally Hershel had enough.

"Okay Magda, fine," he said, "let's buy a house and try to start over."

For just one glorious minute, Magda felt the tiniest spark of hope. If they moved out and Hershel took responsibility for the breakdown in their marriage, she would try her best to become slim again. It seemed that that's all that mattered to everyone she knew.

Beyond her family, for whom appearances were all that mattered, Magda had friends who took anti-anxiety pills to stay calm, friends who were never home, drinking way too much, leaving the care of their babies to their mothers or nannies, and none of that mattered, because when the couples went out on a Saturday night, it was only Magda who was uncomfortable and miserable in her body. None of her beautiful wedding outfits fit her and Ava refused to buy her new clothes. Magda went to Mr. Martin, Loehmanns, and Shoppers Club, taking Suzi with her to help her find new skirts and tops to cover what she saw as her swollen body.

12

> "Just as despair can come to one only from other human beings, hope, too, can be given to one only by other human beings."
> —Eli Wiesel

Suzi was in shock. How could Hershel have betrayed Magda like that? She knew Magda could be obnoxious and annoying but from the moment Hershel proposed, Suzi saw a change in her sister. She was in love and happy and only wanted to make Hershel happy. According to Magda, they were happy, in the bedroom and everywhere else. Suzi felt sick thinking of how Hershel had taken away Magda's happiness.

She decided then and there that her marriage was going to be different. To begin with, she would marry someone less charming, someone who was more sensible, less adventurous and superficial than Hershel. Maybe it was because he was an only child and his mother acted like he was a god? She vividly recalled one of her mother's Sunday morning marathon conversations with Zita, followed by a similar one with Kati in which they dissected how Ruchel raised Hershel to be superior, smug and a *shvitzer*, someone who was a showoff. Suzi deduced from these conversations that being a *shvitzer* was despicable and nearly the lowest level a man could sink to, just slightly ahead of being mean, cold or poor. Suzi felt sorry for Magda who Ava firmly pushed into the marriage, advising her to grab Hershel because her options were limited due to her weight problem, which Mrs. Berger, the matchmaker corroborated. Suzi remembered Magda's sad expression and determination not to let Ava's words wound her. But later, when the two of them were alone, Magda poured her heart out to her sister.

"Suzika, do you think Mommy is normal? Who talks like that? I don't believe for one minute that Kati or Zita *nene* would be so mean? Why is Mamuka so obsessed with thinness?"

Suzi had no answer in which she could comfort her sister. It was then that she decided that under no circumstances was she ever going to let her mother rush her into getting married at age 18.

To Suzi, this was half the problem. What was the rush? How could anyone be mature enough to get married at that age? Suzi began to wonder what her mother's motive was. Was it simply to follow in the family tradition that Orthodox children had to be married before they became dissatisfied and started to look outwards and seek what the larger world had to offer? What destiny, wondered Suzi, did she and her sisters need to fulfill for Ava that stipulated they must get married and have a child before their 19th birthday? Was this Ava's way of repopulating the family that was murdered in the war? Suzi couldn't sleep. At night she tossed and turned. She looked at *lemala* in the bed next to hers and envied her naivete. Being Magda's confidant certainly had an effect on Suzi. Lately, she hardly felt like singing anymore and that worried her. Singing had always been the one thing that made her feel special. Suddenly it felt like an awful lot of effort to open her mouth.

When Ava finally noticed that Suzi appeared lethargic, she invited her to skip school so that they could spend the day together. For Suzi, these rare but highly anticipated days were the highlight of her existence. The day would start after *lemala* left for school. Then she and Mamuka would drink coffee and have a slice of Mamuka's hidden linzer cake. Suzi remembered when she accidentally discovered Mamuka's stash of treats and guessed that Mamuka hid the sweets so that Magdushka and Tatuka wouldn't be tempted.

Although cake was strictly forbidden during the week and reserved as a rare Shabbos treat, on these special days, Ava relented. After coffee, the two of them would get dressed and leave for downtown Brooklyn to A&S and May's to shop. If Ava did not get a headache, the plan was to continue the day by taking a train to Manhattan, go to the Guggenheim or Frick Museum and then have lunch. For Suzi, putting on her beautiful pink wool Shabbos coat, her black velvet beret and angora gloves was a wonderful feeling. It made the day even more special, as was watching how people on the bus gazed at her beautiful mother.

Suzi was honest with herself. Neither she nor her sisters were anywhere near as beautiful as their mother. Ava simply was a beauty, with no makeup or effort. Today, she was wearing a fitted black wool coat, her Shabbos *sheitel* which had fringe bangs and a soft flip. She wore kid gloves of the finest Italian leather and a kitten heel shoe. Ava did not often indulge herself by buying extravagant clothing, often saving up money for years until she could afford something grander. If she resented the fact that Lajos could not buy her pretty things or a bigger house, she only shared that with her sisters and Magda who eventually shared it with her. Looking at her beautiful mother as they sat on the bus, Suzi felt a pang in her heart. Would there even be one person sitting on this bus who could ever begin to understand what her mother had suffered during the war?

Suzi remembered once going with Ava to the dentist at 1 Hanson Place in downtown Brooklyn. Dr. Terman was an endodontist and Ava needed three root canals. Mamuka had trouble with her teeth, likely from the starvation she endured in Auschwitz. It would be 25 years before researchers would link cortisol, the stress hormone, to a host of illnesses and disorders. She recalled with absolute clarity how the dentist turned pale when Ava innocently raised her arm, and he saw her tattoo. While Suzi played in the corner of the office with her drowsy doll, Ava in her heavily accented English that Suzi hated, confirmed to the gentile doctor that indeed she had been forcibly taken to Auschwitz as a teenager. The doctor was effusive in his words.

"Mrs. Rosenbaum," he stammered, "it is an honor to meet you. I am so sorry for what happened to you. I..." The dentist could not continue.

Ultimately, Ava wound up comforting him, assuring him that she was okay, that life had given her a husband and children and she was fine. Suzi always thought that the Ava the world met made it very lucky indeed. Even with her accent, her words were intelligent and clearly revealed that she was refined. Suzi was enormously proud of her mother and hoped that she could make her mother proud of her as well.

When Ava and Suzi arrived in the city, Suzi drew in a huge breath. Manhattan was the most incredible place on earth, and she loved being there! Suzi vividly recalled so many wonderful moments. On occasion, she and her sisters and her cousins got to ice skate at Rockefeller Center around Christmas time, instead of at Prospect Park. Skating at Rockefeller Center was a privilege, Mamuka reminded them, and they were grateful. After skating for two wonderful sessions in which the girls felt like they were famous because of all the tourists watching them skate, they would ruefully leave the rink and enjoy delicious hot cocoa with whipped cream. Then they would walk around the promenade, peeking in the windows of the shops and then cross over to Saks Fifth Avenue, the famous department store.

For some unfathomable reason, Ava and her two sisters madly adored the lights, the Christmas tree and the holiday windows ornately decorated in revolving tableaus symbolizing the Christmas holidays at Saks Fifth Avenue, B. Altmans, Lord and Taylor, and Bonwit Teller. It was only when they headed to 34th Street to Radio City Music Hall or to Macy's that Ava often got panicky and anxious as the size and smells of the crowds enveloped her. Then, if Ava couldn't catch her breath, they had to leave. While ordinarily they would end their day at 3:00 p.m. to allow enough time to get home before *lemala* got back from school at 4:20 p.m., with Magda living downstairs, it gave them more time as *lemala* would go straight downstairs to play with baby Dani. Although Magda and Hershel were actively looking for a house, so far, they were still living in Ava's house.

13

"The way to get started is to quit talking and begin doing."
—Walt Disney

Gradually, Magda forgave Hershel and life resumed. She didn't trust him and barely looked his way but was willing to put up a facade for the sake of her daughter. Although it hurt her to the core, she never forgot her mother's words and, in time, recognized the wisdom behind her mother's dire warning that in the event of a divorce, her precious Dani would indeed suffer the most. Magda allowed Hershel back into her bed. She wanted Dani to have a brother or preferably a sister far more than she wanted to have sex with Hershel. But she knew, as Mamuka had pointed out on only one occasion that she could recall, that a wife has certain obligations.

Eventually Magda figured out on her own what those obligations were, as she did when she got her period or went to the ritual bath, the *mikvah,* before her wedding. Maybe it was European mothers who were uncomfortable talking about sex? Magda didn't know because there was no one to ask. She fantasized about having a grandmother whom she could call up and complain to, someone who would take her side and understand that just like *lemala,* she too was sometimes scared of both Mamuka and Tatuka. Being that she was the oldest, she had no choice but to maintain an aura of strength. To Magda, it was as if the entire family's stability rested on her oversized shoulders. If she wasn't there to keep it all together, how would they manage? It would be decades later in therapy that Magda would come to understand the nature of the complicated relationship between survivors and their offspring who functioned as support staff to their parents, ahead of their own developmental, social and emotional needs.

And lately there were some benefits coming her way from caring for *lemala* all these years. As much as *lemala* used to annoy her when she, as a 10-year-old, was assigned by default to be her babysitter and playmate, she had since become invaluable as a playmate and babysitter for Dani. The freedom this afforded Magda allowed her to slowly heal. She had time for herself, and without any fanfare or anyone's permission, registered for courses at Brooklyn College in the night school program. She resented having to quit school after only one semester, when she got married and now not really caring enough to coddle and nurture the marriage, Magda wanted to get smarter. More than that, she most certainly did not want to be home when Hershel came home and be receptive to his needs. She would faithfully leave him a lovely dinner, but she did not eat with him or ask about his day. By the time she came home from her classes at 10:45 p.m., Dani was fast asleep and so was Hershel.

Naturally, when Ava found out about Magda's nighttime program on Mondays and Wednesdays, she was hysterical. "Magda, what is the matter with you," she pleaded. "You can't abandon your husband and daughter like that. He will get lonely and look for company elsewhere, and Dani will think *lemala* is her mother."

It seemed as if Mamuka always knew best. Yet, shockingly, Magda did not back down this time. She was getting very tired of her mother running interference in her life, of not ever letting her make a mistake on her own or simply making decisions for her own family.

It seemed like the only area in which her mother did not meddle or interfere was in her sex life. Then, Magda was on her own. She remembered sadly not having a clue what intimacy was, until she discovered Cosmopolitan magazine and started to read every article that Helen Gurley Brown printed. Maybe all Hungarian mothers were like that, but Magda was adamant that when her daughter turned 11, she was going to explain things to Dani about her body and would make herself available for questions. Maybe Ava was European, but she, Magda most definitely was not. So, Magda continued in college. No one paid much attention or even asked her what she was learning, least of all her husband or father. But Magda knew this was good for her.

In class, Magda felt free to express her opinion. In her sociology class on women, she found to her utter surprise that she was a closet feminist. It led her to the library for books by Betty Friedan, Simone de Beauvoir, Gloria Steinem, and Bell Hooks, leading feminists who made it patently clear that all women had rights to equality on every issue that affected them. It inspired her so much that one fine day Magda opted to take Driver's Education. She remembered how disappointed she was when some of her classmates took driver's ed in their junior year of high school, but she was denied permission. Tatuka said no and Ava was in agreement.

"Why would you need a driver's license?" she had asked at the time. "Your husband will take you wherever you need to go and if not, New York City has wonderful buses and trains."

With that, the topic was closed. Magda fleetingly thought of asking her *nenes* to intercede but felt uncomfortable as she reached out to them both, all the time. Magda was willing to accept that she couldn't take driver's ed, but what was unacceptable to her was the excessive amount of fear and anxiety that the lecture Tatuka gave her.

"Magdushka," he began reasonably, "it's not you I'm worried about, it's the *meshuganas* out there, the crazy drivers, drunk or stupid who might hurt you."

Magda just nodded because the extent of fearfulness that both of her parents routinely demonstrated made her feel sick. Did Mamuka not think she didn't hear Tatuka scream in his sleep? Did anyone besides her think that the iron bars welded onto every window in their house, in addition to an alarm system was a little excessive or was she the only one who knew that not every family was so scared? She would get her driver's license now and make up for lost time.

For starters, Magda wanted to drive herself to school rather than wait for the bus. Many days, Hershel left the car at home and it just sat there in the driveway all day and all night. When Magda let everyone know that she passed the road test on her first try, it was the talk of the whole family! Magda drives, just like Kati. They were the only two women in the family to be so bold and daring! Ava unfortunately could not get past her anxiety; similar to Lajos, she was skeptical of Magda's ability to drive a car responsibly. She never said a word to her daughter and even when Magda had the car at her disposal and offered to drive her to Kingston Avenue to do her grocery shopping, she refused. To Magda, this was very hurtful. Finally, she could do something to make her mother's life easier and Ava refused. In fact, she was adamant that Magda not take Suzi or *lemala* in her car either. Magda was astounded, but reluctant to confront her mother. In her mind she envisioned what she would like to say.

"Mamuka, are you that old-fashioned? Do you think women are inferior drivers to men? I am an excellent driver, even Hershel says so."

But those words remained in Magda's mind only. Ava was steadfast in her refusal to set foot in any car that Magda drove. The hypocritical fact that she allowed herself to be driven by Kati was difficult for Magda to handle, but she let it go. This was the landscape she was familiar with. No boundaries, few rational decisions, and periods of highs and lows. She had enough to deal with.

14

"Every moment is a fresh beginning."
—T.S Eliot

The Nutcracker was coming to the New York City Ballet and Ava decided this was a serious enough occasion to pull all the girls out of school so that they could attend. For Ava, ballet, along with theater, classical music and museums was the culture she fundamentally found so lacking in New York and was determined to inculcate in her daughters and even in their best friends. Ava's mission was to raise upper-class girls in what she considered a low-class society in America.

She recalled with revulsion the first time she ever went with Lajos to a supermarket, dazzled and nauseated at the sight of so much food. Rows and rows of bottled and canned foods followed by aisles loaded with dozens of types of frozen foods, from tv dinners to vegetables and breads, snacks, drinks, dairy foods and meat for those who were not kosher. She watched as the many overweight American housewives loaded their wagons to the brim, thinking they must be preparing for a famine. She accurately foresaw that America would alarmingly become a nation of hypertensive, insulin dependent people from all the processed foods they ate.

She utterly hated their informality, shopping with hair curlers in their hair, chewing gum and speaking loudly. Her next-door neighbors refused to call her Mrs. Rosenbaum as she introduced herself and laughed when she couldn't bring herself to call them by their first names. It wasn't the gentile neighbors though whom she had a hard time with. Rather it was the Jewish neighbors, the Berliners and Markowitzs who upset her. Calling her and Lajos "*de greena*" right to their faces, implying that they were naive, uncouth, and as green as unripe fruit, while they, second or third generation Americans, were that much more sophisticated. Ava often laughed to herself. She spoke four languages and yet in the eyes of her neighbors, it was she who was not worldly or sophisticated. She vividly remembered telling Zita and Kati who by that point were both newly married and living in their own apartments, that she would never forget what Mrs. Berliner shamelessly told her the day they moved in.

"Well, you know Eva," pronouncing Ava's name like the Anglicized version, "we also had it very hard during the war; we couldn't get things we needed for years, because everything went to the army."

Ava remained tight-lipped and never responded. Instead, she continued wheeling Magda up and down the block, lost in her maudlin thoughts. Magda, shockingly for five whole minutes, wasn't shrieking. No matter what Ava did, from the old-fashioned remedies of putting a piece of paper in water to ward off the evil eye, to putting a drop of whiskey on her baby's tongue, to holding Magda for hours at a time, from the minute Magda was born she didn't stop crying. And while there were a few other newborns in Bergen Belsen, who also cried, none of the women appreciated Magda's howling all day and all night. Most of the women, weak and fragile like Ava, Kati and Zita were there because they had no plan, other than waiting for exit visas or sponsors who would vouch for them on arrival in a host country. They were Holocaust survivors, with nowhere to go and no clue on how to resume life. Sometimes Ava thought that Magda must have felt her pain, that somehow, she knew her mother was weak, broken and sick. Maybe too, baby Magda missed her two *nene*s that doted on her?

All Ava knew was that she couldn't handle Magda's wailing and finally had to get medication to calm her nerves. She did not give the doctor details and he asked for none, used to housewives who needed a boost. She never once told anyone that when Magdushka cried, it reminded her of the babies in Auschwitz, in particular her older sister Surika's children, her precious Naftuli-Binyumin and Malkala, who she was told, were brutally snatched from their mother's' arms, thrown like useless trash against the wall, by laughing Nazi officers who wanted to silence them forever. That memory was enough to make Ava want to die. How, she wondered, could any person who belonged to the human race justify such horrific cruelty?

She begged Lajos that first year in America, when they lived in Bay Ridge Queens, in a one bedroom walk up apartment to take her and Magdushka back to Hungary. America was too big, too noisy, too dirty and too diverse, she would never find her place here. Of course, there was no way she or her sisters could or would ever go back to Hungary, but that first year was exceedingly difficult for Ava. In fact, it took Ava the longest to acclimate, to adapt and adjust. She stubbornly clung to her mother's ways, trying always to live up to her mother's expectations of how she should be, and she was relentless when Kati or Zita started getting too comfortable in America. It seemed especially like Kati with her new friends, always laughing and planning a party, was eager to shed their past. Zita was obsessed with her own daughters and that's all she wanted out of life, to make them happy.

Ava felt it was her responsibility and would grimly remind them often of what happened to them and six million Jews and that it could happen again. She firmly believed that it was their mission to educate the world about all that had befallen innocent good people who had the misfortune of being born Jewish. When Eli Wiesel, a Holocaust survivor from the town of Sighet in Romania where her grandfather was born, became a world-famous spokesperson determined to educate the world about the genocide that happened, Ava was elated. Finally, a person who would speak on behalf of the dead and on behalf of the living. To look into the critically acclaimed Nobel Peace Prize writer's sad tormented eyes was to feel his pain.

Ava followed Wiesel's career, was ecstatic when he became a Professor of Humanities at Boston University. When he met presidents, prime ministers and members of the monarchy and mostly when he spoke on behalf of helpless innocent people being murdered, tortured, starved, uprooted, and displaced in Cambodia, Rwanda and Darfur, she was genuinely relieved. Finally, here was a man who commanded respect, who used his suffering, his losses, his pain to assure that the world knew what happened when no one stood up to stop blatant hatred and racism.

Mrs. Lieber, their next-door neighbor whose family emigrated to America before the war and someone Ava admired for her polite distance, her religious principles, as it applied to her everyday life, happily agreed to babysit Dani so that Magda could join Ava and her girls along with Kati and Zita and their daughters, for this lovely event. For Suzi, this had to have been the most spectacular day of her life, second only to Magda's wedding. To watch the spectacular George Balanchine choreography was a dream come true. Suzi was in heaven and Ava was pleased.

All the girls were dressed in their Shabbos clothes finery and when Zita took a group photo, she hoped that in Gan Eden, that special place in heaven where only the righteous rested for eternity, that her parents both knew that their daughters and granddaughters would always be loyal and true to what she and her sisters had been taught in Baia Mare. While the Reiss girls did not attend the opera or ballet in Budapest, they did in fact have a tutor, who taught them the German language, literature and poetry, and introduced them to great works of art and classical music. They were raised to be refined, *eidel*, genteel girls and living in America, a cauldron of unsavory types of people was not something Ava ever wanted her daughters to be exposed to.

Ava was extremely cautious about who her daughters could mingle with, not wanting others to unduly influence her daughters. She knew Magda was loyal and attentive and Judyka was a good child. She worried most about Suzi and her ridiculous dreams of becoming a famous singer. She would have to quell that burning desire in the same way that she ended Magda's harmless flirtation with the Gross boy. She and she alone would steer the course for her daughters so that they were happy and, more importantly, that they kept the legacy of their heritage intact. Suzi was not going to become a famous singer and that was final. She would get married just like Magda and she could sing to her babies. Ava was never more certain of anything. She had to assure that her future generations would turn out right. It was the least she could do to honor her own beloved revered mother.

Though Ava herself was a Holocaust survivor, her deference to the memory of her own beloved mother bound her to survivor's guilt that dictated how she would live. Often, she felt burdened by the guilt but had no words by which she could effectively deal with it, so it sat inside her and rarely allowed her a reprieve. It moved with her from season to season, dominated her thoughts and oddly, comforted her when she felt sad. At a minimum, she believed that her mother was watching her from heaven and expected that she, Ava of the three surviving sisters, would always behave properly, and motivate and inspire everyone around her.

15

"Everything you can imagine is real."
—Pablo Picasso

Judy had a crush. His name was David, and he was new in the neighborhood, his family newly arrived from Israel. He was tall, slim, had dark hair and a great smile. Every time Judy saw him her heart beat a little faster. He reminded her of Jeff Stone, the son on *The Donna Reed* show. Unfortunately, every single girl in her grade also had a crush on him and he didn't notice her. He walked past her house every day never looking for her, oblivious to the fact that she adored him.

The stress of hoping David would pick her out of all the other girls who openly smiled at him when they walked on Eastern Parkway every Shabbos was starting to get to Judy. At first, she couldn't sleep, then she lost her appetite, and then it escalated to where she would cry for days on end, utterly devastated that this boy didn't even know she existed. His lack of interest pierced her very being and simply corroborated her worst fears that she would never be special to anyone. Magda was the first bride in the whole family, already had a child, so no child of hers would ever be the first grandchild and if Suzi had her way, she was going to become rich and famous and give Mamuka a maid and a bigger house and a new car and tons of diamonds. So, what would she ever do to stand out?

Judy worked herself into a terrible state of mind. In school, she presented as alarmingly lethargic and listless and two of her teachers were very concerned. The principal, Dr. Rose Seltzer called Ava and requested that she and Lajos come to school for a meeting. Ava was terrified, having never before been summoned to school. What, she asked her sisters, in a state of panic, would this woman who was a doctor think of her and Lajos? Would she think they were terrible parents? Ava had to take a whole Valium that night so that she could get a decent night's rest. She dreaded going to school and facing the principal. It seemed as if anyone in a uniform or position of authority made her very nervous.

Once, Ava had a flashback right in the A & S department store on Livingston Street. She was shopping with Kati when suddenly they heard the security guard yell "STOP" as he began to chase a teen whom he suspected of shoplifting. Ava turned pale as the security guard firmly held the young boy who clearly was terrified and likely, in her opinion, targeted because of his skin color. In her mind, the security guard looked evil, and he could have been a stormtrooper SS Nazi. Ava started hyperventilating and thankfully took the water her sister offered her.

"He," she said and trembled.

Kati just stroked her hand. "Avala, *drágám biztonságban vagy, itt vagyok veled* [please darling, I am here with you, you are safe]."

Ava smiled weakly. "Okay," she joked. "I'm turning into Lajos."

The horrible memory moved past her, and the sisters left the store. Kati steered them out of the store quickly. She did not want Ava to see what happened next. She was very protective of her sister, then and now.

Dr. Seltzer was a plain no-nonsense shrewd woman, who ran the school with an iron fist. When she met the Rosenbaums, though, she was surprised. Based on how Judy appeared, particularly in the past two months, she was expecting to find parents who she would have immediately recognized as the source of their child's problems. She had seen many in her day. Overbearing parents, authoritarian parents, permissive parents, neglectful parents. But the Rosenbaums were lovely. Mr. Rosenbaum was sincere and heartfelt and very concerned about his daughter, while Mrs. Rosenbaum was clearly a caring devoted mother, albeit nervous.

Dr. Seltzer cleared her throat and hesitantly began her rehearsed speech, concerned that she was going to upset the Rosenbaums.

"As I am sure you are aware, we have been concerned about Judy for quite some time. In spite of her shyness and her reluctance to speak, she has done well in school. She doesn't have many friends but that's by choice."

Then, she leaned in and asked, "To your knowledge, has anything happened recently to upset her?"

Ava and Lajos shook their heads.

"Actually," Ava said, "Judy has never been happier since her married sister had a baby. She is always downstairs, playing with the baby, happy to babysit for her older sister." Just saying those words "her older sister" brought an immediate flashback to Ava. The image of her own beloved older sister Surika, who along with her mother, infant nieces and nephews and brothers did not survive Auschwitz. Surika was the apple of their mother's eye. She could do no wrong and was Ava's role model growing up and every day since. She felt a pain in her heart as she remembered those wonderful days at home. How she loved going to Surika's apartment down the street at 29 Hodes. She happily helped Surika with her two babies, sweeping, cleaning and preparing food. As Lajos coughed pointedly, she realized she had skipped a piece of the conversation.

"I'm sorry," she said.

Dr. Seltzer softened, which was rare for her.

She was aware that the Rosenbaums, like many of the parent body, were Holocaust survivors. Most of the time this had nothing whatsoever to do with her management of the school. On the contrary, these particular parents assured that their children treated the teachers with great respect, as they had been taught in Europe. But today, for some odd reason, she felt kindly towards this woman who sat in front of her. She relaxed her posture and what for her was a sympathetic tone inquired again,

"Did Judy mention any feelings of nervousness or anxiety about perhaps the summer? Many of the girls talk about sleep away camp all year long. Perhaps she feels left out in those instances?"

Ava just shook her head. Magda never wanted to go to a sleep away camp and Suzi loved it from the first summer when she was 12 years old. Judy being the baby was not yet a consideration. Was it possible Judy was jealous of her friends? She decided to talk to Zita and Kati and get their opinion. She hoped that they were ready to consider the same camp for their daughters, so that all the girls would be together. For Ava, by extension of her relationship with her sisters, she assumed her daughters and her nieces would take comfort if they too were all together in the same camp.

"Dr. Seltzer," she responded slowly, "camp is a luxury. My husband and I are not looking for another expense right now, but if you think this might be good for our Judy, we will look into it right away. We very much respect your opinion."

Mrs. Seltzer was taken aback. Very few people spoke to her with such charm, sincerity, candor and honesty. This woman was indeed unique.

"Well, in that case, let's do the following. You think it over and if you believe this is a good fit for Judy, call me. I know the Hausmanns, the owners of the camp, they are neighbors of mine, and I have recommended many girls to their camp. I am sure that with already having one camper from your family, that I can persuade them to reduce the camp fee. Then, start to talk to Judy about how she might feel going to camp. Make lists of what she will need to bring. Let's meet again in three weeks. In the meantime, I will speak to Judy's teachers and have them give her extra attention and see if that helps."

Ava was simply astounded. This was the first time since arriving in America that anyone outside of her great uncle who had sponsored them, had spoken so kindly to her. It was also her first encounter with Dr. Seltzer as her girls as well as her nieces, always behaved in school. The children in the family knew that at home they could "let loose" as Kati referred to it, but in school they were expected to remember where they came from and who in heaven was watching over them. Ava practically burst out crying and had to take a deep breath before responding.

"Dr. Seltzer, I cannot thank you enough for your wonderful advice and kindness. My husband and I are very grateful," she ended humbly.

Dr. Seltzer, a rather unattractive woman who had her own fair share of problems with twin sons both diagnosed with neonatal encephalopathy, smiled. Her face practically lit up as she let Mrs. Rosenbaum's kind words seep into her tired soul.

"I am happy that I could help. I have enough to do answering to an all-male board and dealing with 200 active children every single day, so I don't often find the time to chat with parents. Nevertheless, this meeting was important, and I am hopeful that Judy is simply being a pre-teen. We will get through this together."

With that, the much less formidable principal rose to signal the meeting was over. The Rosenbaums did the same and exited her office.

Ava could not wait to get home and call her sisters. She was almost in a daze from how incredibly nice Dr. Seltzer was. What an honor to actually be in the same room as a Jewish woman who became a doctor, who devoted her life to the education of Jewish children! Ava was noticeably impressed. Lajos of course was already tuned out and she could barely get a reaction from him. But the girls, her sisters, they would understand her. They always did. Ava allowed herself permission to rest in the car until they reached their house. This had been an extremely emotional morning.

16

"All limitations are self-imposed."
—Oliver Wendell Holmes

As soon as Ava got home, she immediately called Kati who conferenced Zita onto the call. It was much simpler this way than Ava repeating herself twice. This way they all heard the news at the same time and discussed it at length until they reached a consensus. Many times, Suzi would find Ava on the phone in the kitchen, exactly where she left her at 8:05 a.m. Lajos was nearly out the door and on his way to Williamsburg where he could always find a *minyan*, a quorum of 10 men needed to pray. He smiled to himself when he heard Avala tell her sisters about their encounter with Dr. Seltzer. He didn't smile though when he thought about his sisters-in-law. He didn't always appreciate their *eitzas* [advice], but accepted that they were Ava's closest family. Overall, he loved them and was glad that Ava had them to lean on. Much as he would have liked a little privacy from them, he was resigned to the fact that Ava was never going to make a move without them. He knew how the three sisters survived together and nothing was ever going to break them up.

Ava made the executive decision that Judy needed to go to camp because that's what Dr. Seltzer suggested. She didn't think she needed to have a discussion with her daughter, because both of her sisters agreed and that was enough. Her immediate challenge was going to be to save up money. She would not let Zita help her this time. The fact that Zita quietly paid for many things bothered Ava a lot. The more important thing was to call Dr. Seltzer and hope that she could get her a discount because not only Suzika was going, but now her two nieces as well.

When she met them for the interview, Ava planned to ask the Hausmanns for a monthly payment plan. She hoped they would agree. That would hopefully give her sufficient time to grow her *knippel*, her secret savings fund. Ava felt happy knowing how incredibly lucky her daughters were, to attend a prestigious sleep away camp like Camp Rina, where they would have the opportunity to make new friends and get out of the stifling heat of the summer. Ava planned to tell Magda to have a talk with Judy and remind her that camp was a privilege that not every girl was lucky enough to get. She was positive that the excitement of getting her own trunk, and new shorts and tops would snap Judy out of her mood. It actually made Ava happy as she and her sisters started to make lists of what the girls would need. Zita and Kati were also sending their oldest daughters who were close to Judy's age, for the first time and they were all excited, if not a little nervous. Knowing that Suzi, the oldest cousin, was there to look out for the younger ones was comforting to the mothers.

Magda was still active in the role of Ava's chief advisor, especially now that she was married. Oftentimes when she was studying or playing with baby Dani or even on the rare occasion when she and Hershel went out to the movies by themselves, she felt irritated when Ava called to talk. Didn't Mamuka realize that she was grown-up, wondered Magda or did that not matter when Ava needed her? Magda wondered if moving into their own home might be the answer. She decided then and there to cozy up to Hershel. Lately things were a lot better between them. Hershel was trying and even his mother grudgingly acknowledged what a wonderful mother

Magda was to baby Dani. Magda felt slightly hopeful that things could get better, if only Ava would just cut her some slack and not need her quite so much.

17

"Try to be a rainbow in someone's cloud."
—Maya Angelou

Magda did not get her wish. Over the course of the next two years, after Judy's attempted suicide, Ava was a total nervous wreck. Not only was Magda unable to move into her own home, but she also became a permanent fixture once again in her parent's home while Ava attempted to recover from Judy's near fatal suicide gesture. Judy herself, following a three-months inpatient stay at the exclusive highly recommended psychiatric institute Care Winds in Connecticut, actually recovered quicker than Ava. She met with a psychiatrist daily until discharge and then was scheduled to see him monthly to review her medications. She would also be referred to a psychologist for intense psychotherapy. It was Ava who took to her sick bed, devastated by what she felt was Judy's perfidy.

"How," she cried to her sisters who faithfully visited her every single day at lunchtime, in the first three months after the incident, "could my own daughter do that to me?"

Ava was beside herself and, once again, it was Magda who ran the household, driving Judy to her appointments, going grocery shopping, doing laundry and clothes shopping for the holidays.

There were days when Magda felt very sorry for herself, but of course all the sympathy went to Mamuka, not even Judy got half as much attention as Ava. For Lajos, this was the straw that broke the camel's back. He was oblivious to anyone but Ava and relied even more heavily on his Rebba and his larger evening glass of whiskey. He no longer made any effort with his children or granddaughter. Magda started eating again, late at night when she finally had a minute to herself, she ate to comfort herself. Mostly junk food seemed to calm her. In addition to the worry about Mamuka and Judy, Tatuka's excessive drinking and Hershel staying out late again, Magda was furious that she was forced to drop out of school.

At first, she took a leave of absence for the fall semester when Judy almost died, but then when she couldn't find the time or energy to register for the spring semester, she simply gave up. She punished herself for not being strong enough and fighting for herself by doing what felt comforting, she ate large quantities of food after Hershel went to bed. In a matter of three months, she gained 20 pounds on top of the baby weight that she never lost. Worse was that Mamuka didn't notice or seem to care. Everything was on pause, all because of Judy. In time though, Judy began to speak. She learned relaxation techniques with her therapist, made an effort to eat right, took her antidepressant medication faithfully and learned to articulate her feelings, something that no one else in the Rosenbaum household knew how to do.

Magda watched her little sister in amazement. Was it possible she wondered that a suicide gesture could possibly have a silver lining in its dark devastating cloud? It gave Judy the opportunity to learn more about herself and to work towards a goal of finding balance, and for Mamuka it brought a best friend which surprised everyone that Mamuka would allow Rose Seltzer into her inner circle previously only open to her two sisters? Magda wholeheartedly endorsed this friendship, seeing it as a sign that Mamuka was allowing herself to trust other people besides her family. But her aunt did not agree. Kati *nene* called her up one morning and preempted the conversation by insisting she was not jealous or threatened by Rose Seltzer.

"What is your mother thinking," she said. "Doesn't she know that telling a stranger what happened is not smart? In a few short years, Suzika will need a *shidduch* and what good family would want a girl whose sister is not 100% well? This is a mistake, mark my words. Please Magdushka put a stop to this friendship, I beg of you."

Magda did not know how to respond to Kati's bizarre thinking. Was that the issue? What the neighbors would think? That Judy's suicide attempt might bring shame on the family's good name?

Magda struggled to understand how her aunt, whom she adored, could be so ridiculous. Wasn't it a little more important to understand what drove Judy to such desperation? To understand why she cried every single night in camp, and no one thought to bring her home? The fact that, yet again, it was her responsibility to fix things simply infuriated her and left her feeling even more powerless and helpless than usual. The only thing that consoled her was her determination that she would do better with her own daughter. Never would she make Dani into her confidant or expect her to understand grown up issues. Magda just wanted her daughter to be a child, have friends and be happy, something she was deprived of.

Poor Dani, she was too young to know about all these problems swirling around her. But Magda was determined to make sure that Dani, and hopefully more children, had a better future than she did. Here she was in her early twenties stuck in a loveless marriage, unhappy with herself, nowhere to go, and no one to turn to. It would take Magda another 25 years before she was ready to even contemplate going to therapy. It was when she watched Judy take control of her life and move outside of Mamuka's orbit, eventually divorcing her husband, and deciding to make a new life for herself that Magda finally gave herself permission to put herself first.

Magda was glad that life had at the very least given Suzi a break. When Suzi started dating Zak Zweig, she knew immediately that Suzi would have a good life. Zak was slow and steady. She and Judy would laugh behind Suzi's back, exactly like Mamuka did when talking to Kati and Zita, that Zak was an insufferable bore, but if he was good to Suzika that was all that mattered.

And Suzi was happy. She loved her home that she decorated with Mamuka's help. She had a keen eye for color, and her daughters were her happiness, always making their home a fun place for them, where they could bring their friends. In fact, she adored Faygala's childhood best friends May and Ray. Though they were from very different backgrounds, and far less observant than the Zweigs, Suzi didn't care. The girls were darling, loved coming to the house, and were important to Faygala. Suzi practically made a vow on Yom Kippur that she most definitely was not ever going to be as judgmental as Mamuka, who never thought anyone was good enough to be her friend. That she occasionally exploded was something Suzi was aware of, particularly when she picked on Bethie and Dini, but practically worshiped Faygala, her first-born daughter. She knew it wasn't fair to always give Faygala special privileges, but couldn't help herself.

Later in life, when Suzi began therapy, she realized that choosing Faygala as her favorite was her subconscious desire to imitate her own mother, who turned to Magda for everything. But Suzi knew that Mamuka's favoritism came with a price. One only had to look at Magda, diagnosed with pre-diabetes and hypertension in her thirties, to know that she couldn't handle Mamuka's attention. Suzi tried often, offering to go with her older sister to Weight Watchers meetings. At the end of the month, Suzi lost three pounds while Magda shed not an ounce. Suzi signed up to a gym with Magda and changed her cooking style, while Magda dropped out after two weeks. Someday, thought Suzi, Magda will be ready. In the meantime, Suzi tried her best to be supportive. loving, understanding and considerate sister to both of her sisters. Mamuka may not have done everything right, thought Suzi, but Suzi loved the bond her mother had with her sisters and felt it was essential for her to have that same one with her own sisters and hoped her daughters would one day too. For Suzi, that was the essence of life, family.

18

"We must accept finite disappointment, but we must never lose infinite hope."
—Martin Luther King, Jr.

Ava was simply enchanted with her new best friend Rose. Rose was like a tour guide, opening Ava's mind to new ideas and possibilities she never dreamt of. She began to influence her friend too, inviting her to go shopping on Sundays, carefully and sincerely helping her pick dresses that fit her properly. Rose was beyond grateful for her European friend who inherently had so much style. She even shared her copy of Rona Barrett's Hollywood magazine and Ava was fascinated, poring over the pictures of Marilyn Monroe, Ava Gardener, and Elizabeth Taylor with great interest. Oddly she didn't share any of this with her sisters. She tried a few times and neither sister was receptive, so Ava dropped it. But she liked her new American friend whose life was so different from her own.

Rose spoke flawless English and understood Yiddish, fondly recalling her Zayda Avram, a dignified man who wore a top hat on Shabbos, who came to America from Russia in 1902, and who never spoke English. Rose also wore hats, but only on Shabbos and Yom Tov because it was respectful to cover one's head when walking into a house of worship, but she did not wear a *sheitel* like Ava. The wearing of a wig, Ava learned, was a Hungarian custom imposed on married women. Although she knew it was unkind, Ava thought Rose would look a million times better in a human hair sheitel, as opposed to her sparse pixie haircut. But she didn't want to offend her friend and had no one with whom she could indirectly send a message to Rose, as Magda would certainly never get involved, as she always did whenever Ava wanted to change something about Suzika or Judy. It was just simpler if it came from Magda. Ava decided that if she was asked, she would offer her honest opinion and take Rose to Malkala Fox for the nicest *sheitel*.

The bonus to this unusual friendship was that they talked English all the time, and that pleased Ava who decided to try and read a few of her favorite books in English. When she finished reading Theodore Dreiser's *An American Tragedy* in English, Ava was pleased. If Kati and Zita couldn't understand what an achievement this was, she was thrilled that Rose, who was so educated, obviously did. Ava desperately wanted to be more proficient in the English language so that her girls would be comfortable talking to her in English. After all, her girls were American and even she was, having become a naturalized citizen along with Lajos and her sisters. Ava loved the President and avidly discussed politics because she was proud to be an American, though she would always be a Jew first. Her tattoo reminded her every single day, even if she could forget. Now, all she had to do was keep practicing her English. It was hard, because Lajos, her brothers-in-law and sisters only spoke Hungarian and occasionally Yiddish if they were joined by Roszi *nene* who refused to speak anything but Yiddish. In fact, Roszi *nene's* 10 children all spoke Yiddish as their primary language, minimal English and no Hungarian whatsoever.

One evening, as Ava sauteed onions to make *káposztás tészta*, Lajos' favorite dish of noodles and cabbage, Rose told her how she landed in Brooklyn. Ava was simply fascinated and even put her cooking on pause as she cradled the telephone to her ear not to miss one word of Rose's story. Rose was born in Milwaukee, a city in the state of Wisconsin that Ava had never heard of before. Rose's father,

Rabbi Avigdor Schneiderman was a well-known and beloved scholar and Rabbi in Sherman Park where the Orthodox Jews primarily lived. In the small community, the Shneidermans lived next door to the prominent Shoyers, Adlers and Weil families. They were all immigrants who eventually established themselves as grain dealers, merchants, manufacturers, tradesmen, craftsmen and professionals.

When Rose turned 17, her father began to seek a suitable match for her. She married her husband Shmuel, who was already in a *smicha* program at Yeshiva University in New York City and expected to obtain his rabbinical degree and become a pulpit Rabbi. With a stellar reputation, Rabbi Seltzer was immediately offered a job and after they married, the Seltzers moved to the Bronx which was where the *shul* was within walking distance. Rose thought she was going to hate living in New York but found it fascinating. She particularly loved the museums and proximity to the Yeshiva University campus, an institution pioneered by Dr. Bernard Revel whose ideological vision made it possible to synthesize the study of Torah and the arts and sciences. When she and her husband had to face the reality that their infant sons required institutional care, Rose decided to get a teaching degree. It was not the life she expected but it was her life. It took Rose 14 years to receive her doctorate in Jewish education. She rose in the ranks and was offered the prestigious position as principal of a very fine co-ed yeshiva in Brooklyn. She was the first woman to head a yeshiva and she knew that her father of blessed memory would have been very proud of his only child. There, at Yeshiva Crown Park, she finally felt at home. She ran the school strictly but fairly. If it was painful to see 200 healthy children every single day and not feel resentful that her twin boys would never walk, run, play or go to school, she kept that to herself.

19

"Our greatest glory is not in never falling, but in rising every time we fall."
—Confucius

Judy was extremely nervous about going to camp but didn't want to spoil the mood. Apparently, she was the odd duck. Her cousins Elyse and Rochelle were eagerly counting down the days until they were leaving for camp and Suzi was busy day and night composing songs for color war. It was only Judy that couldn't cope with the idea of being that far from her mother and trapped in a bunkhouse with nine other girls for eight long weeks. Knowing that Suzi would be in camp was a small comfort, because she worried that if she was not popular or bothered Suzi too often that Suzi would get annoyed with her. It seemed as if her whole life was about pretending to be one thing while really being another. And why? She still couldn't get David's attention or any other boys for that matter. Judy was honest with herself; she was no better or worse than any other girl. She knew the only thing that made her different was the fact that she was chronically worried. Maybe that's what kept the boys away, she wondered?

Just like that school was over and camp was starting. Judy

watched her trunk loaded onto the truck and felt queasy. The next time she saw her clothes, her favorite stuffed animal, her new Shabbos dresses and favorite bathing suits would be at camp. Judy couldn't look her mother in the eye at the bus stop. There were so many girls, laughing and calling each other's names. But no one called her name because she was new. Finally, she spotted her cousins coming over with their mothers. Judy actually was thrilled to see that they too were a little nervous. But to her consternation, as soon as they were introduced to the other girls in the bunk, they were fine and ready for their mothers to leave. They hung on every word their energetic red-headed counselor named Lucy said and just adored their junior counselor Mimi who was from Florida and so much fun. Judy watched all this and longed to be as carefree as everyone else but try as she would, it didn't happen. She was the outsider, exactly like at home. Everyone paired off and she was left outside the circle.

All summer Judy wrote letters to David. She knew that he was at a sports camp, probably 40 minutes away from her camp in Liberty, New York. If only he would answer her letters, or they would meet at Dorney Park on trip day. If anything kept Judy going, it was the notion that David would see her and fall madly in love with her. She was positive it could happen; she read so many amazing novels where the girl always got her guy. It happened in every Gidget movie too, so why couldn't it happen to her? Being a smart girl, she also knew that most girls didn't marry their crushes. Magda didn't, and Suzi had already dropped Chaim Leifer. So maybe, David wasn't the boy she thought was destined to be her husband? Nevertheless, all summer she wrote letters to him, expressing her feelings, her yearnings and desire to be connected to him. Not once did she write to her parents and cringed at the thought of them coming up on visiting day.

In camp there were fewer girls of the same background as her, her sister and her cousins. A large majority came from Manhattan's Upper West Side Jewish community. Many of their parents also were immigrants who came to America before the war. Some were Holocaust survivors but not necessarily of concentration camps or slave labor. On Tisha B'Av, the day in Jewish history that fell in

August most years, a day every person fasted, beginning at age 12 for girls and 13 for boys, commemorating the destruction of the Temple, people shared what they considered to be equally as tragic moments in Jewish history. Judy was mesmerized; she knew her bunk was not invited to these lectures, but since her counselors were fasting and there were no scheduled activities, she was free to roam around and entertain herself until the 25-hour fast was over. She snuck into the large room where the campers typically gathered for night activity and sat all the way in the back. She listened for hours as the older girls talked about the war.

It was an eye-opener for Judy. It was the first time she ever heard of the partisans, Jews who hid in the woods and fought back. What was even more astonishing to Judy, who was so captivated that she forgot she was fasting, was when Miriam Belsky got up and talked about her uncles who had established a school, an infirmary, and a society in the woods for over 1,000 people who were determined not to go to their death like meek sheep being led to the slaughter. When Judy thought about how sheep, actual *lemalas* docilely went to their slaughter, it snapped something deep inside of her. She was not going to be a *lemala*. She would fight for what she wanted, and she would be heard.

Ironically, while for almost every single girl in camp, Tisha B'Av, the ninth day in the Hebrew month of Av was the worst day of camp, for Judy Rosenbaum it was the best. The day inspired her in ways she didn't know was possible. She determined that when she got home from camp, she was going to read about the partisans. She would ask the librarian at the newly opened branch on Maple Street to help her and she would lie if necessary, saying the books were for a school project, in case Mrs. Deutch thought she was too young to read those books. But first she had to deal with visiting, which she dreaded.

For some reason that she couldn't quite understand, Judy didn't want to see her parents, her aunts and uncles. If anything, she wanted to see Magda, Hershel and baby Dani and hoped they were coming up to see her. After a Shabbos in camp that was full of fun for most of the girls, like her cousins and sister Suzi who was the most popular girl in camp because of her voice, Judy, along with her bunkmates, vigorously cleaned her cubby. She rearranged her sweaters and folded her shorts so that when Mamuka came in she would be enormously proud of her neat shelves. She ran to the area where the girls kept their hanging dresses and assorted shoes and boots and did the same.

Sunday morning, ridden with anxiety, Judy woke up at 4:00 a.m. She wrote six letters to David and paced up and down the bunkhouse numerous times, counting to herself. She watched in envy as everyone around her slept peacefully and resented bitterly that she wasn't one of them. Finally, it was 7:00 a.m. camp time, and everyone rose when they heard the camp director Barbara Hausmann's cheery *boker tov yeladot* [good morning girls]. As the somber nine days leading up to Tisha B'av was over, music blasted throughout the camp. Even the lazy girls got up, eagerly anticipating seeing their parents.

And then it happened. The grueling day was finally over, promptly at 4:00 p.m. The Hausmanns followed a strict schedule that they felt was best for the girls. It was at 4:05 p.m. when everyone returned to the bunk that Judy felt like a freak. She was the only girl in her entire bunk who did not come back with *nosh*, the proverbial chips, candy, chocolate, cookies and drinks that every other camper had on their bed. Judy was in shock. Didn't Mamuka know she was supposed to bring her pretzels and licorice? Even Hershel, who was like a big brother, didn't he think she needed something? And worse, even her two cousins had *nosh* on their beds! It seemed as if even her aunts didn't subscribe to her mother's rigorous health plan. Judy was livid! She never fit in.

In a flurry of tears, she ran out of the bunk so that hopefully by the time she got back, maybe the *nosh* parties would be over. That was the tradition in Camp Rina, there was no canteen, so this was the one night when all the girls celebrated and obviously their parents got the memo and brought more than some hot cherries. Yes, she admitted to herself, she did love cherries, but they were hot from sitting in the car for two hours and didn't come close to being what everyone else was unfolding on their beds. Judy walked aimlessly, not caring when it started to rain, or that night activity was announced. It seemed that when visiting day was over, the camp always had a wonderful dinner and a great night activity. Judy heard the head counselor announce that Suzi Rosenbaum was going to give a concert.

"What else?" groaned Judy.

She could not and would not sit through a Suzi concert. Girls envied her that Suzi was her sister, but aside from waving to her, Suzi was simply too busy having a blast in camp. Suzi and her friends, as waitresses, were on their own schedule and actually had a day off. Judy wondered if she would ever make it to being a waitress or a junior counselor at camp. Maybe, if she survived these miserable years, she might be okay.

Judy returned to the bunk and a miracle happened. The *nosh* was all cleared away, the perishables eaten or thrown away and the rest put away. Judy breathed a sigh of relief. Nearly everyone was still at night activity. She took a shower and went to sleep. Seeing her parents, particularly Tatuka who was sweating and looked pale, was harrowing. She wondered why Ava's health plan didn't seem to work on the ones who needed it the most, Tatuka and Magda. Judy started sweating, terrified that Tatuka was not well and Mamuka didn't notice. As tired as she was and secretly terrified that her counselor would come check up on her, Judy got out of bed and took another shower. Then she went through her numbers routine again where she counted all the members of her family, including her cousins and their parents, Hershel and baby Dani, in addition to her parents and her sisters. This ritual seemed to relax her.

Settled once again in bed, Judy was pleased with herself for telling her counselor she was sick and needed to go to the infirmary. Lucky for her, neither her counselor or junior counselor checked up on whether she was admitted to the infirmary or not. Judy adored momma Rachel, the camp nurse and actually enjoyed going to the infirmary when she had a cut, sore throat or mosquito bite that sometimes, because of her excessive scratching, turned into a wound. But her counselors were busy celebrating the tips they received and ecstatic to hear Suzi sing. No one noticed Judy.

When the girls came in, seeing her in bed, they all tiptoed and tried to be as quiet as possible, not to awaken her. Judy was in fact up and touched at their consideration for her. She happily drifted back to sleep but not soon enough, when she heard Bayli say, "It must be awfully hard to be Suzi's younger sister."

Immediately all the girls chimed in. "I'm so glad my sister is just boy crazy," said Gabby.

"Yes, how awful that one sister is so talented and the other, well you know..." said Dassy.

Judy felt her face burning. Could it be possible to die of shame and still be alive? She was humiliated beyond belief. She didn't want anyone's pity at being the superfluous add-on in her family that no one needed? She would show them all, and with that she fell asleep dreaming of barbed wire, running for her life. Though Judy herself, like all children of Holocaust survivors had no first-hand frame of reference for what happened at Auschwitz, what she absorbed in her home environment was sufficient to transmit the trauma her own parents had witnessed and endured to her own subconscious, as if she too had gone through the experience.

20

"The greater the obstacle, the more glory in overcoming it."
—Molière

The campers came home, taller, suntanned and, in some cases, full of freckles. While Judy was hanging on by a thread, no one seemed to notice except Hershel, whom no one really paid attention to. While it was true that Ava did not sanction divorce, she also did not sanction betrayal of any kind. Passively, as was her style, she was aggressive. Hershel was persona non grata. He could stand on his head for all his mother-in-law noticed him. Naturally that meant Kati and Zita too. So, when Hershel called both of Magda's aunts voicing his concern about Judy, beyond her shyness, both of them brushed him off. Zita practically laughed out loud.

"Hershel," she said, "that's all that worries you these days, our *lemala*?"

To which Hershel had no answer. Indeed, he had plenty more to worry about than a moody teenage sister. His latest business venture was not going well, and his investors were impatient, forcing him to take on more investors whose money he used to placate the previous investors. It was surely enough to keep him busy, and Hershel put Judy out of his mind, especially after he got the identical response from Kati, whom he always thought was a bit more open minded. He should have known better. Crossing Ava was crossing her sisters. Those were the unspoken rules.

As the children got back to the routine of a new school year, the mothers began their shopping expedition for the coming holiday season. Rosh Hashanah was a major event. It was the time when the entire family was together, first in *shul* and then for all the meals. The mothers took the shopping very seriously and most of the daughters looked forward to the trip to Williamsburg to Borland. Once the younger girls were outfitted from head to toe, the mothers took the bigger girls to Loehmanns and Mr. Martin and to S&V in Manhattan.

Lajos knew the owners, both Sam and Volvie from the Baia Mare *shul*, and wanted Ava to patronize their store. Surely if Avala wore a dress from S&V other women would follow suit. Lajos gave his word to his friends and when they became very successful, they never forgot who got them started. Ava got a huge discount every single time she stepped foot into the small store on the corner of 7th Avenue and E. 26th street. Ladies she didn't know sought out her fashion advice, including her friend Rose and Mrs. Hausmann. In a matter of months, religious Orthodox and Hasidic women from New York and New Jersey began flocking to S&V. It got to a point where Sam and Volvie offered to pay Ava just to come into the store and be available to advise customers. Ava did so at least twice a week, happy to add money to her thin *knippel* and also because she genuinely enjoyed it. On those days, her headaches miraculously were managed by the new medication her cousin Libu sent her from Sweden.

On those days when Ava wasn't home for the girls, Magda magnanimously offered to be upstairs and get dinner started. When Ava was happy, so was her family, and everyone wanted it to continue that way forever, regardless of who had to sacrifice what.

Things were certainly looking up in the Rosenbaum household on a financial level too, thanks to Lajo's brother Rummy who never forgot his brother and sister-in-law's small but steady help, unequivocally for 25 years. When he arrived in America and arranged to *daven* together with Lajos over Rosh Hashanah and Yom Kippur in Williamsburg, he told his brother about a big business opportunity.

Lajos believed his brother and immediately after Rosh Hashanah, approached Cheskel Lefkowitz, an enormously successful Baia Mare Hasid who was extraordinarily generous and lent him the start-up money needed. Lajos gave his brother $300,000 for a 50% ownership in a new candy company in Israel. Although Lajos didn't live long enough to realize his foresight in backing his brother, his investment allowed Ava to pay off all of Lajos's loans. It sustained her and his children after his death, even after Ava agreed to marry Imre two years later, a close friend from home who had never married and adored Ava.

21

"I am a slow walker, but I never walk back."
—Abraham Lincoln

Ava liked her brother-in-law Rummy far more than her own sister's husband and was happy to have him in their home for the 10 days between the holidays. She admired his approach to life and his implicit faith in God, the same God who had abandoned them in Auschwitz. Being in his presence was comforting and when Rummy mentioned that he was concerned about Lajos, Ava got scared.

"Lajos," she anxiously asked her husband later that evening, "are you feeling okay? I noticed you couldn't catch your breath after you picked up the baby?"

"Avala, I'm fine, *Kedvesem, teljesen jól vagyok, nincs miért aggódni,*" Lajos said, emphatically reassuring Ava that he was fine. The last thing Lajos ever wanted was to aggravate his wife.

The next day, without telling Ava, sure that he had heartburn, Lajos made an appointment with the doctor and decided to take a taxi to the office, rather than battle parking. He left his car in Williamsburg and Rummy assured him that he would drive it home. In the doctor's waiting room Lajos began to sweat, felt slightly nauseated and within a second, he slumped over. The doctor attempted to revive him, but it was too late. Lajos had suffered a massive heart attack in the doctor's office.

22

"Our dead are never dead to us until we have forgotten them."
—George Eliot

"It's not possible!" Ava kept screaming hysterically. "I just spoke to him. It couldn't have been him."

Lajos never took a taxi in his life or went on his own to a doctor. Her brother-in-law Rummy, her sisters and their husbands all sat around her dining room table as Ava rambled on, refusing to accept the inevitable. Finally, Kati brought Ava two Valium pills, begged her to take them and go lay down. Ava refused.

"Kati please, you would never lie to me," she screamed. "Tell me this is a nightmare, please Kati. I beg you. Tell me the truth, is Lajos in the hospital? What happened to him?"

Kati just shook her head slowly, looking to Zita for help. It was Rummy who finally got through to his sister-in-law, as he gently knelt in front of her.

"It's true, Ava. We got the call from the hospital where they brought Lajos, and the *chevra kadisha* [burial society], are with him." Rummy gasped, unable to continue.

Ava looked at him as if she didn't know who he was. "Didn't I give enough in Auschwitz for 10 generations," she pleaded wildly to her sisters. "Didn't you both force me to stay alive? For what? To see this day? So that my children should be orphans? Why, why, why?"

She repeated these words brokenly over and over. Because none of them had an answer that would placate Ava, they simply surrounded her and tried their best to comfort her. The children had all been sent to Zita's house. No one noticed that Judy was seriously not doing well, far worse than her sisters and even her mother.

23

"You see, I usually find myself among strangers because I drift here and there trying to forget the sad things that happened to me."
—F. Scott Fitzgerald

The day of Lajos Rosenbaum's funeral was sunny, and Ava was irrationally irritated. Far better that the *himmel*, the very heavens, should have been crying and sending buckets of tears down to earth. Weren't her parents and Lajos's parents crying and beseeching the heavens on this day? Ava and her daughters went through the motions, sitting in the first row of the chapel, not hearing one word of the eulogies spoken first by the Rebba himself who openly cried for this Hasid who felt like a son and a brother. His *hespid*, long and lengthy eulogy was followed by Rummy's heartfelt words of gratitude to his brother and concluded by asking his brother for forgiveness on behalf of himself and the entire family. Sobbing, he let those gathered know what a selfless man his brother was. In a matter of minutes, it was over, and the men prepared to take the *aron* [coffin], for burial.

The women were not permitted to escort the casket to the cemetery for the burial, as was the Orthodox custom. They instead returned to the house, where candles were lit, the mirrors were covered as a symbol of the mourning that would take place and Ava and her three daughters sat on the low chairs where they would sit *Shiva* for the customary seven days of mourning, in their torn garments that symbolized their mourning status. For Kati and Zita, seeing their beautiful nieces in mourning was unbearable and unthinkable, but it was seeing Ava, eyes glazed over from the Valium, sitting as still as a statue that penetrated their hearts. They were well acquainted with this Ava, and they had hoped never ever to see her again. Yet here she was again, the Ava who robotically lived at Auschwitz.

The sisters never left her side, sleeping for a few short hours in the study on the pull-out couch, ignoring the fact that they had children of their own at home. No one noticed that Judy stopped eating altogether and sat in her designated low chair by her mother's side, looking equally as glazed over. People who came to pay their respects remarked at Judy's devotion to Ava, sitting there for hours on end without moving a muscle. It was the first time in her life that Judy dared to speak up, but she did.

"My chair is going to be right next to Mamuka," she told her sisters. "I don't care where you sit, but I am sitting right there."

She pointed to the spot by her mother. Although everyone thought Magda as the oldest, would surely be needed by her mother, would sit there, there was something desperate about *lemala* and she nodded her head in agreement. This was definitely not the time to have a fight.

During the Shiva, the shock that reverberated throughout the family was that Hershel volunteered to say the *kaddish*, the mourners prayer, three times a day for the full year of mourning, as there was no son to do so. While privately his own parents were less than thrilled, somehow fearful that their only child saying the mourners' prayer for a parent would God forbid give them an *ayin hara*, an evil eye, they had no choice but to be proud of their son. In this way, Hershel slowly edged his way back into the bosom of the family. Later in life, he thanked Magda profusely for staying with him, recognizing what he might have lost.

Yom Kippur was upon them, and it was difficult. Rummy did not go to Williamsburg to the Rebba, instead, he stayed in his brother's house, trying his best to be of comfort to his sister-in-law. When it was time for him to return to Israel, he felt torn. NechaLiba, his wife, had even told him that should he decide to stay for the Succos holiday that she would go to her sister in Bnei Brak. NechaLiba's younger sister was married to Berish Shanzer, a very learned man who was eager to help his sister and brother-in-law by opening his home to them. But Rummy refused, knowing that his place was with his family. After the *shloshim*, the marking of 30 days of mourning, as a brother, he was technically no longer in mourning and was permitted to resume life. As Rummy prepared to leave America with a heavy heart, he reflected on the bitter irony that in the coming months, it was he who was sending checks to America, after so many years of receiving checks from America.

24

> "I have learned now that while those who speak about one's miseries usually hurt, those who keep silent hurt more."
> —C.S. Lewis

How the family got through that Succos holiday was unfathomable. It was probably Dani who slept with Bobby Ava nightly and insisted daily on baking cookies with her and decorating the *sukkah* that got them through what should have been a wonderful holiday. Kati and Zita took the girls to the park for a picnic on *Chol Hamed,* the days between the Succos holidays and took them out to lunch. It was Magda of course who was left to deal with Ava, and she did so admirably, with all her heart. She tried everything in her power to please her mother, going so far as to get diet pills and lose weight again. But sadly, it was wasted on Ava, who saw and heard nothing.

Suzi, of course, was excused from all choir practice and would not be in the January production. Instead, she would help with scenery, discovering that in addition to singing, she was quite talented at drawing. It was only Judy who couldn't find her place. She mechanically went to school but could not focus. One night, a few months after her father's death, after everyone went to bed, Judy took her mother's bottle of Valium and swallowed 10 pills. She just wanted to sleep and make the pain go away. It was just too much. Rejected by David, who finally let her know that she was crazy for writing all those letters, made it untenable for her to go on. She was sure people at school were talking about her because David had a sister in school who made a point of laughing whenever she saw Judy in the halls.

Judy started to drift off, still conscious and feeling overwhelmingly sad that she would never see Dani grow up or live to have her own children, when suddenly she felt Suzi pushing her, slapping her face and screaming for her to wake up. Within seconds, Hershel called 911 and EMS came to pump her stomach. It was touch and go on the ride to Bellevue Hospital, but Judy pulled through. Many years later, after extensive therapy, she jokingly told her sisters, in a rare conversation about that terrible time in all their lives, that she was afraid Ava would never let her rest in peace if she died.

The road back to health slowly started for Judy. On the rare occasion someone tried to call her *lemala*, they stopped in their tracks, remembering Judy's hysteria in the hospital, screaming at the top of her lungs that she was not a *lemala*, she was a resistance fighter. Though no one knew what she was saying, sure that she was hallucinating or delirious, Judy knew exactly what she was saying. She was given a second chance, and she was going to be different, no matter how many years it took her, she would never ever give in to being insignificant. It indeed took many years for her to evolve; she was reserved and calculated, thinking before speaking, considering before acting. She made good choices in her life, including the man she married, who was good for her until he wasn't.

25

"Tears come from the heart and not from the brain."
—Leonardo de Vinci

Judy's suicide attempt was a scandal of epic proportion that Ava and her sisters did not know how to deal with, and it defined the Rosenbaum household and took the spotlight off Lajos' death. Even though Ava was in her sick bed most days, it was Judy who got all the attention. Being in therapy helped not only her but even peripherally her sisters. It would take years for things to settle down by which time Ava realized that she would marry Imre.

It was after a trip to Israel when Ava sat with her brother and sister-in-law, Rummy and NechaLiba, asking for their guidance, permission and blessing that Ava decided to say yes. In marrying Imre, who was realistic enough to know that Ava was not in love with him, Ava changed. Suddenly material things that she only cared about on major occasions became important to her. Imre who adored her was only too happy to indulge Ava, hopeful that one day she would come to love him. Slowly, life changed. Ava and Imre moved to a bigger house in the neighborhood and Magda moved into her own home nearby with Hershel and Dani. Judy was doing well, and Suzi was Suzi, philosophical about life's blows, and able to look ahead to better times. She also knew that she was never going to sing again. She loved her father unconditionally and when he died, her voice evaporated. She had no desire ever to sing again.

26

"You know you're in love when you can't fall asleep because reality is finally better than your dreams."
—Dr. Seuss

Imre loved his life with Ava. He was finally married to the only woman he ever loved, and her happiness was all that mattered to him. He took on her children and grandchildren, sisters and nieces as if they were his own. He bailed Hershel out to help him avoid lawsuits that could have landed him in jail, but by the same token, threw his hands up in resignation when the exact same thing happened 20 years later.

Imre was no one's fool. He was a very respected real estate developer in all of New Jersey and worked very hard for his money. He gave charity and treated all his employees very well. Now that he was married to Ava, he was happy to semi-retire, travel, and enjoy life with her. He knew that she had not had an easy life with his dear friend Lajos. Now that he was married to her, the sky was the limit. Every time Ava smiled it made up for all the years that he had suffered during the war. Life was very good, and Imre increased his charitable donations as a way of thanking God for his blessings.

When Suzika got engaged, Imre threw a huge *vort* engagement party for her and Zak. It was the party that everyone was talking about. He bought all his girls new dresses and gave Ava a blank check to prepare for the wedding. Ava, at least once a week, asked him to pinch her, to make sure she wasn't dreaming. Could God really have sent Imre to somehow make up for her losses? She was shocked to find out how much she loved money and all that it could buy. With Magda expecting a third child and Suzi almost married, she gleefully anticipated everything she would buy for them all. Yet, there were somber days, such as Lajos's *yahrzeit* , the anniversary of his death, when she needed to be alone and Imre, ever the gentleman, understood. He made himself scarce on that day and Ava was free to lovingly reminisce with her sisters, pay tribute to the father of her children, and simply remember her husband.

On his *yahrzeit*, Ava remembered to send a check to his Rebba. The Rebba, according to Imre, was a very wealthy man with his own vast real estate holdings, but nevertheless it was Ava's way of honoring Lajos. The first year, she ordered dozens of *sfarim*, Hebrew Biblical books, inscribed with Lajos's name so that when anyone picked up a *siddur*, *chumash* or a *tehillim* in his beloved *shul*, they would remember him too. The second year, she donated brand new chairs at the Kotel's women's section, so that women would have comfortable chairs while praying at the Western Wall.

When she and Imre celebrated 10 years of being together, they commissioned a Torah to be written in memory of their respective parents, Lajos, and all their siblings that perished in the war. On the day that the Torah was completed, a procession marched from their home to the *shul* that would receive the Torah. People gathered on the streets to participate in this ancient custom; treating the newly written Torah as if it was a bride being escorted to the chuppah canopy where she would be married. When the Torah reached its destination, a number of men carrying other Torah scrolls came out to greet and welcome the new Torah. Those invited for the final letter writing ceremony and sit-down dinner indeed felt like they were witnessing a special moment, one that had not been done in any Orthodox community. Rummy and NechaLiba came in from Israel to be part of this celebration and Ava's heart filled with joy.

Seeing Rummy reminded Ava of her Lajos and she never wanted to let go of the past. She missed Mamuka every day of her life and often told Zita and Kati that for her, as she got older it didn't get better. It finally dawned on Ava that maybe it was time for her to take a trip to Hungary to visit the graves of her grandparents who died before the war and see the house where she grew up once more. Naturally, her sisters would join her.

It was a memorable but difficult trip for the three couples. Imre made all the arrangements, hiring a comfortable bus to take them to all the towns they would visit on arriving in Budapest. It was a long journey, going from town to town, village to village, from Csenger to Szeged and Debrecen where relatives once lived and died. In each town the villagers came out to greet and gawk at the "millionaire American tourists", shocked to hear these rich fancy ladies speak Hungarian and claim to be as Hungarian as them. At some moments the three sisters were giddy, walking arm in arm, laughing as if they were teenagers, while other days they could barely talk. It was 30 years since they had emigrated to America; they had lived more years in Brooklyn than in Baia Mare. After spending three days and three nights they reached the end of their itinerary. Zita uttered exactly what Ava was thinking. It was time for them to go home to their families and try to make peace with the ghosts of the past that still haunted them.

The three sisters knew that they would never in their lifetime go to Auschwitz as many of their contemporaries were doing. Ava, in particular, strongly felt visiting Auschwitz was on some level disrespectful to the millions of people who had been abused and defiled, tormented, experimented on and murdered there. She knew that if she saw the barrack that they slept in that she would never be able to go on with her life. So, they visited Baia Mare, Hunyad and Dej, going from cemetery to cemetery. Imre promised that he and his brothers-in-law would leave money to repair all the broken headstones, some nearly 100 years old.

Ava and her sisters lit candles at every grave they visited and said prayers. They were stoic and did not cry the entire time they were in Hungary and Romania; not even when they visited the tiny apartment Ava and Lajos lived in when they were first married. Cluj, in comparison to Baia Mare, looked devastating to Ava. She held onto Imre's arm and just wanted to leave.

The hardest part of the trip was when they arrived in Baia Mare. Kati knocked on the door of their childhood home which looked so tiny to them while Ava hid behind Imre. Kati went in with Shlomek, but neither Zita nor Ava could bring themselves to join their sister, though the owners were happy to oblige. All that Ava wanted was to see her mother's garden. It broke her heart to see her mother's carefully planted flowers still growing.

The three women were silent on the bus that evening. As they approached Budapest in preparation for their flight, they stopped at the Hanaj restaurant to have a final meal in Hungary. The Hanaj was the only kosher restaurant in all of Budapest. The men ate heartily while the women just stared at their plates. Once they were back in the air and on their way to Israel, they all sighed in unison. Knowing that Israel was their homeland made it that much easier to put this trip in perspective. When they got to the Western Wall, there at the Kotel, the three sisters cried their hearts out, for what was and what would never be again. It was cathartic, and Ava was glad that they finally performed the *mitzvah* of *kever avot*, visiting the graves of parents, or in this case, grandparents.

Ava was wildly grateful to Imre for caring enough to give her this trip and for truly understanding her needs. Sometimes she didn't know what she wanted, and he never took offense or got angry. By nature, he was entirely different from Lajos and Ava was grateful for who he was. Without knowing it, she slowly began to fall in love with Imre. It happened without her noticing, but Imre was well aware that it wasn't his money or his looks, it was his patience and kindness that finally gave him the prize he sought. He would have gladly waited another 55 years but was very grateful that the moment had arrived.

27

"When it is obvious that the goals cannot be reached, don't adjust the goals, adjust the action steps."
—Confucius

1972

Suzi graduated high school, distraught that her father was not there to see the moment when she began a new chapter in her life. She felt the same way the day she married Zak. Of the three sisters, she had the hardest time accepting Imre, regardless of how well he took care of Mamuka. For Magda, there was a sense of relief that she would no longer have to be Mamuka's go-to person, though it hardly let her off the hook with Mamuka still, habitually asking her to run interference. For Magda, knowing that Imre was there and giving her mother unlimited attention definitely was a game changer. Judy felt the same way and looked to Imre for advice, as he was a very successful businessman and was the catalyst behind Judy's foray into real estate, eventually becoming a very successful broker, who closed deals on many homes in the six figures. It was for Suzi alone, a bone of contention when she saw Imre sitting at the head of the table; it actually made her angry.

The first time they gathered at Mamuka's gorgeous new house, it was Chanukah the Festival of Lights. Ava's new home sparkled, ready to receive and indulge the family gathered together to celebrate. Ava made her incredibly thin but delicious chewy potato pancakes, the *latkes* that everyone loved. When Imre got ready to light the menorah, Suzi felt a fine rage simmering inside her. It should have been her father standing there, doling out the extremely lavish gifts on Hanukkah. The worst part was that Imre was kind, he expected nothing in return. When they sat down at the table, Suzi had to excuse herself. She was livid, eying Imre sitting so comfortably at the head of the table, where her father once sat. Were they all crazy, she wondered?

Magda came looking for her and found her on the back porch. "What is it Suzika?" she gently probed. "Are you and Zak arguing? What's got you so grouchy?"

"Well, Magda," fumed Suzi. "I can't believe that you don't see the utter disgrace and disrespect to Tatuka. Why is that man sitting in his seat?"

Magda nearly burst out laughing but seeing how upset her sister was, controlled her impulse. "Suzi, you are not going to like what I'm about to say but please listen to me. To begin with, this is Imre's house, his table and his seat. He bought this house; he has the right to sit at the head of the table."

"You know what I mean, please don't treat me like a fool. Why is he here and Tatuka isn't," she sobbed.

"Because Tatuka died," said Magda. "Imre had nothing to do with that. Come on, you know that."

"But Mamuka always told us when we were children that she 'paid in' for 10 generations in Auschwitz. How could this happen in our family?" she sobbed.

"Suzika, I am sorry that you believed Mamuka's words in that way. Probably she needs to believe that to somehow help her make sense of her tragic experience. But if we are religious women, then we have to accept that this was Hashem's plan. We have so little control over anything that God decrees," she concluded.

"So, you have no problem with your children calling him Zaydy when he is in fact not their grandfather," Suzi shrieked, "because I will not allow my children to do so."

"Suzika," said Magda sternly, "this man is so good to our mother. To begin with he indulges her every wish. And he is incredibly good to all of us too in case you haven't noticed. Why be angry at him? Or is that just a good excuse to be angry?"

"I don't know what you are talking about," answered Suzi. "Ever since you went back to college you seem to think you are better than the rest of us. Even Hershel told me the same thing last week!"

"Now you are just being plain mean Suzika," said Magda, "and I can't bear to think that you would talk about me behind my back to my husband. Let me guess? Is it my intelligence or my being overweight that bothers my wonderful husband?"

Suzi was silent, recognizing that her sister was right. She was angry; it seemed to her that for no reason, she would simply blow up and find herself unable to be rational and calm. It wasn't Zak, she had a happy life with him. It was her.

She looked at Magda who was really a wonderful big sister, an amazing aunt to her baby daughter Faygala, and felt sad that she hurt her.

"Magdushka, please forgive me. I am an idiot. Really. It's true, I did talk to Hershel, but I promise you, it will never happen again. It was wrong and I feel sick that I betrayed you like that."

Magda looked at her younger sister and felt the sincerity of her words. Suzi was her sister. She loved her, but that didn't mean she didn't see where Suzi was not always as nice as she should be.

"I forgive you," said Magda. "Just please remember this. Our childhood had its ups and downs because of what our parents suffered in the war. But we don't have to bring that into our lives. We have choices. We need to stick together, always be united and supportive, but we must truly recognize in what ways we want to be different. And maybe most importantly, we have to communicate, use our words to express how we feel."

"Magdushka," sighed Suzi, "I think you are reading too many

books. Why think so much? Is it going to help us, if you keep looking at the past?"

"Actually yes," said Magda emphatically. "I recently read an incredible book by a woman named Helen Epstein, who herself is a child of survivors. Do you know that she traveled around the world to interview children of survivors? She had this burning need to find out if other people like herself were also consumed and affected by a history that they themselves had actually never lived."

Magda took a deep breath and continued. "We are not alone Suzika. This brave woman took it upon herself to travel to many countries, to meet and hear the stories of many children of survivors. In her own words, she said something I always felt, that we, in our generation somehow knew that we had to make up for those who died. We always went out of our way to make Mamuka smile. Helen wrote in her book that her two grandmothers whose names were hers, lived through her, and that her parents also were living through her because they saw in her life the years they themselves had lost in the war and the years they had lost in emigrating to America. Don't you see Suzika? There are many children of survivors who grew up with the same concerns we had, the same anxiety, worry, fear and unanswered questions."

Then, lowering her voice Magda added, "Are we to ever forget what happened to *lemala*?"

"Hold on a second," retorted Suzika. "Are you going to blame what Judy did on the fact that our parents were in the war?"

"Yes, I am," said Magda, brooking no opposition with her fierce expression. "There are children of survivors who, how can I put it, absorbed that horrific pain that their parents suffered, as if they themselves were in the war. Please believe me that secondary trauma is real or read just Epstein's book and see what she has to say. There is a connection. Most people don't want to talk about it because they are scared it will upset their parents. You know how we worry about Mamuka? Lots of children of survivors are also like that. But normal daughters whose mothers weren't in the war do not worry obsessively about their parents."

"Wow," said Suzi slowly, "I guess you and Hershel aren't busy having a good time anymore or you wouldn't have time to go over this stuff so much. Me and Zak never talk about the past. I like his family, he likes mine. We love each other and that's it. I just think you are not happy and are looking for some big reason to let you off the hook."

"You mean, why I am fat," asked Magda.

"Exactly," said Suzika. "Look I don't want to hurt your feelings, but it's not normal that you can't keep the weight off. Do you know how terrified Mamuka was when you were pregnant? I don't think a day went by when she didn't tell me."

"That's my point Suzika, but sadly you are in denial, or you just don't want to understand. My weight is 100% connected to Mamuka. Not because she's a Holocaust survivor, but because her way of coping after the fact, was to be in control of everything. And growing up like that, made food so much more important to me because of Mamuka's using it to feel in control. Never mind that our father was heavy and maybe just maybe I inherited that fat gene?"

"Sounds like excuses to me," said Suzi. "All I know is that Mamuka might drive us all a little crazy but I kind of think every mother does. Why is she so different?"

"Well, Suzika, I don't agree with you. It might take you a while and I'll be here whenever you want to talk to me. Let's go back inside and please, if you so highly respect your mother, then be courteous and pleasant to her husband, whom she adores, if you haven't noticed."

Suzi shook her head in disagreement. Magda read too many books but there was no denying she was smart. The anger had simmered and Suzika put her arms out to her sister. As they hugged, she whispered, "I love you Magdushka, even when you were mean to me, you were the one I always needed. I'm sorry if I hurt your feelings, I just want you to be happy."

And Magda, still in her sister's embrace, whispered back, "I also want to be happy. I hope one day that I will find out how to make that happen."

As the sisters walked back into the dining room, Ava looked up quizzically at Magda, but Magda didn't say a word. The women sat down next to their husbands and Magda laughed out loud. On her plate was a large serving of salad, steamed vegetables and a very small slice of Ava's minute steak. Every other plate had mashed potatoes with sauteed onions, stuffed cabbage with rice and a pureed chicken liver crepe with mushroom sauce. Mamuka was still watching her weight for her, as if what she ate at that one meal might make a difference. Some things would never change.

28

"Kindness is the language which the deaf can hear and the blind can see."
—Mark Twain

Judy could not believe that both of her sisters were married and had daughters of their own. While Judy desperately wanted to join the club, and be a married lady, coming into *shul* with a freshly styled *sheitel* on her head, with an adorable baby in her arms, waiting for Mamuka's approval, she knew she wasn't ready. She still was working on herself, though it was years since she had seen Dr. Steiner, the psychiatrist who painstakingly prescribed medication, adjusting it and fine tuning it so that she was able to work through in therapy with Dr. Brody to uncover what had brought her to the point of not wanting to live anymore. No one ever referred to it, but she knew no one forgot it. Along with the unspoken topic of her suicide gesture, no one ever called her *lemala* to her face. In therapy, she learned just how much that bothered her. Ever since she learned more about the partisans, she decided that she was going to marry someone from a Polish or American background if she had any say in the matter, at the right time, when she felt ready to commit to another person.

Perhaps marrying someone altogether who was not a direct descendant of Holocaust survivors might change things.

For now, she loved being an aunt to the little girls, but she had some concerns about Dani. In fact, Dani reminded her of her younger self, and she made a note to reach out to her eldest niece. In the same way that her *nene*s were always there for her and continued to be, she wanted Dani to know she could count on her Aunt Judy.

For Judy, the fact that she lived in the basement of their old home which Mamuka refused to sell even when she and Imre bought a new house, gave her a measure of comfort. The downstairs reminded her of Magda's early married years and when she felt like she needed to connect with the past, she could go upstairs. In fact, the basement suited her just fine. It was comfortable, it was roomy, and she had the solitude she craved, the space just for herself so she could be alone with her thoughts, some of which were difficult, even these many years later. Ava repeatedly thanked Judy for living in the house, thrilled that the house did not seem abandoned and therefore vulnerable to vagrants or thieves.

Certainly, her life was not what Mamuka had in mind, but ever since the incident, Mamuka treaded very carefully with her. It was possible her best friend Rose gave her advice. It seemed that whatever Rose Seltzer said was taken very seriously by Mamuka. So maybe one day she would have to acknowledge Dr. Seltzer for being in her corner. She liked the woman a great deal. Had she not been Mamuka's best friend, Judy knew she would have enjoyed being her protegee. What an incredible woman! Judy was in awe of Dr. Seltzer's achievements, her status as a lecturer and writer, ever since she had retired as principal of Yeshiva Crown Park.

Judy was not the only person who was mesmerized with Rose Seltzer. People came from all over to hear her speak. She was dynamic and thanks to Ava, she was now incredibly stylish and well dressed. Rose barely recognized herself when she got dressed. She adored her classic clothes, the navy wool Bill Blass suit that Ava of course got her at a discount along with her very fashionable Jackie Kennedy felt pillbox hat in the same matching blue that Ava assured her was a necessity to pull it all together, giving her a sophisticated look she never imagined could ever be her. Her husband loved her new look, even after these many years of marriage. Rose was delighted with the friendship!

29

> "The pessimist complains about the wind, the optimist expects it to change, the realist adjusts the sails."
> —William Arthur Ward

Judy was right. Hers was not the same path most girls took. She proudly did not get married until she was 26 years old, way past her prime, as told to her by her mother for six years straight. But she didn't really much care what Ava said, because she was in love. It was a love that was not obsessive or needy as in past relationships. It was simply about loving this person and wanting to be with him all the time. When Judy invited him to her basement apartment, she knew she was ready to commit to him. He was the first person that she could share her space with, without fearing he would deprive her of her freedom. Shlomek, who preferred to be called Jack, was perfect for her. He was tall enough, smart enough and rich enough to impress her mother, he was kind like Imre Baci and nothing at all like her father. Judy thought she had found Nirvana and anticipated her life with Jack Dembrowsky. Within five years she had three babies and finally she could keep up with her sisters.

30

"Life isn't about finding yourself. Life is about creating yourself."
—George Bernard Shaw

Ava now had nine granddaughters, more than she ever thought possible. In her estimation, eight of them were adorable and sweet and connected to her. Only Dani seemed distant and not at all receptive to being part of the family. When Dani insisted she wanted to go abroad for high school at the prestigious Gateshead School in London, no one was surprised. Magda cried for days that her Dani would miss out on so many precious family moments, but Dani seemed oblivious to whatever Magda tried to foist upon her. Magda, determined not to repeat history, did not badger her daughter, remembering her very own pledge. But it backfired on her as she found herself begging her daughter and even trying to guilt her into coming back to New York. But Dani wasn't having it. She had already decided she would live in England, intended to go to college and get married to the first man who proposed to her. She was especially anxious to get to know some of the city's most eligible Jewish bachelors like Charles Benadin, who was ten years her senior and poised to go into business with his uncle who was making a name for himself as an incredibly generous charitable man who was also immeasurably wealthy.

For Dani, while her family was in the U.S., her life was in Europe. She loved exploring different cities. She worked as a waitress through college until she got her law degree and visited Ireland, Scotland, France, Belgium, Germany, Holland and Italy with her school mates. The day she arrived at a youth hostel in Berlin, she felt absolutely no guilt at being in Germany, though this nation had singlehandedly and systematically destroyed her ancestors. The day she first ate *treif*, non-kosher, she felt a small sense of remorse but decided that she needed to be herself and not adhere to ancient dietary laws. Maybe one day that might appeal to her, but right now, this was the life she wanted and was going to have. It was a far cry from the life her sisters and her cousins were going to have, and she knew that. She just needed to get out from under, from the ghetto-like cult that was her family from as far back as she could remember. And moving 10,000 miles away was definitely enough distance, even for her.

To say that Magda was conflicted was an understatement. On the one hand, she was enormously proud that her daughter was going to become a lawyer; but on the other hand, knowing that she was not observant or keeping Shabbos was extremely painful to her. Why, she agonized, did Dani choose not to embrace the *Yiddishkeit* that Ava survived for? Wasn't that why Ava survived? Magda hid this from her mother, pretending that she supported Dani's desire to be European, almost as an homage to her grandmother, but somehow the fact that Ava very seldom asked about her first granddaughter seemed peculiar to Magda. Ava, who had her pulse on everything that went on, who she and her sisters laughingly wondered had a bulletin board with all their names pinned on so she could keep track of who was where and doing what, was she the one who didn't ask about Dani? Was it even remotely possible, wondered Magda, that maybe her mother didn't badger her to spare her feelings? Magda hoped that was the case; if Mamuka cared enough about her feelings to actually not comment or criticize her, then it was almost worth it to her that her eldest daughter, her shining star, chose to abandon her.

Nevertheless, the fact remained that Dani did not reconnect with any family member until by coincidence she met Ray Salem, her cousin Fay's best friend who was married to Charles' younger brother Sammy. When Ray found out she was Magda's oldest daughter, the floodgates opened as Ray knew more about her family than she did. For Dani, it was the first time in years that she admitted to herself that she missed her family. Her reunion in Israel at Fay's epic wedding to her beloved Baruch, with her parents, her sisters, aunts and grandmother Ava was indescribable. Seeing her 90-year-old Bobby Ava made her cry.

Dani wondered for the first time if she hadn't made a mistake. Though she had vowed to marry the first boy who asked her, in fact, she was afraid to get married. In therapy, she discovered that her father's betrayal so soon after her parents had married was the reason. As angry as she was at her father, she was even more angry that her mother had confided in her when she was a child and ill-equipped to comfort or bolster her heartbroken mother. Long after her parents had reconciled, she remained the keeper of the wound in their marriage, the ugly scar that never healed properly. Seeing her cousin Fay and learning how she had overcome far worse adversity, made her reconsider. She thought that if she moved to Israel, perhaps she too might find a wonderful man and get reacquainted with her religious upbringing and with her grandmother, who still remained a force to be reckoned with, still eager to live another day, for the next chapter in her life.

Yes, Dani, I will consider working in the Tel Aviv branch of the law firm. After all, if Bobby Ava could rise again, after living through the Holocaust and burying two husbands, to taking an active role in the global AvaFay, Fay's clothing company, then what the hell was her excuse?

31

"Creativity takes courage."
—Pablo Picasso

When Ava was reunited with Dani, she felt a weight lifted from her shoulders. The fact that Fay had moved to Israel was always a source of agony for her, but Fay frequently came to America and maintained a strong bond with her. That was not the case with Dani. Ava knew from the time Dani was a child that she was entirely too mature. She never acted like a child. She wasn't surprised that Dani could not find one high school that she wanted to attend, even though her parents offered her the option of any school in any borough. I am certain that she wants to get away from us, Ava recalled telling Imre. "I think she doesn't want to be close to us."

Ava remembered being startled when Imre agreed with her. Normally, he was the one who reassured her that her speculations were simply a manifestation of her worrying too much, but he did not.

"I think, Ava *dragam*," he began, "that living with Magdushka has affected her."

In a rare moment of insight, Ava remembered laughing and saying to Imre, "And living with me was easy on my girls, you think?"

Imre, loving his wife, did not point out the obvious, that indeed Judy had nearly died, not because Ava was a bad mother, but because the trauma of what she went through became part of the family legacy, woven into the fabric of their family, from generation to generation. That was what he believed Dani had to get away from. Imre was right, concluded Ava.

How ironic that now in Israel, in her 90th year, she would get to spend time with her two beloved granddaughters, Fay and Dani, both of whom now lived in Israel. Almost weekly, one of her other granddaughters was calling from America to plan a visit. With Suzi and Zak already owners of their own apartment nearby, and Judy considering buying a condominium in Herzliya, Ava felt marvelous. She would, as long as she lived, believe that family mattered the most. All she needed was strength and good help to manage the linens and meals.

It was only when she went to *Amcha*, the social services agency in Israel, that for the first time in her life Ava found out how her trauma irreparably was generationally transmitted biologically, environmentally and psychologically. It was almost traumatic finding out that her girls struggled because of what happened to her. Ava was so overcome and distraught with what she discovered that she immediately called her sisters Zita and Kati, hoping she could make them both aware of the depth of their life experience too. But neither were that interested, both not being in the best of health. Kati had developed a weak heart, and Zita was in remission from breast cancer.

Ava worried day and night about her sisters and spoke to her nieces daily to make sure no one was hiding anything from her, simply because she was 10,000 miles away. Ava remembered grimly how her precious Fay hid things from all of them and she never wanted to be in that position ever again. When the time was right, if it ever would be, she would share with her sisters what she had learned. For her, it was a game changer. If they never wanted to go down that path, that was fine too, as long as they were okay and continued to visit her at least three times a year in conjunction with Rosh Hashanah and Yom Kippur, the High Holy Days, Shavuot and summer. When her sisters and brothers-in-law came, they stayed with her for four or more weeks and Ava loved having them. She prayed that both of her cherished sisters would ultimately decide to join her in Israel, so that they could be reunited once again. In the meantime, Ava decided that she would immediately share her revelations with her own girls, Magda, Suzi and Judy. If anything, they were the ones who needed to know what she knew.

32

"Tell me and I forget. Teach me and I remember. Involve me and I learn."
—Benjamin Franklin

When Ava finally got the opportunity to gather her very busy daughters in her beautiful apartment in Rechavia, she started the conversation.

"So, girls, I asked you here for a reason," she began.

"What is it Mamuka?" asked Suzi, her voice unnaturally high. "Are you okay?"

"*Persze, határozottan* [of course]," replied Ava in Hungarian. Before she could continue, it was in that instant that Ava realized just how much her daughters worried about her and always had. It broke her heart and for a minute, she looked her full 90 years. Taking a deep breath, she began.

"After Fay's wedding, you know I became very close to Rabbi Shanzer. I knew the minute I saw him that there was something familiar about him. Oh, how I hoped that maybe he was a long-lost blood relative. He is not actually, but close enough. He is my sister-in-law Necha Liba's nephew. What an unusual, kind, brilliant man."

Her daughters looked at her, wondering where this story was

going. Magda had literally just gotten off the plane, greeted by Dani at the airport and came straight to see Ava who had insisted on this reunion. She couldn't wait any longer.

"Mamuka, honestly, none of us are young and I for one am *nagyon kimerült*. Can you kindly tell us why you wanted to see us?" she pleaded.

Ava again took a deep breath.

"Yes, Magdushka," she said crossly. "A little patience please. I was just getting to that. Rabbi Shanzer recommended that I go to Amcha, which I had never heard of. As you know, in the months since I moved here, he became like a son to me, and I didn't hesitate. I thought he wanted me to give my testimony or to speak about AvaFay and how so many Hasidic women are employed by the company. Little did I know this social services agency is run by therapists who are all children of survivors, and they provide a range of services to survivors and their children."

She paused and her hands trembled as she continued. "I learned a lot when I went to Amcha. I want to ask the three of you to join me and meet my therapist, Dr. Chagit Levy."

Suzi nearly fell out of her chair as she absorbed her mother's words. "Mamuka, you have a therapist?" Then turning to face her sisters, she said again, "Our mother has a therapist? I believe *moshiach* is coming, the messiah is on his way."

Suzi began to cry. Judy and Magda raced to envelop her, and soon they were all crying while Ava tried to understand what she had said to cause such a reaction in her daughters. Didn't they understand that this was a good thing she was proposing?

Ava cleared her throat and her three daughters, middle-aged women whom she loved beyond measure, looked at her. "May I know why this is such an emotional moment," Ava asked timidly. "I have so much more to say."

This time Judy took the lead, cutting away from her sisters to hold her mother's hand. "Mamuka, the three of us have been in therapy for years. Not just me because of what happened, but Suzi and Magda too. I think Suzika cried because this is something we've hoped for and never dared to ask you to do for us."

Magda and Suzi shook their heads in agreement.

"Mamuka," said Magda, "we never ever blamed you or Tatuka. A lot of the time we thought we were different because you were European. And let's be honest Mamuka, when we were kids, you had some pretty serious standards of what you expected from us. And while that didn't help the situation, the real truth is that we were deathly afraid of what you went through... to hear you say that you want to go to therapy with us so that we can all come to terms with what happened, is beyond belief."

Now it was Ava who was sobbing uncontrollably, and her daughters surrounded her.

"Please Mamuka, Imre would kill us if he knew you were crying," said Suzi trying to lighten the mood, "That man loved you more than any woman, even you Mamuka, deserved."

Ava stopped crying and looking at her daughters and in a rare moment conceded, "Oy, but did I make him sweat until I could love him back."

Once again, her daughters were astounded. Their mother was so real, was it age, thought Judy? Was Mamuka losing it and unable to control what she was saying? But looking at her mother, Judy knew for sure that Ava's cognitive skills were not on the decline whatsoever. Ava was simply reaping the benefit of intense cognitive behavioral therapy and happy to put into words all that she had uncovered and what she knew she had to share with her precious daughters.

"So, the plan is," she said briskly, "before Magda falls asleep, is for us to meet with Dr. Levy and just talk. And why Magdushka, you can't stay with me here, I'll never know."

"Mamuka," said Magda, patiently and lovingly, "Dani wants me, and I have plenty to make up with her. I know I am the reason she left and the fact that she wants me in her life..." Magda started heaving.

"Please *dragam*," said Ava, "don't cry. It's my fault, I know it is."

Suzi, ever sensible Suzi, intervened. "From this day forward, we never use the word blame. We all have our feelings and our histories, but please let's remember, no one was to blame for anything. And honestly Mamuka, you gave us so much that we in turn gave to our daughters. That's what matters."

They all agreed to continue the conversation with Dr. Levy.

Ava led them into her beautiful dining room which was elegantly set for lunch with cloth napkins and Limoge china. When Ora brought in the first course, a delightful cream of asparagus soup with freshly made garlic bread croutons, Magda started to laugh. "Shouldn't I be getting a salad," she teased, looking at her mother.

To her surprise, Ava's face turned bright pink. "Oh Magdushka, can you ever forgive me, all those years, how I must have embarrassed you all those many years."

Magda looked at her mother, completely stunned. "Mamuka, in my entire life, I never thought I would live to hear you say that."

Magda hesitated, wanting to continue to tell her mother how awful she felt at every meal, at every family occasion for disappointing her mother, because she was too big, but she did not. There would be time to unpack all of that with Dr. Levy. Instead, she took a deep breath and lifted her silver spoon.

The ladies enjoyed Ava's fresh salad, quinoa and grilled salmon and were stunned when Ora brought in coffee and tiramisu for dessert. Ava laughed out loud as her daughters' jaws all literally dropped at the same time.

"Life is too short," she said gaily, "to worry about cholesterol and calories. And anyways, look at my beauties, every one of you can afford to have dessert."

"Mamuka," said Judy, "I speak for my sisters. I am sure when I tell you that I cannot wait to meet Dr. Levy. The change in you is incredible!"

"Well, my darling you will have your chance tomorrow. Now," she said, rising from the table, "you will all excuse me. I need to place some fabric orders for the factory and Magda needs a nap more than I do."

Then, she said under her breath, to no one in particular, though they all heard her, as she intended, "When did they all get so old?"

All three women burst out laughing at the irony of their mother's jab. Ava wasn't old, she never would be, with her zest for life, her facials and exercise. She had enormous stamina and vitality and truly looked remarkable. But her daughters were getting old!

33

"If something is wrong, fix it now. But train yourself not to worry, worry fixes nothing."
—Ernest Hemingway

The very next morning Ava and her daughters had breakfast at Ava's home. Once again Magda was amused and amazed at the change in Mamuka, who not only didn't care what Magda ate, but actually ate her own breakfast with gusto. Magda recalled all the years when Ava would simply pick at her food, barely eating, seemingly repulsed by food. Was it possible that Mamuka in those years had a hard time eating because of her wartime experience? Magda decided, as she ate her eggs benedict, that she didn't really care. Not only did she enjoy her food, but it was a joy to see Mamuka enjoy her meal too.

Suzi, dressed in a new turquoise knit outfit, perfect for Jerusalem weather, looked at Mamuka's sideboard groaning with the amount of food it was holding. It looked almost identical to the lavish hotel breakfast that most of the Israeli hotels laid out for their guests. The smoked cheeses, the fragrant fruits, the fresh baguettes and rugelach, salads, cereals, and fishes so artfully laid out and large enough to feed at least 20 people.

"Well," said Suzi laughing, "I see some things haven't changed. Mamuka, how much did you think we were going to eat?"

To which her elegantly clad mother, dressed in a simple pale pink silk sheath dress with a matching kitten toe heel, replied, "First of all, Suzika, I want you all to have a nice breakfast, because as you know, breakfast is the most important meal of the day and second of all…"

She was interrupted by the peals of laughter, from all of her daughters. "What is is so funny?" she asked. "Or are you three so simple that you don't know that breakfast is important to properly give you energy for the whole day?"

To which the girls erupted into shrieks of more laughter. Mamuka looked at her daughters and tears rolled down her face. In her entire life, though there had been numerous wonderful moments while the girls were growing up, she did not remember ever hearing them all laugh with such wild abandon. Apparently, life then was not so hysterically funny. As Ava listened and loved the sound of their laughter, she noted her thanks to God. How incredibly lucky was she that life had brought her, at this stage in her life, to a moment in time when she could see her daughters feel so happy?

Drying her tears which not one daughter noticed, Ava continued. "If I may remind you three that this is a breakfast table and not a hoedown in a barn?"

Again, three pairs of luminous, expressive eyes stared at her.

"Mamuka," gasped Judy, still laughing, "I feel like we are girls again and you are so desperate to instill good manners in us, trying so hard to fight the American culture which you found so beneath your European standards."

Ava replied stiffly, "I suppose it's never too late if I haven't been successful at illustrating how young ladies should compose themselves at the table." But she said this while broadly smiling, so that the girls would know she was joking.

"Actually," she continued, "you three could do no wrong. You are perfect the way you are, and every one of my granddaughters is so fortunate to have you as their mother."

Magda's butter knife dropped out of her hands as she fully absorbed her mother's words. "Mamuka," she whispered, trying hard not to cry, "I never ever heard you say anything remotely similar to what you just said. I wonder if you know how I longed, all my fat years, to hear you say that you loved me, admired me and accepted me, exactly the way I am."

"Magdushka, you have daughters of your own," said Ava wistfully. "Surely, even living as an American, you must know how terrible it is for their long-term development to over-praise them? I always told Kati and Zita and your father of course, but I wasn't going to ruin you girls by telling you how perfect you were. Think of those Loman boys in Arthur Miller's *Death of a Salesman*, over-praising them to the point that they were failures all their lives."

"Mamuka, I think," said Judy, trying to steer the topic from getting too serious, "that we are meant to enjoy this extraordinary morning together. Plenty of time for serious talk. Let's just agree on something we've known all our lives, and I hope you are ready for this revelation."

"Judyka, don't be silly, at this point in my life, after all that I have lived through, I promise I can handle whatever you are going to say. Honestly, it is just so wonderful to hear you talk, so say your truth my darling, I want to hear it."

Each of Ava's daughters sat in near shock. Their mother had evolved in her advanced age into a woman who was aware, humble, articulate and capable of hearing them.

"Well," drawled Judy, "here it is. There is a cultural divide between us. Yes, Mamuka, we are American, our daughters and grandchildren are Americans as will their children be. You on the other hand, while a beautiful, sophisticated elegant Hungarian woman who became a citizen of our wonderful country, is not, in fact, American."

This time it was Ava who set off the laughter, literally howling with glee, a sound that was rare for her.

"That's your *Gemara* [Biblical commentary] on what divides us Judyka? I know you may not believe this, but I am grateful to God that you are Americans! And yes, I will admit," she said reluctantly, "I don't love everything I see and hear, not from you girls, but from let's just say, your daughters... but I know it's not my place to say anything and for sure to stop judging."

"Okay," said Suzi, dramatically rising, but really getting up to hug her mother, "who are you and what have you done with our real mother?"

The four of them laughed until they couldn't laugh anymore, and, in the kitchen, Ora smiled at the sound of their voices. She loved Mrs. Kertesz fiercely and knew firsthand how much she had struggled. She herself was a daughter of Yemenite Jews and remembered stories of survival from her own mother.

"Ladies, it is time for us to leave," said Ava, "but I did want to tell you all that I never in my life ever wasted food, not since 1945 and I'm not starting now. So don't worry about the leftovers. In five minutes, Ora will start packing everything up and delivering it to the nearby *yeshivot*. The children in the local schools love my food and the Rabbi luckily knows me and trusts me that everything is as kosher as *Bdatz*, the highest kosher certification here in Jerusalem."

"Mamuka," said Magda, "you never cease to amaze me. I have no words. Quoting Arthur Miller, extending yourself to the needy... All I can say is that I'm glad that I have your DNA and I hope when I grow up to be exactly like you."

"Magdushka," said Ava lovingly, "don't be silly, you are the best of me and your father. Don't ever try to be anything but yourself."

As the four of them quickly said *Birkat Hamazon*, the blessing after eating a meal, each in her own way felt gratified and happy. Could the day get any better, they wondered?

34

> "The question isn't who is going to let me; it's who is going to stop me."
> —Ayn Rand

The day was in fact the catalyst for much good that would ultimately become a vehicle for Suzika to start a new career as a writer and lecturer for thousands of other descendants of the Holocaust to hear first-hand how it was possible to move past the generational symptoms of trauma that reached undoubtedly to the next generation.

At Amcha, the three women sat in silence as they took in everything Dr. Chagit Levy, in perfect English, explained to them. She gave them a brief history of what Amcha attempted to provide to its clients, how the social service agency became a leader in developing unparallelled psychosocial support for Holocaust traumatization, including its long-term implications and far more long-lasting, delayed-onset reactions. The women were in awe at the range of services that were available to individuals, couples, families, and groups to help them cope with anxiety, depression, loss and bereavement. Rabbi Shanzer, in sending their mother for grief counseling to get help dealing with Imre's death, had unwittingly changed the landscape not only of Ava's life, but of theirs.

The three-hour consultation was an intense but deeply meaningful experience for all four of them. The comfortable chairs were arranged in a circle so that each participant could maintain eye contact and derive support from each other. Dr. Levy, a lovely woman in her mid-forties, was originally from Sydney, Australia, where her grandmother was born. She disclosed her story to Ava's daughters, choosing to illustrate to them that she too came from a family of survivors. She explained to the women how life had been good to her great grandparents when they were taken by transport to Australia, but within a matter of a few years, decided they wanted to live freely as Jews in their own homeland. The ladies were drawn to this incredible woman who had devoted her life to interacting and working with survivors and their offspring. As they left, Ava lingered for a moment.

"Dr. Levy," she said, "what did you think of my beautiful daughters?"

"Ava, all of them are rare, strong, unique women. You can rest assured that in spite of all the trauma you dealt with while trying to be a mother, you succeeded. I am so happy that this day has come."

Ava nodded, knowing if she spoke, she might lose herself. She had held herself together all of her life and Dr Levi's validation that in spite of what happened to her, that her daughters had triumphed made her happy.

"I look forward to seeing you on Thursday," she finally replied. "And please make sure all the staff will be hungry. I am bringing lunch."

Ava recognized that her largesse was her innate nature and in therapy also came to understand that it represented far more to her than merely to feed people. It gave her the opportunity to do her *tikkun olam*, repairing the world, feeding people, to make up for the emaciated, bone-wasting starving lager sisters in Auschwitz, nearly all who would have killed for a crumb, who traded their bodies and their souls for an ounce of gruel.

Ava could still recall how one night, shortly before the Death

March in the winter of 1945, when she started crying in the middle of the night. Zita held her, terrified that the cruel Jewish *kapo* in charge of their barrack would happily make an example of Ava and silence her for good.

"What is it, my precious?" asked Zita.

"I want rice," said Ava, barely speaking at an audible level.

By now Zita was up and right next to her sisters on the wooden rack that was supposed to function as a bed.

"Ava," she pleaded, "please, we are going to get beat or shot if we don't stop talking."

"Maybe that would be better," said Ava bitterly. "If I can't have some rice, I am going to die right now."

Zita rose and Kati nearly shrieked.

"Zita, where are you going? Please come back," she begged. "Please, I will die right here with Ava, if something happens to you. I promised Mamuka and Surika, right before they were separated from us, that I would take care of you. Please, please!"

But it was too late. Zita walked swiftly out of the barrack, in her rags, with no shoes to protect her feet and made her way to the camp kitchen where she worked during the day. In years to come, when she shared the story with her own daughters, she swore it was only Hashem, one God, who protected her so that she could get to the leftover rice that she often hid, to bring back to Ava and not get shot in the process.

When Ava saw the rice, she looked at Kati to tell her she wasn't hallucinating. Kati just looked at her sisters and said, "Zita, you are my hero."

Ava ate rice until there was none left and never ever again in her life could she eat rice again.

35

> "Enlightenment is always preceded by confusion. "
> —Milton H. Erickson

The sisters looked at their mother, trying to take a cue from her. They wanted to go over every single detail that the session had uncovered. But for Ava, who started the day promptly at 6:00 a.m. in her garden, followed by her flower arranging, yoga and *tefila*, it was time for a nap.

"Girls," she said reluctantly, "I wish I could join you. I know you have a lot to talk about. How about you all go to the newly renovated spa at The King David Hotel, have a light lunch, massages and then we will have dinner together later?"

The women looked at their beloved mother gratefully. At 90 she was still so intuitive, so empathetic, understanding exactly what they needed.

"Yes, Mamuka," said Magdushka. "I think that is a perfect plan. You rest and we will do the spa!"

Ava's driver took her home first and then drove the ladies to the hotel. On the brief ride to the hotel, Judy requested a small detour.

"Girls," she said, "would you be okay if we went to the kotel first? I really want to *daven* and pray at The Wailing Wall right now."

Magda held herself back from making any unkind or judgmental remark, wondering to herself when her baby sister had become so spiritual? Was it after her divorce when she had a series of relationships with various inappropriate men? Or was it at menopause when there was nothing left anymore? Magda wisely kept her thoughts to herself. If she had learned anything in therapy, when she took control of her compulsive eating and steered herself into a healthy body that she loved, it was that she didn't always have to share every single thought she had. She remembered sharing this revelation with Suzika.

"Suzika," she said at exactly 8:04 a.m. when the girls had left for school, "why do you think we always felt like we had to say everything we thought, as kids?"

Suzika, herself a veteran of years of group therapy and extensive research, reading every book related to the transmission of trauma from survivors to their children, simply replied, "I'm not exactly sure, Magdushka, but maybe it was something we picked up from Mamuka, Kati and Zita, who felt, after liberation, that it was their right to talk, to breathe, to scream without fear of dying? And as little girls we internalized that and believed that was how it was supposed to be."

Magda remembered clapping excitedly.

"Yes, *dragam*, I think you are right, dearest."

Magda learned from that day forward that she could not only control her mouth, but she could literally also control her thoughts and her mood. Often, she looked back and wished that she had had the ability to do so before Dani was impacted. Magda vividly recalled the day she was writing in her journal when it occurred to her that she had made Dani into her confidant exactly like Ava had done to her, burdening her with details about her traumatic discovery of Hershel's infidelity, something she had no right to tell her young impressionable daughter just because she was socialized to believe that her daughter was there to absorb all of her pain. Magda remembered screaming and crying, closing her journal, sick with shame and anger, repulsed by her own behavior. Why hadn't she recognized that she had overstepped a boundary and turned her darling Dani into her sounding board the same way Mamuka did to her, the difference being that Mamuka was a Holocaust survivor and in attempting to cope with her survivor's guilt and anxiety, depression, headaches and often crippling fear couldn't possibly shield her. But she should have done better and that was why she never imposed any of her problems on her other two daughters. They were just her daughters, not her friends.

36

"The purpose of our lives is to be happy."
—Dalai Lama

The three glorious hours that the sisters spent at the spa was exhilarating and rejuvenating. Judy insisted on treating her sisters to the decadent facials and deep tissue massages.

"It's my utter pleasure, girls," she said when each insisted on paying their share. "I just got an exclusive listing at the insanely opulent new condos going up in Herzliya and I have three solid prospective buyers lined up from New York, L.A., and Montreal."

Suzi and Magda were proud of their baby sister and though they never revisited the harrowing events that brought Judy to near death, both were ecstatic that she was at the very least successful in her career and could afford to live life on her own terms. It had been a shock when Judy and Shlomek had divorced. They of the three couples seemed to be the happiest and yet Shlomek couldn't handle Judy's spectacular success, or so Judy told them.

Judy loved her life. She had the financial freedom to live her life as she pleased, and if she was lonely, she knew how to distract herself. Her dear sisters still considered her fragile, she was well aware of that. They were always available to her and so were her nieces, more so than her own daughters. Judy accepted that because she wanted her daughters to live their own lives. In true American fashion, she invited them every year for Thanksgiving, and they almost always attended with their friends or boyfriends. Would she have liked more, like her sisters appeared to have with their daughters? Suzuka had her hands full with Bethie having babies every year and Magda was constantly babysitting for her daughters or going on cruises with Hershel and their friends.

Of course, she might have liked more of that, but she was never going to make her daughters feel in any way responsible for her happiness; only she was responsible for that. When she had too much time on her hands, Judy got on a plane, called any number of old discarded boyfriends, sponsored a charity lunch, had some cosmetic surgery or shopped. Altogether not a bad plan and she had no regrets. That none of her daughters was married yet or indicated that they ever wanted to have children was something she never allowed herself to dwell on. They could choose whatever life they wanted; how observant or not observant, whether they wanted to be straight or gay, live in New York or Hong Kong, smoke pot or cigarettes, have long hair or short, was all fine with her. Judy was certain that this was how the legacy of both her mother's and father's trauma would end; they who fought to live, never realized that they inadvertently took over the lives of their own children. Now, these many years later, stepping aside and knowing her children did not have to compete with her for their lives, gave Judy a great sense of satisfaction.

37

"Freedom is the oxygen of the soul."
—Moshe Dayan

What happened that day in the City Center at Amcha didn't stop there. For Ava it was liberating, gratifying and exhilarating to address the past and know that it was finally over. She and her daughters met with Dr. Levy for many weeks in person and then segued into conference calls which were not as effective but kept the dialogue going. For Suzi, it was everything she ever wanted, to put her parents' wartime experience in perspective.

When she returned to New York, after asking her mother and her sisters for their permission, she began to speak to other people, to share what she, her mother and her sisters learned in session. It began in her home innocently enough on a Shabbos afternoon when she invited eight women, all of whom were her contemporaries and children of Holocaust survivors. They talked until the sun went down, not one single person willing to end the conversation. It seemed as if not one person in the room had ever connected that suppressed emotional pain often manifests physically as an eating disorder, anxiety, a phobia, physical pain, migraine headache, chronic stomach issues, eczema, psoriasis or other skin eruptions.

Not one person in the room ever knew that there could be a powerful link between their present-day thoughts, behaviors, adaptability and emotional dysregulation to their childhood exposure to traumatized parents and grandparents. And they were grateful for the knowledge. From there, Suzi began to speak at schools, both yeshiva and public schools, at Jewish centers and Holocaust museums across many states, on Yom Hashoah and before Yom Kippur.

The reception was staggering. It seemed like everyone was either a child or grandchild not just of Holocaust survivors, but of trauma. People wrote and messaged her day and night with their stories. Suzi began to keep a record of some of their stories and within 18 months she wrote a book. Each chapter, simply and unembellished, detailed a story of survival post-Holocaust from both the survivor and their children's perspective. The book was met with great interest and enthusiasm by thousands of people.

For Suzi this was a turning point in her life. Meeting with people, some who traveled from overseas to attend one of her workshops, was an eye-opener for her. How was it possible that neither she nor her sisters had ever considered that thousands of people in their generation, whose parents were Holocaust survivors, might also have experienced much of what they did?

One night, after tossing and turning for hours, Suzi tapped her husband's shoulder. "Zak," she whispered, "are you awake?"

"I am now, Suzi. Are you hot? Do you want me to lower the heat?"

"No, no, no," she said, desperately trying to hide the irritation in her voice. She hated menopause and just wished it would go away. Even Zak's being solicitous of her night sweats was annoying.

"I figured it out," she started again.

"What might that be Suzi," asked Zak, who was used to many proclamations and announcements that his wife made.

"I figured out," she began. "The puzzle. I think I always believed that my being raised religious was somehow the reason my parents didn't get help. But now, after talking to so many people, from Germany, Holland, Belgium, Italy, France and Greece, I realize that being religious had nothing to do with how we the second generation were affected by what happened to our parents because most of their parents, most of whom were Jewish in name only, also had parents who acted just like my parents, overprotective, overbearing, moody, hypervigilant, depressed, anxious, and a bundle of contradictions."

"You figured that out, Suzi," said Zak in awe. "That is really impressive. Maybe it's because I'm half asleep but I'm not sure I get your point."

"Seriously Zak," said Suzi, this time not bothering to hide her annoyance, "I'm trying to share with you, this means so much to me!"

"I hear you Suzi," pleaded Zak, taking her hand, and attempting to hold her. "Can we try this again in the morning?"

Suzi relented. He was a good man, more than she deserved, for putting up with her moods, for agreeing to going to couples counseling when neither of her two brothers in laws would consider it. Not even Jack, when his marriage to Judy was blowing up.

"Okay Zak," she said, turning to face him. "Time enough in the morning. Sleep well darling."

For Suzi, being able to finally let go of the learned behavior of her beloved Tatuka, the explosive anger he couldn't control, that used to accompany most exchanges with her husband, was an unparalleled victory. Years of therapy and working on herself, forcing herself to a level of self-awareness had helped enormously. What gave her equally as much satisfaction was that both of her sisters had done the same for themselves. By the time they met Dr. Levy, collectively they had been in therapy for 25 years.

But it was that life changing experience, going with Mamuka to therapy and witnessing Mamuka's utter dejection at how her daughters had inadvertently absorbed her trauma was truly the moment Suzi became whole. All the years of therapy, all the years of reading the voluminous research that she couldn't quite piece together finally crystallized and came together when she, her sisters and their mother sat in that circle with Dr. Levy. It was as painful as childbirth, agonizing waves of pain, terror and anxiety that coursed through her. Pained by the knowledge that she and her sisters never had a fighting chance. They were already compromised by their mother's cortisol level in utero. At birth and beyond, during their critical developmental years, their needs, she learned, were automatically put on hold, as the family collectively and unconsciously adapted to the needs of two parents who were nobly doing their best to cope with PTSD, all while trying to forget the past, acclimating themselves to a host country that wasn't very accommodating, raising a family, dealing with marriage and financial woes. And terror, Suzi remembered, morbidly afraid that her mother would have a heart attack and die, right there. And anxiety, that maybe no amount of denouement could ever undo the impact on her own daughters as they also were forced to adapt to growing up with parents who were children of Holocaust survivors.

Suzi remembered thinking, but not sharing, that on some level she felt her parents had a better chance of resuming life because they had had 20 years of a foundation in which they acquired the values of their religious belief system, their cultural norms and an environment that supported their growing needs, while she and her sisters and most likely thousands of other children of survivors were born into an environment loaded with trauma symptoms that invariably shaped them from the moment they were conceived.

38

"Success is to be measured not so much by the position that one has reached in life as by the obstacles which he has overcome while trying to succeed."
—Booker T. Washington

Zak sighed as he rose from his bed. He loved his wife and tried hard to be the kind of husband that she craved. But he knew that he fell short because he was not a financial success in the years when Suzi desperately wanted a bigger house, a country home, and a Florida condo, even though her mother and Imre had a condo big enough to accommodate the entire family. How ironic he thought, as he headed to the shower, glancing at Suzi fast asleep, the love in his heart making him smile as he looked at his bride of 35 years. Suzi was no longer young, but in his eyes, she was and would always be beautiful. Now, when Suzi was so much less materialistic, now, when she no longer had the drive to clothe herself in designer fashion, on her own, through her book, lectures, and workshops, she could afford to indulge herself and did not. He was so proud of his wife, for sharing her knowledge and experience with others. In fact, although he would never admit it, he read her book and found it to be illuminating and thought provoking. It caused him to do some reflection and try to understand his own parents and the family dynamics that impacted on his own emotional growth.

Growing up, Zak instinctively knew that his father was not okay. He just wasn't. He never smiled and hardly spoke. He never ever played ball with his sons because he was always working. He worked day and night like many fathers in the neighborhood and Zak mostly got to see him by the Shabbos table. He didn't have much to say to his father, he recalled, because his father seemed distant and tuned out most of the time. It was his mother whom he relied on for emotional sustenance and she was happy to oblige, up to a point, because she too worked and took care of them, leaving her with little time for indulging her sons. Zak also understood that his mother felt that boys needed to be raised with a strong hand. Zak very vividly recalled trying very hard to please his parents to somehow make up for their six long years of suffering, in five different concentration camps and he wanted his daughters to know that. He remembered one YomTov meal at his in-laws' house during Pesach at the Seder when he tried to teach his daughters about the magnitude of the redemption the Jews experienced in Egypt and tried to describe to them what his own parents had endured before their liberation. It was a complete and total disaster. For whatever reason, it was not what his in-laws were prepared to hear. His mother-in-law shut him down and he never ever dared speak of the Holocaust ever again. Being quiet was something Zak was all too familiar with. At an early age he learnt that he was far better off keeping quiet. His older brother Mendy was the one who tried to assert himself and got shot down time and again by their mother. Zak, watching this unfold, realized soon enough that it was hopeless. Neither of his parents knew how to be parents. They, like other survivors, without the benefit of resources, family or enough stamina to wade through ordinary conflict, simply did their best to get through the day, the week and the year. When both died tragically in a car accident when he and his brothers were teenagers, Zak felt like his world had ended.

They had no grandparents and the only relatives they had was their mother's first cousin who lived about 40 minutes away from their home, in Queens, New York. For Zak and his brothers, living with Edie and her husband Benyak and their two boys was both disconcerting and hopeful. In this household, the father was a very large presence, constantly reprimanding his sons, raising a hand to them when their behavior didn't meet his standards. But Edie and Benyak were good to him and his brothers. They had a roof over their heads, and they assimilated into the family. On one level it was fun having two more brothers. All five of them understood what was expected of them. While they may have had friends who left home, experimented with alcohol and drugs, they knew they had to become professionals; it was that simple.

Benyak, a manufacturer of feathers, would stress the importance daily to all the boys and indeed, even while going through hard teenage years without their parents, Zak Zweig and his brothers, alongside their cousins became respectively an accountant, a lawyer and three doctors. Edie beamed with pride at his graduation and Zak was eternally grateful to them. He appreciated what they sacrificed, so that he and his brothers would survive the trauma of losing their parents. Zak wholly and without reservation, considered them his parents and while he never asked much of Suzi, on this one thing he was adamant, that she allow them access to his daughters and treat them like revered guests in their home.

39

"For what it's worth... it's never too late, or in my case too early, to be whoever you want to be."
—F. Scott Fitzgerald

Magda and Judy flew back to New York after three incredible weeks in Jerusalem with their mother, Suzi, Fay and Dani. As the two sisters settled into their business class seats, Judy smiled at her older sister. "It wasn't a dream, right Magda," she asked.

"Absolutely not," said Magda. "It was actually the best thing that could have ever happened to us."

"Yes," said Judy, "I believe that Mamuka at heart is really open minded. I just think that her life experience changed her, but somehow after these many decades past the war, she was somehow ready to reclaim her real true authentic self."

"Judyka," said Magda affectionately and excitedly, practically forgetting that they were sitting among people who would not appreciate their raised voices, "I think you described it very well! Mamuka had so much pain and so many horrific memories to deal with, of course her real self got buried under there. But what a person she is! I am so proud of her. At her age, to put herself out there, to attend those intense two-hour sessions no less than six times while we were there, who else would do that?"

"I know," said Judy, nodding her head in agreement. "Granted, I had a lot of issues growing up and dreamed of just getting away from everyone, like–"

"Like Dani," said Magda.

"Oh Magdushka, I'm sorry," said Judy. "I didn't mean to–"

"It's okay," soothed Magda. "To begin with, Dani and I are in a much better place now and she is planning a visit to New York as soon as she can get away. In the meantime, she is almost certainly going to go for therapy, and I will certainly join her as soon as she wants me. I am ready, willing and able."

"You know Magda," said Judy, "I can accept that we were affected by what our parents went through. After all, we lived with them and indirectly absorbed all that they were desperately trying to put behind them. But it just kills me to think that our children, two generations from the Holocaust, also have inherited trauma symptoms."

"Wait a minute, Judyka," interjected Magda. "You heard Dr. Levy. The research is overwhelming and yes, most definitely points to transgenerational transmission of trauma but also, thank God, also speaks to resilience and growth. That has to be a comforting thought, right?"

"And," continued Magda, "when I see my darling Dani living her best life I will celebrate. The fact that she left London, the life she made for herself there and simply moved to Israel just warms my heart. I know that she is getting very close to Fay. Did you see the two of them at lunch yesterday? And with Mamuka in the background, she is bound to come back into the fold."

"On her terms," said Judy. "Please Magdushka, don't try to force anything. Nothing good ever comes from that."

"Look at you my baby sister, all grown up, smart, sophisticated, successful, and most importantly assertive. I can't tell you how much it means to me to see you happy," said Magda sobbing.

"Thank you, Magdushka. You were my rock. Even living in your basement apartment after you and Hershel bought your home gave me comfort. Babysitting for baby Dani really saved my life!"

"I can't even begin to imagine how Mamuka survived what happened back then," said Magda. "The fact that she was able to go on, after Tatuka's death, just tells me that the resilience factor in our DNA is stronger than the vulnerability one."

"I would have to agree," said Judy slowly, "but this bonus of Mamuka, at this stage in her life to be able to look at her own behavior openly and honestly, just so that we could benefit from it, is nothing short of a gift. I am positive this is going to give us closure and allow the three of us to live our lives in a far more meaningful way, and that too will benefit our own daughters and grandchildren."

"Yes," said Magda, "I agree, and Suzika's plans to share our understanding are wonderful too. I don't know how many of our friends or cousins or peers will ever have the good fortune, the *mazal* that we had to sit with our mother in a safe therapeutic environment and work through what was so difficult for us."

"I agree with you, Magda. The more we do for others just shows that we are okay with ourselves. I've been involved in many charities, mostly writing checks but I'm going to do more. I think that I am going to volunteer to work with special needs kids in some capacity. I don't have any training or background, but I have money," she laughed. "And if I find the right school and they allow me to interact with the children, I believe I can make a difference."

"I love that plan, Judyka," said Magda softly and gently. "It just feels very right to me. Your girls are doing their own thing and marriage and babies don't seem to be the path they are choosing. For you to interact and love these children who could use as much attention as they can get, would be so amazing and a huge mitzvah too."

"My thoughts exactly," said Judy. "And I know a great deal of corporate people whom I can tap to make donations. I would love nothing more than to help any school whose special ed teachers dedicate themselves to these kids! They are the real heroes, day in and day out. And trust me, from what I've gathered so far, the compensation is hardly earth shattering."

"I'm curious," asked Magda, practically laughing, "have you mentioned this to Mamuka yet?"

"Magda, you really surprise me. No, I have not. Do you think I need her permission?" she asked.

"No, no, no," said Magda, realizing she had just reverted into old behavior patterns that Dr. Levy painstakingly pointed out to them. "Please, forgive me, that was totally inappropriate, and I don't know where that came from!"

"Actually, I do," said Judy. "We both know how judgmental Mamuka is. Even at Fay's wedding, a moment she waited for, she was still looking at how your girls were dressed to see if they were dressed according to her standards! So of course, she is going to have an opinion about this; if Mamuka didn't, I would seriously be nervous that she's getting old."

"Well," said Magda, "she's not a spring chicken, no matter how fantastic she looks. But maybe she will surprise us with her reaction. She is hardly as one dimensional as we thought. She was positively fantastic with Dani, so supportive, so interested in her law cases. And I saw how thrilled Dani was. So, let's give her the benefit of the doubt that therapy and time has given her an enormous opportunity to reclaim her prewar self."

"Oh Magda, you were always so smart," said Judy. "I'm so glad you are my sister."

"Don't be silly," said Magda, dabbing her eyes. "I'm the lucky one. You and Suzika were my anchors. I always felt that if I took good care of both of you that Hashem would help me with my struggles. And guess what? He did and I did. I am really in such a good place."

"Nothing makes me happier," said Judy, "Now, let's enjoy these lie-flat beds. I used a lot of miles so we could go home in style."

"Judy darling, thank you," said Magda.

"Quiet," said Judy warmly. "Now you listen to me. I never forgot what you did for me and even Hershel too for that matter! I have more than enough money to buy myself comfort and luxury. If I can't do that much for my own sisters, then who am I and what am I?"

"I'll tell you who you are," said Magda, beaming with pride. "You are an extraordinary human being and I love you beyond words."

The two sisters rested for the duration of the flight. It was a moment in time that cemented a relationship born of challenges, tragedies, and triumphs.

40

"A girl should be two things: who and what she wants."
—Coco Chanel

For Dani, living in Israel opened many possibilities that previously she herself had chosen to close. It began with her cousin Fay whom she learned was a survivor of rape and severe trauma. When Dani found out to what lengths Fay went to protect her family from ever being hurt by her personal tragedy, she was astounded. But as Fay revealed the details of what happened to her and how she chose to live her life in the aftermath of rape, Dani was in awe of Fay. There was Fay at the age of 19, having the wherewithal to move, on her own to Israel, establish herself in the business world of fashion, connecting to a family that provided her with emotional stability and support, and she persevered.

To Dani that Fay, her contemporary, could take away such an incredible amount of resilience from their family history was beyond her comprehension. By comparison, her own life was simply a breeze. Yes, she had a mother who was devastated by her husband's infidelity and maybe invited her to be her confidant, but what was that compared to what happened to Fay?

Dani could not get enough of her cousin. She wanted to be in her presence every minute of every day, to absorb her energy. And she simply adored Baruch, Fay's husband, the lovers who weren't meant to be married until 20 years had passed and Fay achieved closure from the stranglehold Danny Salem had on her psyche.

When Fay suggested they have Shabbos at Bobby Ava's house, Dani agreed, far more eager now to see her grandmother, the one she learned who inspired Fay!

Ava was delighted to host Fay and Baruch and Dani for Shabbos. A week did not go by when someone wasn't with her for Shabbos. Rabbi Shanzer and his wife came often, as did his children and grandchildren who simply wanted to be in her presence and hear stories about her life, her parents, her city, and her life in prewar Europe. Neither of her granddaughters lived within walking distance of her apartment and secretly Ava was thrilled that they would be under her roof for two nights. She and Ora planned the menu a week in advance. Ava saw to it that her guest bedrooms were properly prepared with French soaps in the bathroom, flowers, bottled water and chocolates by the bedside, magazines and newspapers in English and exquisite Frette linen on the beds. She wanted her granddaughters to be comfortable and pampered.

At exactly 12:00 p.m., the kitchen table was set with delicious baked goods from the famous Marzipan bakery in Machne Yehuda, brewed coffee, fruits and yogurts for when her guests arrived.

When her doorbell rang, Ava was as excited as a young girl. "My darlings," she called out, as she walked quickly across the hall to where they stood. "Shalom to you. I cannot tell you what joy this gives me, Fay, to see you married and settled and Dani, to have you here." Ava hugged the girls, and it was Dani, shocking herself, who refused to break away.

Baruch stood by, regretful that his religious standards precluded him from joining this circle of love but sure that those who respected him for the life he chose would certainly accept the fact that the only woman he ever touched in any capacity was his beloved wife, Fay. As the three women finally separated, he cleared his throat and acting as the male host, offered to escort them all into the kitchen.

Ava was thrilled beyond measure. She loved this boy to pieces and often wondered how Fay could ever have thought for one minute that she would disapprove of him because his parents were allegedly Polish? In therapy she repeated this to Dr. Levy who did not make any comment but gently reminded Ava of patterns of behavior that resurfaced which were entirely compatible with being judgmental. Ava shamefacedly admitted it was true.

Ava sighed and thanked God that fate and determination by Baruch to never give up on Fay had brought these two together. If only they would have a child immediately, she thought wistfully, somehow, instinctively not quite sure that was in the cards for them. As they sat down, Ava quickly redirected her thoughts to the present.

"So tell me, all of you, how are you?" she began with a huge smile on her face.

Dani looked at her grandmother and started crying. "Oh my God, Bobby, I am so sorry. I am just so overwhelmed and grateful to be here, it's like a dream come true that I didn't know I was missing," she gasped.

"Please darling," said Ava. "Don't cry, or I will too. And at my age, it's not very attractive to see my makeup start to run down my wrinkled cheeks."

Dani jumped up and wrapped her arms around her grandmother. "I love those wrinkled cheeks," she sputtered. "Oh Bobby, can you ever forgive me for disappearing?"

"And here I thought we were just having a simple Shabbos," said Ava. "If I knew that we were going to revisit the past, I would have asked Dr. Levy to join us."

"Honestly," said Fay, "the way my mother talks about that woman, I'm starting to wonder if I'd like to meet her?"

"I can't speak for Dr. Levy," responded Ava seriously, "or how many generations of my family she can manage, but if you girls want to talk to me, I'm ready."

Dani took her seat again and while nibbling on a cinnamon *rugala* said, "I have an idea. Why don't we hold off a bit, let's enjoy coffee and gossip a little and let's see where Shabbos takes us in terms of conversation."

Fay looked at Dani and tacitly agreed. She wasn't sure what she could contribute and wanted to simply let whatever had to come out, come out organically. Ava, ever practical, literally clapped her hands. "Vonderful idea. Dani darling." She took a slice of caramel cheesecake onto her plate while Fay stared at her plate and started to laugh.

"Bobby," she said, "cheesecake? I figured for sure all the pastries you so lavishly laid out were for Baruch. I'm shocked."

"Vell darling," said Ava as she reluctantly put down her fork as she took the time to explain herself, "I think at my age I can afford to indulge. Don't you agree?"

Fay understood that Ava was not really ready at that moment to talk about her food issues and Fay respected that. In her heart, she was ecstatic that Dani wanted to be part of the family, but certainly Bobby's involvement in her evolution and understanding of the generational transmission of trauma didn't necessarily have to implicate Bobby as if she was on trial or responsible for all their challenges. That would not be ethical or fair. Bobby after all was over 90 and while blessed with good health, did not necessarily have the stamina to revisit the past repeatedly.

For the next 45 minutes, the three ladies and Baruch Natan chatted. Baruch was working on a huge new project which he was reluctant to take credit for. Dani was acclimating herself to the firm's Tel Aviv office and Israeli cultural norms so different than her London office and Fay was busy expanding AvaFay's online presence, working with influencers and e-commerce specialists so that customers could easily shop online day or night from anywhere in the world with ease and the click of a button on their screens. What Fay was not prepared to share yet with her family, was that she was seeing a fertility specialist. Given her age, she wanted to assure that she would have every advantage to conceive and have a healthy pregnancy. It was what she and Baruch *davened* and prayed for daily. The only person who knew was her beloved friend ChavaSara, whose married daughter Esti was unable to carry a pregnancy to term and she referred Fay to the renowned Dr. Fuldhamer. Fay was hopeful that soon she too would be blessed to be pregnant with Baruch's child.

41

"When you trip over love, it is easy to get up. But when you fall in love, it is impossible to stand again."
—Albert Einstein

After coffee, the ladies went upstairs to unpack and relax. Five hours later, Baruch left for *shul* for Kabbalat Shabbos. Fay was still napping but looked up when she saw her husband getting ready to leave. Her heartbeat rapidly as she stared at her husband of 18 months. He was so splendid, a fine specimen of a man she thought. Baruch looked at his wife and smiled. He bent low to kiss her and to tell her he loved her. He was determined to make up for all the lost years when Fay was in exile, ironically right here in Israel. How he needed her then, ached for her. When he read the court transcript and Fay's impassioned speech for justice, he cried. He, who never cried in his life, was overcome with grief at how much his beloved Fay had suffered. He would never get over what happened to her and that he had not been there to shield her, to comfort her and love her after what happened to her at the hands of Danny Salem. He was indebted to his best friend Sammy Benadin for all the support he had provided to Fay at the trial.

"Shabbos Shalom, my husband," said Fay, as she quickly rose

from the bed, put on a lovely AvaFay floral robe and silk scarf to cover her hair and went downstairs to light the Shabbos candles.

Fay met Dani and her grandmother in the dining room. If Ava was surprised that Dani, an unmarried woman, lit Shabbos candles, to her credit she said nothing. This, thought Fay, is what my mother must be referring to. Bobby had evolved into an extremely considerate person who understood boundaries. She was so happy for Dani, who confided in her that the path to becoming religious was one she would take slowly and at her own pace, but that she was on the right track. If Dani wanted to light candles, even though this was a custom reserved for married women, who would be cruel enough to stop her as she evaluated her religious options?

As the three women closed their eyes and made the ancient hand gesture of gathering the Shabbos close to themselves, there was utter silence, each woman immersed thoroughly in her *tfilot*, her prayers and wishes as they lit their candles. When Ava opened her eyes, she simply reached for her two eldest granddaughters and cradled them both. She didn't say a word and neither did they.

42

"Saying nothing sometimes says the most."
—Emily Dickinson

When Baruch walked back into the house after the evening services concluded, he was not alone. Ava looked at her grandson in law and the guests he invited to join them for Shabbos dinner. "Shabbos Shalom," she gaily greeted, a tall slim man and his two twin boys.

"Shabbos Shalom," said Eliyahu Klein. "Allow me to introduce my sons Akiva and Benjy."

The handsome boys stood at attention and greeted their hostess.

"Bobby," said Baruch, "I was sure you would have invited your new neighbors had you known they just made *aliyah* and literally moved down the block."

And Ava, ever the consummate hostess, and far more relaxed at this stage in life about socializing with strangers, agreed immediately. "Of course, it is my absolute pleasure to welcome you to my home, to the neighborhood and to Yerushalayim."

Within seconds, three place settings were discreetly added to the resplendent sparkling glimmering Shabbos table. The guests enjoyed Ava's rendition of an elegant, healthy, delicious Shabbos dinner from the challahs to the assorted Israeli wines, the fish, chicken soup and choice of Cornish hen stuffed with spinach, standing rib roast with grilled vegetables, potato kugel, many *salatim* and an assortment of Hungarian *linzer* tart cookies and *dobos* torte cake with herbal tea for dessert.

While Ava could no longer stand on her feet for the hours it would have required to execute the lavish meal she planned, Ora and her two younger sisters Bathsheva and Simi executed it all to a tee. The girls felt privileged to work in the house and admired Ava beyond words because she took the time to listen to them. Whenever they came to help Ora, Ava genuinely inquired about their life, what they were studying, how they felt and what their future plans were. To Ava, they were Ora's sisters and therefore of interest to her.

The older she got, the more Ava appreciated what money could do, not for her, but for others. For her part, when she did not have company, Ava ate very simply and only indulged when in a social setting. Ava never divulged a word to anyone and arranged payment for all three Nachmani sisters to attend Hebrew University, so that they could eventually hold positions at AvaFay rather than remain domestic workers. She also helped pay for all the expenses of marrying them off and setting them up in their first apartments as she knew how poor their parents were, because Ora told her that all nine children in the family were tragically at some point in time, due to parental physical and mental illness, placed in foster care.

Her charity did not end there. Every other Sunday, she briefly visited the children at the Zion Orphanage, the oldest orphanage in all of Israel. She tirelessly raised money for them by writing to every business contact she had. In addition to establishing a sensory playroom and food garden in memory of Imre, she distributed baskets of fruit to the children. Not one person in her family knew of her endeavors and that was exactly how she wanted it.

Within hours, after the guests departed, Baruch explained to the ladies that Eliyahu Klein was a widower from Chicago, a wealthy nursing home operator, who recently made *aliyah* with his young sons, after the sudden death of his wife. It was apparent to Ava within 30 seconds why Baruch elected to invite this young man to join them. He was educated, refined, religious, a gentleman and quite possibly, a perfect match for Dani. Within a few short months, Dani became wife and mother to Eliyahu and his boys and was married in Ava's exquisite garden that was an identical replica of Fay's wedding. Similarly, the entire clan gathered from all over the world to be present at Dani's beautiful and meaningful wedding.

Dani was a radiant bride, nervous and excited but overwhelmingly happy to see her sisters, cousins, and family, all of whom were so accepting of her. She was still finding her way to a religious life, to what she felt made sense for her and Eliyahu was patient and never questioned her. It was Magda who quite literally stole the show, when she got up to speak, shortly after Rabbi Shanzer officiated at the wedding.

"Dearest family," she began, "I certainly cannot compete with the blessings of our dear, wise Rabbi Shanzer. Just a short while ago, Rabbi Shanzer stood right here in front of us and married Fay and Baruch. What I would like to share today with my beautiful daughter Daniella Devorah and her husband, is that I wish you both a life of joy, one in which you raise those beautiful boys with the values that mean the most to you. In our family, we only have to look at our matriarch, our beloved Bobby Ava who by example has always put family above everything else. May you be surrounded with the love of family forever, until Moshiach, our Messiah comes."

Magda raised her glass and proclaimed, "L'chaim."

It was a moment to remember, not lost on her husband, sisters or mother, because it was a conscious decision on Magda's part not to mention the Holocaust at all.

That week, when Suzi, Ava, Judy, and Magda opted for an impromptu reunion session with Dr. Levy, it was Ava who made them all laugh when Magda described her speech to Dr. Levy.

"Thank God!" said Ava sputtering. "Enough already with the Holocaust and the trauma. Let's just live our lives."

As her daughters laughed, Dr. Levy spontaneously rose and clapped her hands. "Mazal Tov," she said, and all four of them thought she was congratulating them on Dani's wedding, until she continued. "Ladies, I am honored to inform you that both Magda and Ava have illustrated right here before us that you all have learned so much about yourselves. You have shown that your identity as survivors of trauma, primary or secondary, need not define you. You are officially discharged from therapy, but not from my heart. You have taught me so much and I am so proud of all of you for choosing to deal with hard truths rather than allow that pain to fester and continue to extend itself into another generation. You have reached a wonderful place as a group and I know I speak for you ladies in saying, we all owe a huge debt of gratitude and *hakarat hatov* to this lady, this warrior, this survivor, pointing at Ava, whose courage and quest for truth has truly *liberated* all of you."

Suddenly the laughter turned to sobs as Ava's daughters took in the gravity of what Dr. Levy had just said. It was not lost on any of them that Dr. Levy chose to characterize this journey they had taken together as a liberation. Ava was liberated in 1945 and now 50 years later, so were Suzi, Magda, and Judy.

It was finally over, they no longer had to worry that the aftermath of Ava's horrific experience in Auschwitz would continue to impact their families. They could rest assured that their grandchildren, Israeli or American, would be whole and healthy, growing up proud of their Jewish identities, living without the burden of a past that traumatized their parents and grandparents. They would ultimately pass on their resilience and growth.

43

"Cogito, ergo sum. [I think, therefore, I am.]"
—René Descartes

For Fay the knowledge that she was never going to be able to give birth to hers and Baruch's child was difficult to accept. For a while, she felt an unbearable sadness that life had been so terribly cruel to her. She pondered over her choices and then impulsively, turned to her childhood friends. She needed them no less now than she had when they were growing up. She invited Ray Benadin and May Weisenfeld, with whom she spoke weekly, to come to Israel for a long overdue face to face reunion. Both of her friends did just that, leaving their husbands and children for two weeks.

Their childhood connection remained strong in spite of the fact that they were now consumed with their husbands, children and stepchildren, work and commitments. When Fay reached out, they did not hesitate to go the distance for her. It would always be like that. When May's eldest daughter and stepdaughter both got married within days of each other, Ray and Fay were there. When Sammy's mother died of lung disease, Ray was inconsolable and reverted automatically back to when her best friends stood by her side. Fay and May flew to London to be with Ray, for the funeral and to pay their respects to Sammy and the Benadin family. It would always be like that; that was a given.

Fay arranged for the girls to stay at Ava's house, simply because she knew the girls would be more comfortable than in her home. The arrangement absolutely thrilled all parties concerned. Ava's guest quarters were large and spacious as if her home was a bed and breakfast, and she absolutely loved having company. She wisely excused herself when she sensed the three old friends needed privacy and the girls were grateful.

For days, the girls talked about the past, reminiscing about good times and hard times, their teen years, their life changing trip to Poland, their unwavering sisterhood, and then inevitably they moved on to the present. For Fay, Ray's logic and May's emotion were exactly what she needed. It was cathartic and healing and helped her make peace with the reality of her situation. But it was watching Dani, who embraced motherhood and loved Eliyahu's boys without any hesitation or reservation, who felt no need to have her own children, that made Fay realize she didn't need to give birth to love a child. Once again, she turned to ChavaSarah who put her in touch with the Central Authority adoption agency in Israel. Over the course of the next three years, Baruch and Fay adopted four wonderful children that enhanced their lives. For Fay to finally have children meant the world to her and she never looked back to what was or what might have been.

44

"Happiness depends upon ourselves."
—Aristotle

Suzi was utterly exhilarated by the reception of dozens of women who clamored to each workshop. Many told her that what they learned had been life changing for them, many began therapy, and many walked out of their own lives to find themselves. Suzi had an encouraging word for each one. But she was also exhausted. This was her third flight in the span of a week. As she sat in her seat, she looked around and her gaze fell on the couple in the row adjacent to her seat. They were roughly her age. What struck her was that they were talking to each other for the duration of the flight, holding hands and finally snuggling together while taking a brief nap. How comfortable they seemed to be and still in love.

It was at that exact moment, that she knew she was no longer in love with her husband. Quite possibly it was in Toronto, when she was walking into the Bathurst Avenue Jewish Center to speak to a group of mothers and daughters, when a handsome middle-aged man offered to show her to the lecture hall. He asked her many questions about her odyssey from housewife and mother to author and lecturer. In a mere 20 minutes, Suzi found out that Tommy

Shuster was originally from Toronto and simply back visiting his sister and her family and about to pray in the synagogue attached to the Jewish Center. He was charming, personable, and as married as she was. As he walked off, Suzi felt the acid rising in her throat. Yes, it was a minor condition associated with age and being a bit overweight, but for her, in this moment, it was also the bitter taste of regret. Quickly, before the auditorium filled, Suzi distracted herself by breathing and practicing positive self-talk. After the lecture, on her way to the airport she would think some more.

By the time Suzi stepped off the plane and arrived at the baggage claim at LaGuardia Airport, she had a plan of action. She was not her mother's daughter for nothing, and she would fix this marriage. It wasn't Zak's fault if things were stale; that was her job and being brutally honest with herself, she knew she had to take responsibility for having fundamentally neglected her marriage. First, always being involved with her mother and her sisters, then with her daughters, then with therapy and finally with a career that had her traveling from city to city, wherever her agent booked her to speak. But if she dared fantasize about a complete stranger, even for one brief moment, then it was time to refocus and take action. This is where Suzi saw the fruits of all the therapy she had endured. When she was tired or did not have the money, she went anyway. When she had to face hard truths about herself, she cried and pushed through. She was no longer passive or aggressive, no longer blamed others for what she needed to do. And she was thrilled with her own analysis! She wanted to be in love with her husband, even more so than when they first got married. Then, she simply wanted to copy Magda and get out of the house. But now, she wanted to feel connected to her husband, the father of her children, the man who could have walked out on her enough times because of her moods and temper tantrums but didn't.

As she exited the airport, looking for her husband, Suzi put a smile on her face. Looking at her tired, graying, and balding husband, she realized regretfully just how neglected he was and remembered with clarity not only how Mamuka took care of Lajos but also of Imre. No wonder both of those men had an unwavering loyalty to her mother; she always put them first. Oh my God, thought Suzi, I have my work cut out!

Over the course of the next 12 weeks, Suzi attempted to implement a weekly date night with her husband with clear ground rules. There would be no talking about the children or grandchildren, parents, her next book, money, health concerns or other people. They were only permitted to discuss current events and Israel of course, their plans as a couple and upcoming holidays. Suzi also started to work on a surprise 65th birthday party for her husband.

As part of Operation Zak, known only to Suzi, on Tuesdays Suzi began her day working out with a trainer, to help her regain her figure. While a part of her railed at the obscene cost of a personal trainer, she forced herself to commit, knowing she could afford it and recognizing that this was the only way to gain muscle mass, which was critical for her golden years. Regretfully, her beloved Kati *nene* was weak and relied on a cane, albeit a stunning lucite one, that practically looked like a fashion accessory, because she was not active enough and Suzi was determined to start planning for her own healthy old age right now. Suzi then ran errands and ultimately arrived home to find Zak ready to take her for their weekly tennis lessons.

She and Zak had recently joined the Woodmere Country Club, which coincidentally was a few blocks from where both Bethie and Dini lived. After playing two sets of tennis, Suzi and Zak took their grandchildren out for a casual dinner. The day was so enjoyable for them both that they each secretly looked forward to it as the best day of the week. For both, it was a milestone. Neither felt guilty at taking off a half a day of work to play tennis and Suzi did not feel the need to justify or pretend that it was anything other than for her enjoyment.

She remembered well what Dr. Levy had pointed out, that her generation, no less so than her mother's, felt obligated to make use of time, perhaps the survivors felt guilty at the thought of wasting time, which was a commodity six million Jews no longer had the luxury of. Or like her beloved father, who filled every waking minute to avoid thinking about the past. And they of course passed that on to their children; that one must be productive at all costs. Her father, she came to learn in therapy, was not only a devoted follower of his Rebba but was also displaying the avoidance so prevalent in survivors of trauma, who used to be busy as a distraction so that they never had time to think about the past. To that end, both Suzi and her sisters daily discussed their concerted efforts to "waste" a little time. They laughed about it, but they believed they needed to do it, to break the mindset they learned from their parents for whom it might have been a necessity but was simply learned behavior for them.

Magda made a point of doing the New York Times crossword puzzle every single day except Shabbos, while Judy guiltily at first, tucked into her comfortable bed at 3:00 p.m. in the afternoon to watch her favorite talk show or Lifetime movie, while for Suzi it was the tennis on Tuesdays and a couples massage with Zak on Thursdays. Suzi learned something valuable. She came to enjoy her time with Zak, on the court, in the car, while having a massage, discussing world politics or in their bed. She realized that for all Mamuka's meticulous devotion including starching and ironing her father's shirts and undershirts, she could barely remember her mother talking to either of her husbands. How fortunate was she, thought Suzi, to have reclaimed an important part of her happiness and be able to have a different fulfilling experience with her husband, rather than simply duplicate her mother's marriages and settle for mediocrity at best.

45

"The unexamined life is not worth living."
—Socrates

The day Hershel finally paid back every cent that he borrowed and owed was a day Magda would never forget. Finally, they were debt free thanks to the money she inherited when Imre died. It took five long years to sort out all the debts and make good on them, but finally it was behind them. Magda realized that she needed to take stock of their financial health and do something. She tolerated her husband, certainly did not love him the same way Suzi loved Zak but more like her mother. Hershel was her husband, a constant in her life, the father of her children and she would live with him. That she had no feelings for him was not important now. Now, what mattered to her was financial security. She was not going to rely on either of her sister's generosity any longer and certainly did not expect her mother to support her. If she learned anything in therapy, all those many years of addressing her issues to rid herself of her dependency on food, it was that she needed to accept and make change. It was time for her to find a path to financial stability.

The thought of earning money was almost intoxicating in that Magda never realized how much she hated being dependent and scared of the IRS, debt collectors, and acquaintances who time and again invested in Hershel's latest business "opportunity" in the stock market. That he did not go to jail was only a miracle, one that cost hundreds of thousands of dollars in legal fees. How Magda hated herself then, for being married to a schemer, for not having the guts like her sister Judy to pull the plug on a marriage to a man who humiliated her time and again? First with his cheap affairs, then with his gambling and then with his fraudulent stock schemes. Why she still put up this facade and stayed with him she knew said more about her unwillingness to be alone and less about him.

She owed him nothing. When she toyed with the idea of leaving him, she worried about him. Where would he go? His own daughters would hardly welcome him, his own parents had written him off when he took out loans using their names as guarantors and pleaded with the court for mercy so as not to hurt his Holocaust survivor parents. No, only Magda found it in her heart to stand by him. Was it possible there was still a kernel of love, she wondered or was it simply because she was afraid to be on her own?

Magda, like her mother and her sisters had the same drive, ambition, and determination to make change, albeit hers was laced with low grade depression which she hid from everyone. When she found herself in bed day after day when Dani was a little girl, she knew she needed help. Long before therapy, Magda was taking an antidepressant so that she could get through the day. But now, she was in control of her mind and her body and ready to do what she needed to do. Although Hershel had no idea, she had in fact stashed away a large part of the money Imre left them, investing in blue chip stocks like eBay and Intel simply because as an avid reader she knew these companies would become huge in the coming years. She was right!

Her nest egg had ballooned into a considerable fortune which allowed her to eventually execute a business plan. She was able to take out a business loan and line of credit as well as persuade investors to back her. She read books, listened to lectures and finally she had a plan and a business model. She was going into the grocery business. She thought of Hinda-Baila, the young girl her mother and her aunts adopted in Auschwitz. If she could come to America without the benefit of speaking English and start a very lucrative party planning business, it was impossible that she, with all the advantages of America from infancy, would not succeed. It was not an option for her to fail. Something bloomed inside of Magda; it was hope. That finally the opportunity to do something that she needed, something that she wanted, that would give her pleasure, was going to happen. She was dead sure of it.

Magda was right and the time was right. The kosher food market was exploding into a billion-dollar industry. Consumers wanted high-end kosher from cruises to Passover programs, to destination weddings, to sophisticated wine and liquor to dining out in French bistros. And they had the money to spend. For the generation like her grandchildren, Manischewitz was an outdated relic of the past. This generation wanted to indulge and being kosher was not going to be an obstacle for them.

It took five backbreaking years but finally it happened. Magda, on her 74th birthday became a successful business owner of the very first upscale *glatt* kosher food emporium. Judy of course found the commercial building, Zak helped her get loans as a minority small business owner and she was on her way to creating a store that would make shopping an incomparable experience, the likes of which New York City had never seen. Aside from Jerusalem, where every *makolet* carried only kosher groceries, there was no other place anywhere in the world where kosher consumers could shop and find every item they could only previously dream of with kosher certification.

The concept was brilliant. To offset cost, she rented space in her 250,000 square foot store to nearly a dozen, highly regarded well established kosher brands. Now women who only shopped kosher would have access under one roof to the freshest produce, succulent fruits and vegetables in every variety imaginable, fresh fish, fresh meat with an experienced on-site butcher who was available to prepare medallions of veal, rack and crowns of lamb and standing rib roasts, fresh bakery goods, gluten free and low sugar products, nuts and candies, coffee and teas, hot chocolate and baking necessities, and an unparalleled take-out department headed by five Culinary

Institute graduates, and Ritz Carlton chefs and sous chefs who daily offered a dazzling array of exquisitely prepared foods that ranged from nouvelle cuisine to caesar salads, to eight kinds of rice, to mouthwatering side dishes, to smoked meats and fishes, to Shabbos basics on Thursdays and Fridays, chicken soup and matzo balls, gefilte fish and pickled salmon, broccoli quiches, terrines of spinach and sweet potatoes, roasted potatoes with paprika and chives, homemade cholent, lamb stews, potato, lokshen and noodle kugels, challahs in every size and size and mouth-watering elegant dairy and pareve desserts.

People came in droves, corroborating that indeed the kosher consumer was ready and willing to pay for quality and variety previously not available to them. They came from every borough, out of town and out of state, to shop and indulge at "Magda's Place." Her signature turquoise and orange shopping bags became a status symbol for those in the know. And Magda was in heaven. Finally, all those years of managing Mamuka's household, pinching pennies so she could buy her younger sisters the nicest treats, had paid off.

On opening day, Magda stood in front of her store with Hershel by her side. Ever the devoted wife, because she, as the oldest, still felt bonded to what she observed growing up, that you simply don't throw people away, regardless of how flawed they are, Magda found a place for Hershel. He became the buyer for the store, negotiating with hundreds of food companies under the Rabbinical supervision that assured they were kosher, all vying for precious shelf space, and he was brilliant. He offered incentives and legal cash back rewards to vendors who delivered on time, to stores who placed full page ads week after week in Jewish publications, to the trendy New York Magazine advertisers showcasing Magda's Place as the exclusive location where their products and exclusive items were to be found. In their seventies, while they did not fool themselves that they were young, Magda and Hershel learned to lean on each other. All the therapy in the world did not account for what success did for both. Magda loved how she felt, going to work was a joy, getting dressed was a joy, luxuriating in her brand new jacuzzi was a joy. Her daughters, sisters and mother were simply ecstatic for her.

Ava could not travel for the grand opening. At age 97, after suffering a fall and breaking her wrist, it was simply too much. Magda was heartbroken but philosophical. She would have loved for her mother to be there to share in this moment, but it was perfectly fine even without her. Magda was surrounded by the people she adored, her daughters, sons in law, grandchildren, aunts and uncles, nieces and nephews and her beloved sisters. And Hershel. Secretly, although the three sisters had long since given up gossiping for more meaningful conversation, Suzi could not control the old impulse to bash her brother-in-law.

At the grand opening, she started to rant to Judy in Hungarian so no one in proximity could possibly understand her. On the ride back to their new 2-bedroom condo in Lawrence on Central Avenue, just blocks away from the girls, she continued her rant to Zak. Getting all worked up she rhetorically asked her husband, "Why the hell was he giving interviews to the media? Would you explain that to me? Instead of bragging about his accomplishments, he should be kissing my sister's hands and feet, not acting like none of this could have happened without him!"

Zak couldn't help but laugh out loud, something he had learned in therapy to do, after finally accepting the trauma of his parents' death.

"I agree with you Suzi," he said, laughing until tears came down his face. "He is a very lucky fool, but somehow, he managed to find his way back. Your sister is an angel. But I will say, he is clever and please, don't bite my head off. He did figure out a very sound business strategy."

"Thank you, Zak," said Suzi. "I really and I mean really appreciate it when you validate me, but please don't tell me how brilliant he is after he took millions from innocent people in his stock scams! And right now, I only want to focus on how brilliant my big sister is."

"You know Suzi," said Zak reaching for her hand, as he drove and navigated the conversation to share something he was meaning to tell her but couldn't find the moment. "It only took your love to cure me. How I envied you all those years, that you had the ability to love and even to hate, to yell and scream... to express yourself while I kept everything bottled up inside."

"Where did that come from?" asked Suzi. "Well, dearest husband, don't thank me. Thank my mother. She never stopped nudging me, always on my case about why you were so withdrawn. I nudged you to go to the gym, to talk to your Rabbi and just deal with your repressed feelings because Mamuka drove me crazy with her questions. That woman used to drive me mad. And I am so glad that you are you. For your sake and mine! Even your daughters noticed the change in you."

"I suppose, we are meant to live very long lives," said Zak slowly. "We endured a lot in our childhood, so now this is our time and there is no one I would rather be with than you."

"I feel the same way," said Suzi, tears in her eyes. "We are quite fortunate. And I am thrilled for Magda. As the first child, born in Bergen-Belsen in a displaced persons' camp, and then coming to America with my parents as they started to rebuild a new life, I think she really took the brunt of it. I don't think neither I nor Judy ever appreciated that on days when Mamuka and Tatuka couldn't cope with the demands of being parents to growing boisterous children, she was there for us. She cooked, she cleaned, she did homework with us, she made sure we prepared our uniforms every night, that we showered, and studied with us and made hems on our skirts! That she is today slim and healthy and a success in her own right is the most wonderful justice!"

"Zak," she added breathlessly, "just think, if I don't want to, I don't ever have to cook again for the rest of my life. Hey, you know, rank has its privileges. I am Magda's sister! The food is beyond belief! Who would ever have thought from Mermelstein's take-out on Kingston Avenue that people would want and be willing to patronize a store like Magda's Place? It is incredible. I just wish that I could bring a sample of every single delicacy to Mamuka, although I know Dani and Fay took back a ton of stuff."

Zak smiled at Suzi's exuberance and excitement. In his opinion, she resembled her mother far more than her two sisters and way more than she herself knew, he thought. That enthusiasm and *joie de vivre* zest for life was almost contagious. You couldn't help but be in a good mood when either Suzi or her mother were in the room, and he found his wife's exuberance very appealing. It more than made up for her signs of age, the fine lines, and wrinkles that she agonized over, but that he didn't see. He loved her passion and her generosity which spilled over and over.

And Suzi was still talking. "I know," she said, "that Mamuka tried to hide it, but she was just devastated not to be there at the grand opening but thank God for technology. Can you believe what Akiva and Benjy did on the video? Mamuka saw everything as it was happening, just like a newscaster broadcasting live on television. And did you hear her reaction when the camera homed in on the Hungarian delicacies that were based entirely on her recipes? I'm telling you; Magda is a genius! She really made Mamuka feel wonderful and like an integral part of the day. Seeing her blintzes, her crepes, her cabbage and noodles and *halupchas* on display and people fighting to sample them! I always knew Eliyahu's boys were special, but the way they captured everything, wow!"

"Zak, are you listening to me?" she demanded. "I am thinking we should set up Benjy with one of May's stepdaughters. He is so handsome and brilliant, according to Dani. And I saw those girls, each one a gem. Fay tells me that May has devoted her life to Gabriel's children, raising them with her own daughters." Still reminiscing, Suzi continued. "Was it only yesterday when those girls practically lived in our house, Zak? Where did the years go by?"

Zak started laughing. He knew at this point in the conversation that Suzi didn't even require a response. She was already thinking how she was going to execute this *shidduch*. It was amazing to him, how after all the therapy, insight and awareness and years of straddling between their Jewish and American norms, that the customs and traditions of their religion, that went back hundreds of years, still prevailed. He had no doubt that Suzi would not quit until she brought these young people together. He knew too though they never spoke about it, that Suzi was heartbroken for Judy whose daughters were all single. On some level, making a *shidduch*, a match, ensured that another couple would forge a life together. Not that

Judy's daughters seemed unhappy, just different. One was a Professor at Yale, the other a surgeon at Boston Children and the youngest a social worker, who graduated from the prestigious Columbia University School of Social Work. They had incredible careers, and likely social lives, just not husbands and children. How observant they were was a line that no one crossed, ever.

Therapy had taught them that boundaries were in fact very important, exactly like land boundaries, to keep people in and to keep others out. But having grown up without boundaries, observing their mother and her sisters act in unison, because that was what their mother needed, as she became part of an indelible triumvirate with her sisters, both for physical and emotional survival, was something they all had to consciously work on to change; to respect each other's rights to boundaries and their married daughters as well.

Neither Magda nor Suzi wanted to ever hurt Judy by making her daughter's lives into a topic. If she wanted to share, she would. What each thought on their own was another matter but they respected their sisters right to privacy. Zak, though, was a man who defined himself by his religious principles, as it was a resource for him to deal with the pain of losing his parents. He was simply grateful to God that not only were he and Suzi as observant as the day they got married, but that all three of their daughters were as well. He also truly liked and admired his sons in law, Yossi, Ari, and Binyamin and made a point once a month to have dinner with them in the city, boys' night out. They were all solid good boys, who were good fathers and husbands. How much money they earned mattered to Suzi, but not to him.

46

"You can discover more about a person in an hour of play than in a year of conversation."
—Plato

Judy increasingly found herself spending more time in Israel. She adored her condominium in Herzliya Pituah, a beach resort in close proximity to Tel Aviv, itself a modern city vastly different from Jerusalem where her mother and cousins resided. When she opened the door to her brand-new condo, decorated entirely in white, from the Carrera marble imported from Italy to the lacquered high gloss white walls and furniture throughout the entire 2,500 square feet, a sense of calm washed over her as she looked out at the spectacular Mediterranean Sea. It was a multimillion-dollar view and Judy ached to share it with someone. Yes, the girls came twice a year when they could get away from their busy lives, and she arranged a girls spa week for Suzi and Magda, but they too were very busy, with their new careers and ever-growing family. That left Mamuka, who it seemed was extremely happy in Jerusalem.

Judy knew that she had work friends and she still had a couple of friends from before her divorce, but no one was on her wavelength. So, she enjoyed the apartment by herself. She walked on the beach for hours at a time, sat on her beautiful terrace overlooking the pool and read as many books as she felt like. She ordered food from the magnificent restaurant in the building or from town. But food never interested or excited her. And suddenly, without warning, Judy slipped into a depression. All the years of fastidiously looking out for her mental health came to a crashing halt one morning when she couldn't figure out why she had to get out of bed.

She didn't want to exercise or go swimming, walk on the beach, or eat breakfast, lunch or dinner. So, she stayed in bed, drinking water and coffee. She stopped answering her phone and didn't listen to her messages. It just didn't matter because no one really needed her. Even though her clients were on hiatus, the real estate market was in a slump, though Judy was hardly affected since she saved more than she spent in her very successful years as a top agent for Massey-Green. She didn't need to sell if she chose not to. The question was, what was she going to do for the rest of her life?

Not wanting to worry Magda who always took care of her, or her mother who was extremely anxious about both Kati and Zita, Judy knew she had choices. She could call Suzi or go see Dr. Levy or an associate or she could figure out what would give her pleasure and go get it. She stayed in her bed for another week, off the grid, and spent time thinking, not brooding, weighing her options until she felt like she had a plan. She remembered at some point telling her sisters she wanted to help special needs children and what better place than in Israel? It was time for her to stop the pity party and do something for someone else. In her heart, Judy knew this was exactly what her mother, her aunts and her sisters would tell her to do.

She reluctantly got out of bed and forced herself into the shower. It was hard to be depressed in a bathroom like this, she noted. Then she called housekeeping and room service. In a matter of hours, she was dressed and put on makeup. She felt nervous and scared to even go outside, but she pushed herself. She would go outside for 10 minutes. And that's what she did, increasing her outings in increments of 10, forcing herself to strike up a conversation at the pool or at the art exhibit she went to and then, when she felt a little better, she went to visit her mother and Dr. Levy who immediately referred her to Dr. Heshy Berk, an American trained psychiatrist who made *aliyah* with his family a decade ago. Dr. Berk was quite talkative for a psychiatrist and Judy was pleased at his way of handling her. He didn't merely rehash her old history, but certainly did not make light of her suicide attempt. She felt safe with him and faithfully took the new and improved medication he recommended designed to balance her serotonin level.

Seeing her mother was both good and bad for Judy. In her vulnerable frame of mind, she remembered the agony of her confused childhood. At the same time, there was no one more complimentary or enthusiastic than her mother and Judy felt the love that she still so desperately craved. Mamuka didn't disappoint one afternoon as they drank coffee in her garden.

"Judyka, please forgive me, I'm an old lady and I can't sleep at night. Can you please tell me why you and your three daughters are all single?"

Judy never saw her mother ever so terrified as she waited for her daughter to reply.

"Mamuka, you may not believe this, but I don't ever discuss that with my daughters. They do not owe me an explanation, but apparently, I owe you one," she said smiling, "because now you are using the age card."

"Yes, I am," agreed Ava. "I am 97 years old. I am planning my 100th birthday and I need to know how many rooms you and your daughters will need."

"Mamuka, please," said Judy laughing, "you don't seriously think I believe that? You just want to know why and if I'm happy and I will tell you. I am happy when I am busy and keep moving, but when I stop, it's not good at all. Then I feel scared, not of being alone, but lonely, that I can't share a thought with someone I want to be with, someone to eat a mango with or go to a movie with."

"I understand, my darling," said Ava, choking back tears, "I know it's not me you want, but why won't you let yourself find love? Look at your sisters. Suzi, in this age carrying on with Zak like they would be newlyweds, and Magda has made a lasting peace with Hershel. Why not you, my darling?"

"Because I'm afraid, Mamuka," said Judy simply. "All the therapy and all my success and I'm still afraid of getting hurt. It makes no sense, because somewhere out there, there must be a good man! I look at darling Fay and how long she had to wait... but I'm still afraid. I've thrown away many good men over the years, making excuses just to end what might have been. I might be alone every night but at least I will go to sleep peacefully and that's worth a lot to me."

"Please do it, I beg of you, just think about it. Talk to Dr. Levy, try to get past your fear. I promise you; I will never let anyone hurt you," said Ava passionately, and moved closer to her daughter to hold her.

Her words moved a block of ice in Judy's heart. She would try. This might be the last thing she could do for her mother and yes, she might need a suite for her and a husband for Mamuka's extravaganza celebration of her 100th birthday. She would try.

47

"Sometimes you put walls up not to keep people out, but to see who cares enough to break them down."
—Socrates

The first thing Judy did was arrange to be seen by a nutritionist and an acupuncturist in Ramat Gan. She was a holistic person by nature and wanted to start her quest by being healthy in mind and body. She might need medication to stabilize a chemical imbalance in her brain that she couldn't control, but she could certainly take hold of breathing, positive thinking, eating clean, exercising and the therapies that made her feel better.

Judy decided to stay in Israel indefinitely. She enjoyed the simple life she carved out for herself, in her multimillion-dollar home, as contradictory as it was. She liked being near enough to her mother to visit often, yet still having total privacy and space. It gave her enormous satisfaction to visit her mother multiple times a week, sometimes for lunch or coffee, sometimes to go for a stroll or to pray together at the kotel and ultimately spending Shabbos together. On each of those occasions, Judy felt and often shared with her sisters her adult impression of their mother. Mamuka had so much wisdom and a great sense of humor and always entertained varied friends and family as her guests at her elaborate Shabbos table. Judy felt fortunate that at 97, Mamuka showed absolutely no signs whatsoever of cognitive decline. Weaker and frailer but in body only, the mind—thank God—as sharp as always. Her nieces Fay and Dani came daily to check in on their Bobby and Judy delighted in seeing them. She had incredibly good memories of babysitting both of them.

Slowly Judy started to feel better. She gained eight much-needed pounds, started to color her hair again, having taken off her wig after her divorce and even had Suzi send her some new skirts and sweaters from Saks. Altogether, things were looking up even if there was no man in sight yet.

According to Magda and Suzi, Mamuka told them in her daily phone calls that she was positive Mr. Right was just around the corner. While Judy was not thrilled to know that once again, she was being talked about, she decided to let it go. Mamuka had done everything in her power to help her and her sisters come to terms with being children of survivors. To complain now, that as a 97-year-old woman who loved her, that she expressed her worries about Judy was perfectly legitimate and Judy basked in the love instead of working herself up about boundaries. Sometimes, she thought the therapeutic goal of boundaries had to be put aside for logic and common sense.

48

"As a tree is known by its fruit, so man by his works."
—The Talmud

Judy indeed fell in love with Israel, its people and in particular with the children at Yaldeinu. She started as a volunteer for story time, committing to reading to the children, many of whom were orphans and diagnosed as intellectually and emotionally disabled. Many of the children were bilingual and Judy enjoyed speaking Hebrew while they enjoyed speaking English. Judy committed to visiting them Monday through Thursday and Sundays as well. It served her well.

She began to look forward to starting the day, figuring out how to manage everything she needed to accomplish in a way that didn't stress her out. After three months, she started to wonder if she wouldn't be better off living closer to the school to save travel time. Somehow too, returning to her luxurious condo each day, didn't 100% sit right with her. She wanted to live in comfort, but the apartment was so opulent that it almost felt wrong morally when she compared it to how the children and the staff lived. The thought of buying a huge house, with the profit she would realize from the sale of the condo, which she would convert to a residence for orphaned children started to appeal to her, as she became aware of how dire the situation was, children who had no home and some who desperately needed to be removed from their homes, children with no parents or legal guardians, wards of the state being turned away for placement because there was simply no room, and each state-run facility was at full capacity. If she could find a suitable house and renovate it for 25 or more children, she knew she could make a significant difference in those lives.

She could totally envision the spacious playroom, library, media room, gym, dining room and bedrooms, all decorated in soothing happy colors. Judy knew that had life not presented her with so many challenges, from anxiety and depression coupled with selective mutism, to a marriage destined to fail, she might have had a career as a designer. People noticed her when she walked into a room, not because she was young or particularly beautiful, but more so because of the way she artfully clothed herself.

Depending on where she was going and her mood, Judy dressed with panache. People constantly stopped her on the street or even on a plane to ask her where she shopped. But it wasn't the garments themselves that drew attention, it was the way she styled them, blending unusual color combinations: navy-blue with fuchsia pink or ivory with touches of red or black with Kelly green, always subtle but very sophisticated. She knew she had inherited Mamuka's stylish eye and that she loved fashion as much as her talented niece Fay.

The project started to materialize when Judy actively began a search for a suitable property. It also became a conversation starter with her youngest daughter Hedy, whose considerable training as a psychiatric social worker was invaluable to Judy in planning a living environment for the children that would meet all their needs. Suddenly, Judy felt a whole lot better, able to sleep at night, eat two solid meals a day that energized and sustained her. She was totally determined to open a residence for children, a state-of-the-art medical, educational, and rehabilitative care facility that would ultimately assure that these children would never be forced to spend their lives in hospitals, without the benefit of the type of environment that would ultimately not only provide the services they required but also the love and warmth of a home. The social workers and therapists would provide innovative therapies and services for the children and help promote a pathway to inclusion in society.

While Judy had a concrete plan for every phase of development of the project, she was taken aback at the bureaucracy in Israel. Each time she submitted plans for a potential location, the licensing agencies all found reasons to stop the project. It reached a point where Judy, beyond frustrated, felt like quitting, finding it hard to understand how her project could be stalled for nonsense, when children's lives were at stake. Desperate and determined not to give up hope, Judy reached out to everyone she knew, including Rabbi Shanzer who was the first person able to get things back on track.

Rabbi Shanzer was a very modest man who was much admired by many people in government. Among his closest friends were the Chief Rabbi of Israel and the Minister of Housing, both of whom often sought his advice, politically and personally. And although Rabbi Shanzer was more than willing to help Ava's daughter Judy for no compensation whatsoever, he did make an unusual request. In exchange for his support, he asked Judy to consider the needs of the abandoned Hasidic children in the ultra-Orthodox neighborhoods of Meah Shaarim and Bnei Brak, who might thrive in a residence that accommodated their religious needs. Judy promised Rabbi Shanzer that she would start with a girls' residence and then follow up with a boys' residence and would consult with professionals as well, on how to best serve the population of Hasidic children who were equally as neglected, abused and in need of emotional support as much as every other segment of society in Israel. Rabbi Shanzer was pleased, because at a minimum, the two facilities would of course be strictly kosher and adhere to Shabbos. For him, that was enough, to endorse and use his considerable clout to cut through the red tape. He knew all too well how many Hasidic children desperately needed what Judy's residences were going to provide.

The twin conjoined residences went up and were completed ahead of schedule 20 months later. They were a masterpiece of architecture, form, and function. In the center of the two residences was a common kitchen where daily all the food, including the fruits and vegetables grown in their spectacular garden that the children excitedly daily tended to, was prepared with equal access from both sides. The boys' and girls' homes were divided but the staff, both day and evening, could easily get from one house to the other. The residences were scheduled to open at approximately the same time as Ava's 100th birthday. Ava was perhaps more excited than even Judy. She offered her money; her time and her help and Judy was touched. Ava at nearly 100 years old wanted the opportunity to help heal these children. Was there no limit to her goodness, wondered Judy?

49

"Go confidently in the direction of your dreams. Live the life you have imagined."
—Henry David Thoreau

Ava was actively planning her 100th birthday party. When she peered in the mirror, she smiled to herself. No one, not even her daughters knew that she had had five face-lifts in the past 25 years, choosing to rely on her younger "sister" Hinda-Baila to find her a plastic surgeon in Belgium and make the necessary arrangements. But Ava knew that plastic surgery was out of the question at this point in her life. She could not travel to Belgium, nor did she want to go under the knife and subject herself to anesthesia. She was a realist and accepted that she earned every existing wrinkle, crease and line on her face and body. But that didn't mean she would stop caring. She imported her Hungarian creams and upped her facials to once a week. The owner of the salon, the lovely Penina Sabah, came to her house weekly, so that she didn't have to travel to Beit Shemesh, as did her manicurist Olga and her acupuncturist Debbie, an American girl who lived in Kiryat Mattersdorf, who made *aliyah* 30 years ago and was quite skilled in acupuncture, cupping, holistic herbs and tinctures, which Ava simply adored.

For her birthday Ava wanted to have a meaningful celebration. That of course meant having her family and closest friends. Both of her sisters Zita and Kati, while frail, were scheduled to arrive and stay for at least eight weeks. Ava greatly anticipated spending quality time with her beloved sisters, whom she hadn't seen in over two years, knowing how incredibly fortunate they all were to be alive and able to share this occasion together. While daily her darling daughters asked her if she needed help in planning her birthday, Ava declined. She wanted this party to be her final hurrah. Day after day she made copious notes in her leather journal. Ava wanted this celebration to be one that everyone whose path she ever crossed would remember, as a moment that they felt inspired by her story. For Ava that meant inviting a group of newly graduated young men and women from the IDF, the Israeli army, who would present a video to her guests, showing them completing their mandatory military training at Yad Vashem, the memorial to the Holocaust.

While Ava did not want her past to determine the tone or mood of her celebration, she knew that she needed to connect her experience to the future and allow her guests the opportunity to hear from these young people how their tour of Yad Vashem confirmed and cemented their commitment to their country; it simply felt right to her. Naturally she would ask Rabbi Shanzer to speak as well as any of her daughters and grandchildren who wanted to share their thoughts. Following the dinner for 300 guests, Ava and her sisters would set sail on a cruise. For Ava, the dream of a cruise with Imre had somehow slipped through her fingers and this was to be the moment when she would finally set sail. The cruise would be a week-long opportunity to simply enjoy the bounty, the beauty and the privilege of experiencing something she had never done with her sisters. Both of her brothers in law were more than happy to stay at her house. This was going to be perhaps the last time the sisters would ever go on an adventure and Ava was slightly apprehensive if indeed this was a sound plan. But when she asked her sisters, both sounded as excited as young girls and assured Ava that they wanted to have this special moment.

Ava was not afraid to die. All of her finances and assets were in place; death was inevitable, and she was grateful for her entire life. When Ava sat down to write her speech she began to cry. She wished she could get up in front of her beloved family and friends and say that she not only forgot but also forgave what happened 75 years ago, but that was impossible. While hopefully her daughters had found a way in which to move forward without identifying themselves mainly as children of Holocaust survivors, for her that would always be the center of her existence. It wasn't the numbers on her forearm, it was what was etched in her mind, seared in her memory, and sealed in her heart; the blatant hatred and cruelty of an entire nation, one that ironically considered themselves to be cultured and educated. No, she thought, she was proud of her status, proud to be born a Jew and proud that she never in her 100 years ever forgot who she was, where she came from and what values she learned from her parents.

She wiped her tears and tried again, to compose a speech that would synthesize her feelings, about who she once was and who she became, because Hitler took away the foundation of her very existence, shattered her core into a million pieces that while over time, miraculously reassembled, were never quite the same as the woman she was before she was treated like a slave, one whose very life mattered not at all.

50

"It is better to fail in originality than to succeed in imitation."
—Herman Melville

Dani was happy with Eliyahu, more than she ever hoped for. Indeed, something changed when she connected with her cousin Fay and her beloved grandmother, Bobby Ava. Understanding the complexity and gravity of their relationships provided a window into her own growth. Slowly she found that all the hatred, resentment, anger, confusion and helplessness that she felt as a child, receded. She did not need therapy or religion. It simply happened organically. Suddenly, Dani missed her mother Magda and wanted to spend time with her. That night she talked to her husband. "Eliyahu, I need to talk to you," she began.

Eliyahu looked at his wife and refused to get scared before he heard what Dani had to say. He remembered the exact moment when his wife Rachel told him she needed to talk to him about a lump which she assured him was nothing, but that she'd check out. That 'nothing' turned into malignant cancer which took her away in just under two years. He inhaled deeply and begged God that Dani did not have any such proclamation, which he knew that neither he nor his boys could go through again. Granted they were little boys when their mother died, but they loved Dani and losing her would be a trauma none of them would survive. As he sat in his comfortable chair waiting for Dani to speak, a tear rolled down his face.

"Eliyahu," asked Dani in panic, "why are you so upset? Is there something wrong with you or the kids?"

"No, no," said Eliyahu. "I..." He couldn't go on, too ashamed.

"Then why are you crying," asked Dani with love and concern in her voice.

"I'm worried about what you want to tell me. I–"

Dani interrupted him. "Eliyahu, I just wanted to discuss a trip to America with you. Both of my parents are going to celebrate their 75th birthdays and I want to be there and spend time with my mom, and I want to figure this out with you."

"Is that all?" said Eliyahu in relief. "No lumps or unexplained cough or fever?"

Dani looked at her husband and laughed nervously. "No, darling, none of the above! Thankfully, I come from a line of very strong women. Look at Bobby Ava, almost 100 and *Baruch hashem*, praise God, she is in great health! And Mom is too."

Eliyahu heard Dani's words and wordlessly reached out to pull her close to him. "Dani, our life is a gift, I am so grateful for the home you've created for me and the boys. Forgive my outburst. Tell me what you have in mind, and I will make it a reality."

Dani found herself ready to tell her husband then and there, about her childhood, her estrangement from her family and God. Eliyahu only nodded and held her, stroked her arm, her face and her hair, to encourage her to let it all out. He understood her in a way no one else ever did.

"Then it's a given. You will take some well-deserved time off from work and being a Mommy and go see your mother. The boys and I will join you in three weeks and stay for two weeks, which coincidentally is exactly when the boys are on break from school. I can easily arrange time off from the lab. Okay *motek*, my sweetness?" he asked softly.

"Better than okay," responded Dani, as she got up from his lap. "I am so excited! I want this to be a great experience for the boys. I am going to get theater tickets, and we will take them to Disneyland, and they will meet all their American cousins, and it will be marvelous! And I will go to work with my mother and *shep nachas*, literally, derive pleasure from what she built with my father, after all those unhappy years."

"*Bseder* [fine]," said Eliyahu in Hebrew. "Let's not tell the boys until the plans are finalized. Now, I imagine you have a lot to do as do I. So, let's get moving."

That night Dani slept well. She did not need the melatonin she usually took to help her sleep. She felt elated at the thought of sharing her happiness with her mother and sisters. As she fell asleep, cradled in her husband's arm, she said *Kriat Shema*, the ancient nighttime prayer before going to bed. It filled her soul with peace.

51

"All our dreams can come true, if we have the courage to pursue them."
—Walt Disney

When Magda heard that Dani was coming to New York without Eliyahu, she panicked and assumed the worst. In her usual morning phone call to Suzi and Judy, she shared her feelings with her sisters.

"Why the doom and gloom?" asked Judy. "Is it possible she just needs a break and hasn't been to New York in 20 years? Maybe she wants to shop? Trust me, AvaFay designs are fantastic for Israelis, but not so much for European or American women."

"No," Magda answered, irritated with Judy's logic. She wasn't looking for logic, she just wanted to express the *Sturm und Drang*, the inner turmoil that she felt. Frankly, she was resentful of her daughter coming home potentially to drop a crisis in her lap, now that she was loving life!

"If it was a fun trip, why didn't she tell me?" she asked belligerently. "Granted she's not very talkative, but she would have said so. The absence of an explanation is because it's serious."

Magda burst out crying. "Does anyone realize I'm almost 75 years old?" she exclaimed bitterly. "I am tired of being there for everyone.

Hedy has a million questions every single day and Lisa, while pretty independent, always seems to pop in at dinnertime. Sometimes I think she just wants to raid my fridge, so she won't have to cook. Her children are always hungry!"

"Okay Magdushka," soothed Suzi. "I hear you, let's just wait until Dani gets here before we panic. And as to Lisa's kids, that's easy enough to fix; just bring home food from the store. Why not find a solution? Magdushka, just let your daughter have as much as she wants. If she's not interested in cooking, then be gracious and give her the food. She does not have to be exactly like us. It is not a crime if she doesn't enjoy cooking! I would rather she be honest, than take pills for anxiety, like so many women in her generation. That's not asking too much, is it Magdushka?"

"Oh Suzika, you are right," wailed Magda. "I hate to say it, but you are thinking more like Zak every day and it's quite nice."

"Really Magdushka, really?" asked Suzi with a trace of irritation. "I can't be sensible on my own? Must you give Zak the credit?"

"Suzi," said Judy rather assertively, "please stop. Magda is feeling stressed, please don't look to start a fight, it's unbecoming of you."

"You're right," said Suzi reluctantly, "I'm sorry Magdushka. The truth is, Zak is a lot more logical than me. But please, don't get sidetracked and just give Lisa what she needs!"

All three sisters laughed heartily and the tension in the air lifted. Magda, as the first-born daughter, as the voluminous research on the transmission of trauma would show, absorbed most of their parents' trauma. She was a worrier by nature because so were her parents, and while she had grown so much in therapy, old habits die hard. She also mimicked her mother subconsciously, always expecting the worst.

When Dani arrived in New York, Magda was completely shocked.

"Dani darling, I am so relieved," she exclaimed. "I thought–"

"Yes Mom, I know what you thought," replied Dani slightly sarcastically. "Forgive me for not telling you about my true motive in coming. Maybe it's the trial lawyer in me, saving the best for last. Seriously, I simply couldn't give you more details because I wanted to have the pleasure that I'm having right now. Mom, please focus. With all that you experienced as a child, I know that's a big request, but you can do it. I am here for one reason only, to spend time with you."

Magda sighed in relief. Dani wasn't getting divorced or running off to an ashram and not in need of anything from her, not money or treatment! She simply wanted to be with her family.

The very next morning Dani insisted on going to Magda's Place with her parents. They took two cars so that the ladies would be free to leave without inconveniencing Hershel. Dani was amazed at the behind the scenes look at the business her parents had built in a few short years. It was a lot larger than she imagined and was an enormous operation that was incredibly well run, efficient and organized. She loved watching her mother in action. It was impossible to believe that at 75 years of age, a person could have that much stamina and yet, her mother had come into her own element. She approached problems and situations without catastrophizing, an indication that she, like her sisters, was in control of her thoughts and reactions. Employees and customers adored her.

Over lunch, Magda was happy to share her secrets with her eldest daughter.

"To begin with Dani," she said, "after abusing my body for so long, when I was finally able to take control, I decided to make it my business to become healthy. All the delicacies that we offer our patrons is not what your father and I eat. We eat simply, we exercise, we pray, we sing, we enjoy life, we laugh, and we take vitamins. The rest is up to genetics and God."

"Mom," gushed Dani, "I am in awe of you. But more than that, I flew 10,000 miles to tell you that I too am happy, and I feel so lucky to be part of this family. Practically a day doesn't go by when I don't see or talk to Fay and Bobby and Judy too whenever she visits. What Judy has done with her life is beyond belief!"

"Dani," said Magda, desperately trying to hold back tears, "I was such a mess when you were born. I had no clue how to be a mother or a wife. I did what Bobby told me to do, because that's what girls in my generation were expected to do. How I wish I had had then the knowledge that I acquired only recently."

"Mom," said Dani sincerely, "it's all okay. You did the best you could! Fay told me that you practically raised your sisters when Bobby was incapable of dealing with her physical and emotional pain. I can't even begin to imagine how you must have felt, growing up. Of course, marriage was a way out, in your mind, but how could you know that Dad was in worse shape than you?"

Both of them started laughing. They enjoyed lunch and then drove back to Magda's house. While Magda took a short nap, Dani checked her email and sent instructions to her paralegal and assistant. This was not a total break from the office, but that was fine with Dani. She was used to working and being a trial lawyer was a strong part of her identity, as much as being a wife and mother.

Mindful of the time difference between Israel and New York, she made sure to call Eliyahu so that she could also say good morning and good night to the boys. She adored them and felt very fortunate for the opportunity to be in their lives. Perhaps what she loved most about Eliyahu was his honesty. He reflected on his first wife, their marriage, all of it, never glossing over the facts or revising the truth merely because she had died. Dani appreciated that honesty because she had grown up with so little transparency. No one ever dared speak their truth. Instead, just like her mother did, she too grew up with many inconsistencies in her life. Mainly it was in how her parents interacted with her. Sometimes they were happy but then sad, kind but then mean, distant but then close. It was confusing. Dani came to learn, simply from listening to her mother at their lunches, that this was exactly how Magda herself grew up. Hearing and seeing how much her mother and her aunts and Bobby herself had worked hard to change all of that was enormously reassuring to her, to know that her grandmother's trauma would not continue to impact future generations.

For Dani this trip and this opportunity to sever the last chain of her childhood that bound her to chronic anxiety and fear she could not name, was simply life changing. Eliyahu listened every night as Dani relayed all that she had unpacked with her mother. Dani cried bitter tears for the many years when she—similar to her cousin Faye—exiled herself in London, far from her family, believing too that this was the only way she could get on with her life. Now, she felt she knew the real truth, that this network of amazing incredible women was part of her circle of life, and she never ever wanted to be outside of that circle ever again.

When Dani finally arranged to meet her two younger sisters, she almost made a *bracha* [blessing of gratitude], that's how happy she was to connect with them. She hugged them fiercely. Then the three of them got down to the business of planning a birthday celebration for their parents. As they began to write out the potential guest list, it was Dani who broached the topic of limiting the party just to the immediate family.

"Girls," she said earnestly to her sisters, "I think we need to distinguish between family traditions that are based on our values and not necessarily rooted in what Bobby Ava and her sisters did post-war as a coping mechanism."

Both Hedy and Lisa mulled over their sister's words. Neither had the same exact issues that plagued Dani but seemed to recognize the truth in what she was saying.

"But won't Suzi and Judy be offended if we don't invite them?" asked Lisa. "Mom is their sister, and wouldn't they want to celebrate with us?"

"I think," said Lisa slowly, "that we try to establish something that makes sense for us. We are Mom and Dad's kids and with our husbands and kids constitute their immediate family. We don't have to delve into why Bobby and her sisters were like triplets, that was their history. We are two generations from that."

"Exactly," said Dani. "My first instinct was in fact to call Suzi or Judy and ask them. But then I realized that that is exactly what Mom used to do when she had a problem. She would reach out to Zita or Kati *nene* for help because they had no grandparents and needed the comfort of relying on each other as they did in their darkest moments. So yes, my vote is that we daughters make this our family celebration."

The girls ultimately decided to have an elegant, simple dinner as they had discussed. One in which only Magda and Hershel's daughters, spouses and children would attend. It would be the first event where Magda's sisters, Suzi and Judy and their children would not be invited. It was a new boundary, and they all were absolutely fine with it. It was progress on a macro level and that was a big deal. The work that Ava began at Amcha, then with Magda, Suzi and Judy had taken root and extended itself. They no longer had to hover over each other, huddling together to brace themselves for the uncertainty Ava had experienced in her life.

52

"Strength does not come from physical capacity. It comes from an indomitable will."
—Mahatma Gandhi

Ava wasn't feeling well. It started shortly after she had oral surgery. She was not a stranger to implants, crowns, and veneers, having suffered dental problems her whole life. Most of her dentists, periodontists and endodontists all attributed her problems to the dietary deficiencies she suffered during the war and subsequently in her pregnancies. While Ava was fastidious in maintaining her oral hygiene and in taking calcium supplements, her teeth were weak. After the procedure, she felt weak and began to reconsider the cruise that she hoped she and her sisters would take in honor of her upcoming 100th birthday. If it was too much for her, then how much more so would it be for her sisters, she thought, both of whom were not in good health, but still absolutely determined to come to Israel to celebrate.

Suddenly, the choice was no longer Ava's or her sisters when both of their spouses died within days of each other. The two brothers-in-law had lived long lives, one died in his sleep and the other had a massive stroke. Ava knew that there was no way she could continue planning her birthday, out of respect for her brothers in law and for her sisters. Instead, she made plans to immediately travel to America to be with her sisters, to sit with them during the Shiva, the seven days of mourning. She decided too that on her way back from America she would invite her three daughters to meet her in Hungary and there, in the cemetery of her ancestors, she would celebrate her life, while showing her daughters her hometown, her place of birth, where she lived a very happy life as a child well loved by her parents, siblings and friends. If they were all on board, they would then take three days and luxuriate at the magnificent Széchenyi Thermal Baths.

Ava was positive the mineral baths and medical spa would rejuvenate her. In fact, Ava's new plan felt right for her. Her three daughters were not only on board to travel to Hungary with her, but Judy and Suzi insisted that they too would come to New York to see their beloved aunts and fly with Ava from New York to Budapest. All three were excited to have this opportunity with their mother and felt like it would continue to stimulate and promote the work they did with Dr. Levy.

Beyond understanding intergenerational trauma and epigenetics, now it was also time for them to embrace their roots. Magda was surprised to find out that her great-grandmother was originally from Poland, while Suzi was astounded to find out that on their father's side, they could trace their lineage to King David. Zak made all the arrangements for the ladies. He surprised himself by wanting to join them, partially to protect them all and partially because he too wanted to explore his own roots. But he respected his mother-in-law and acquiesced to her wishes for this to be a trip for her and her daughters. He would approach Suzi and perhaps they could plan a trip of their own to Hungary and Poland.

53

"A dream doesn't become reality through magic; it takes sweat, determination and hard work."
—Colin Powell

The trip to America was excruciatingly hard on Ava. It brought back memories of all that she had achieved in America while forging a life, first with Lajos and then with Imre. The fact that both were taken from her was something she could handle in Israel, with so many distractions, but back in New York, the memories came roaring back. Ava tried hard to control her emotions on the plane. She didn't want to worry her daughters or take away from what lay ahead, both in seeing her sisters and helping them cope with their loss and then when they traveled home. Ava smiled to herself and recalled the day when Suzi, as a teenager asked her why she didn't consider New York home. She remembered not having a good answer, except to explain to Suzi that your birthplace would always be home.

As they deplaned, Ava looked at her daughters and felt grateful for them. They were women of courage, talent, and beauty. She knew that their lives had been challenging, but like her, they persevered.

Magda met her mother and sisters at the airport and drove them to her apartment. She was slightly taken aback at how her mother had aged in the three months since she had last seen her. Nevertheless, Ava surprised them all, eating a hearty meal, courtesy of Magda's Place, relishing every bite she ate which pleased each of her daughters. Four hours later they were on their way to Teaneck, New Jersey where Kati and Zita lived, near their own daughters. It was a very difficult moment when Ava walked in, to see her sisters sitting on the low mourning chairs. As she approached them, and knelt so that she could embrace them, they and all their daughters surrounded them. For Dani that was a moment she would never forget. Not one word was said, but the sisterhood of generations held them all together.

"Suzika," said Ava, "help me up, please."

Immediately, the circles surrounding the matriarchs opened and Ava was in a comfortable chair right next to her sisters. They began to converse in Hungarian and talked, first about their daughters, then about their health and finally about the men in their lives who had stood by them. Ava, having buried two husbands, assured her sisters that they too would be alright. Then she told them how she had altered her birthday celebration. Both Kati and Zita were genuinely sorry that their cruise would sail without them.

"I am sure," said Ava, "we will have many more days of laughter and fun. Wait until you see what Magdushka brought from the store for dinner. In my life, I never saw such unbelievable delicacies!"

Magda, from the kitchen, heard her mother and smiled. Although her mother and aunts were conversing in Hungarian, they sounded so normal to her. It was something in Ava's tone, she simply sounded even and balanced, there was sadness for her sisters, but no undertone of anxiety whatsoever.

Within a short time, Suzi's daughters arrived, along with Bethie and Deenie. Judy's daughters had called and sent enormous food baskets to pay their respects. All the women sat at Kati's table and as they ate, they talked about the past. Ava, Kati, and Zita merely looked in profound gratitude that in spite of the losses they recently endured, they were so fortunate to have survived, these many years older, over seven decades since they were liberated from Auschwitz.

"I wish," said Ava wistfully, "that you two would consider living with me in Israel. I know you would find peace and happiness, in the garden or working with Judy's children."

But neither Kati nor Zita took Ava up on her offer. Neither wanted to be uprooted and preferred to be near their own daughters and grandchildren. The three days that Ava spent with them went by quickly. When she told them she was on her way to Hungary, both sisters cried. Ava left with a heavy heart, vowing to come see her sisters in two months. She would muster up all the energy it took, but she would do it for her sisters. She never forgot the circumstances of their bond.

54

"Peace cannot be kept by force; it can only be achieved by understanding."
—Albert Einstein

Once again, the women were on an airplane. Shockingly they were all sensibly dressed, and Ava laughed to herself, thinking how pleased Imre would be to see her wearing sensible, functional clothing. She remembered being on top of the Jungfrau Mountain with Fay, wearing sandals and a silk dress, and Imre, perhaps one of maybe two times in their married life, actually being irritated with her. Now, as an old lady, she had little choice but to be dressed in a way that enhanced her energy level. They were flying direct non-stop to Budapest. Zak, the family travel planner expert, did not disappoint.

As they deplaned, a driver was at the gate with a wheelchair to assist Ava. Istvan was a delightful gentleman, but Judy was extremely uncomfortable with how easily her mother and sisters chatted with him. He was a man in his forties, she assumed, and she felt sick thinking that his own grandfather might have been a Nazi sympathizer or worse. Later, after eating dinner at the Hanna, while having tea in the magnificent atrium in their hotel lobby, Judy tried to calm herself down, to not allow depressing thoughts creep into her soul. Even if that were the case, she argued with herself, what difference did it make? She was not going to impose her nagging thoughts on her sisters and certainly not on her mother. Ava was already in bed, and they were scheduled to meet Istvan at 5:00 a.m. to start the drive to Baia Mare.

At 3:45 a.m., Ava was completely dressed and tried to rouse her three sleeping daughters. She laughed, hummed and snapped her fingers but not one of them budged. Finally, when room service arrived with breakfast, the smell of the coffee woke her daughters, who each burst out laughing when they saw their mother at the table, buttering a flaky croissant.

"Only you Mamuka," said Magda with love in her voice, "could be dressed at this ungodly hour, ready to rock and roll."

"Vell, my darling, ve do have a plan," said Ava semi-seriously. "But you know what? Take your time. Don't rush yourself."

"Really Mamuka?" asked Judy in amazement. "Aren't you worried we will offend our new friend Istvan?"

"Judyka," said Ava in a mildly exasperated tone, "you are not a child, you are a fantastic woman of age. Do you seriously think I didn't think the exact same things you did when we met him? He is our driver, that's all."

"Oh Mamuka," wailed Judy, "you don't know how much I appreciate that! I tried hard not to show how upset I was. I breathed, I *davened,* and I tried hard to put it in perspective. But I'm so glad it wasn't just me."

"I had the same thoughts," said Suzi, "and I guarantee you Magda, when she gets out of the shower, did too."

"Well," said Judy, "let's be honest, we will always have those moments when certain events or people trigger what is part of our collective subconscious. The point is just to let it go."

"Oy," said Ava, smiling with pride, "a philosopher and a genius right here in Budapest! Who knew?"

"You mean," interjected Judy, "that from a *lemala,* I actually became a whole person?"

"Yes," said Ava, this time with visible tears in her eyes, "I thought I would die when you were a child. I didn't have enough understanding about how affected you all were, and I felt so helpless. I was able to survive the war, but I couldn't protect my baby daughter."

"Please Mamuka, don't go there," said Judy, sobbing too. "I am really okay, you know that! In fact, when we get back home, let's go see Dr. Levy, just me and you. But now, let's get ready and start our journey."

"I'd really love that, my darling," said Ava. "Thank you."

The ladies went from town to town, visiting cemeteries, parks, and synagogues where their ancestors once lived in peace. They all were noticeably emotional when they visited the apartment that Ava and Lajos lived in after the war. It was an experience they would share with their own daughters as well. For Ava that was the critical part, to know that subsequent generations would always remember what happened to her and her family.

When they got back to Budapest, the ladies visited the lovely shops on Vaci Utca, the Dohany Street Synagogue and Museum. Ava was in rare form, excited to show her daughters the best that her country had to offer, from its down blankets to the exquisite hand-painted Herend porcelain and china, to exotics jams and cherry strudel, a cornucopia of delights that they all enjoyed. They ended their walking tour of Budapest by the riverbank, to view the Shoes on the Danube Promenade, a monument consisting of 60 pairs of shoes, an exact true to life replica in size and detail, sculpted out of iron, an unbearable reminder of a time when innocent people were ordered to remove their shoes before being shot. It was the closest they got to any conversation about the war and that too was exactly what they wanted.

As they checked into the opulent well-appointed spa, four weary women felt a glimmer of joy. The trip to all the towns of their ancestors had been emotional, draining, sad, exhausting and at times even exhilarating; but this part of the trip somehow seemed to soothe them. There was always going to be sadness, they agreed, but there would also always be joy.

Over the next three days, Ava took a medical approach to her spa treatments while Suzi and Judy enjoyed Thai massages and Magda opted for deep tissue massages. They swam, they played cards, they napped, and they talked. They dressed for the meals because Ava would not tolerate the sweatsuits she saw the other guests lounging in. They all unanimously adored the delicious vegetarian meals, artfully displayed and elegantly served on the butterfly Herend dishes. The stay was satisfying and nurturing and they laughed heartily in the sauna, as they lay in their towels, inhaling the hot wet steam. Ava emphatically stated that she had reverted to a woman of 70 which made Magda laugh hysterically.

"So Mamuka, if you are 70 then I'm 50," she said jubilantly.

"Fine, Magdushka," said Ava, slightly annoyed. "It's not the number, it's how you feel."

"Yes," said a contrite Magda, holding back more laughter, "I never seem to get it. Promise me Mamuka, you will live forever, so that you can always teach me right from wrong."

"Magdushka," said Ava softly, "I hear you, please *dragam*, please remember you are everything I could have wished for. You don't need me. If anything, I need you."

"Then you shall have me, I love you to pieces. Whatever you need, just say so," declared Magdushka.

Magda impulsively decided then and there to change her itinerary and fly back to Israel with her mother and Judy. She could not bear to leave her mother just yet. At this point in her life, her daughters were all doing well and miracle of miracles, Hershel had evolved into a capable businessman, which meant Magda was free to do as she pleased. She was secretly thrilled though when he called her every day to say he missed her. It had taken a lifetime for Magda and Hershel, but they finally had a relationship that afforded both everything they needed.

The ladies were ready to depart from Hungary. It was a trip they would not soon forget and all four felt that it completely added a new perspective to their lives. They gathered their belongings and assorted gifts and Istvan drove them to the airport. It was then that Judy had her moment of satisfaction with this man whom she believed mistakenly thought he had perhaps because of his Hungarian background made a permanent connection with these Hungarian American women, when Ava dismissed him with a polite but dismissive *elég hosszú* [so long].

Istvan looked mildly surprised that no one asked for his contact information for future trips. Ava merely looked pointedly and asked him to remove their luggage from the trunk of his vehicle, without even answering him. Judy was thrilled, Mamuka, dressed in a beautiful St. John's tweed suit and black felt cloche hat indeed looked like a very successful woman, someone Istvan would have been thrilled to know. But here in an instant, Judy understood that her mother was able to put aside how she felt about Hungarians simply because it was her birthplace. The reality was that the Germans had many allies in their quest to rid the universe of Jews and other non-Aryans, and the Hungarians who betrayed their loyal Jewish citizens was something Judy wasn't willing to overlook, ever.

Somewhere in the recesses of her mind, she knew it was unfair to blame this individual Istvan, who surely did nothing to them, in fact, he was respectful, courteous and professional. But emotions won over logic and Judy didn't care, if just once, she and her family weren't so thoughtful. After all, though she would never really know, the possibility that this man's relatives were collaborators with the Nazis still existed. To forgive and to forget was not in Judy's playbook, at all.

55

"Always remember that you are absolutely unique. Just like everyone else."
—Margaret Mead

When Rose Seltzer and her husband moved to Israel permanently, Ava was elated. The two had remained close friends for many years but having her friend in closer proximity felt marvelous to Ava. They arranged to meet on Wednesdays, for lunch and it was something Ava very much looked forward to. She missed her sisters enormously and wished that they would come live with her. She would do everything for them, even have her nieces and great nieces and nephews visit as often as they wanted to see Kati and Zita, but so far, it hadn't happened.

Ava was aware of her increasing dependence on Ora and wasn't all that keen on accepting advice from someone 60 years her junior. Ava loved Ora and appreciated every sacrifice she made to make her life more comfortable, but she could not be her friend. With the arrival of the Seltzers, Ava felt she would be able to talk to people of her own generation, though Rose was younger than her by nearly a decade. How interesting, Ava thought back to when she first met Rose and assumed she was so much older than her, merely because of her status and education. Ava wondered in that moment, if life had been different what path she herself might have taken? Had there been no war and annihilation of her family and city, might she have made *aliyah* with her husband? Might she have gone to school? Ava knew it was foolish to speculate because how could she possibly figure out who she might have married and where they might have settled?

Not one to mope around, Ava finished her breakfast and waited for Ora to help her shower. She was anxious to get her carefully curated day started, to pray and *daven*, work in the garden, have a nap, do her yoga and acupuncture and then after lunch and another short nap, head over to Judy's Place, where she would be greeted by the children, the staff, and her own daughter. Going to the home had become the highlight of her day and Ava expressed her profound admiration to Judy nearly every day for having the vision to create a facility that was a blueprint for helping children who desperately were in need of a residence that provided a home for them. As bone-tired as she was when she came home, Ava thanked God every day that with a little assistance, she could still get dressed, put on makeup and a lovely suit, and have a productive day. She adored the children, and they all knew it.

When Ava met them in her reading group, her heart broke. She asked and received permission to interact with the children in a way that was meaningful for each. Ava would braid little Lana's golden hair, and baked with the older girls, Rina, Chaya and Chana. She encouraged Kiki and Mendy to write in their journals and found time to listen to Shira tell her about a dream she had. She cuddled with Shlomo, Chesky and Yossi, the three Hasidic brothers who recently arrived at Judy's Place when their mother died, and their father could not cope with his nine children. In the beginning, the little boys, ages four, five and seven regressed significantly. One stuttered, the other refused to eat and the third required diapers though he was seven years old. They cried on and off, long into the night and Malka, the overnight Ima often stayed with them the entire night until they eventually fell asleep. These little boys were vulnerable and scared. Ava would talk and sing to them in their native tongue, in Yiddish, cut their food for them and would hold them in her arms. And slowly, with the arrival of a Yiddish-speaking child psychiatrist and social worker, as well as Hasidic teenage boys to play sports, the children began to thrive.

When Ora lightly knocked on the door to her bedroom suite, Ava felt relieved. Thinking lately had become burdensome. She didn't want to think of the past, except when she was talking to her great grandchildren or the children in the home. Other than that, there was no joy in reminiscing about things that might have been. Far safer to focus on the day in front of her.

Ora looked at Ava and knew that she had been thinking about the past. It was almost impossible, Ora thought stoically, not to have had many tragedies if one lived to 100. But she understood this incredible woman who was already a legend on two continents. Here in Israel, she was a celebrity, after her numerous appearances on the morning news shows, and every year on Yom Hashoah [Holocaust Memorial Day]. Then too, she was widely known as the Ava behind the global, made in Israel AvaFay line of clothing. But perhaps, it was her identity as the matriarch of the foster home, where she visited daily, to see the children, to inspire them and to hand out treats. Her visits made the children feel special and Ora, who accompanied Ava, delighted in watching how all the children, of many diverse backgrounds gravitated towards Ava. How Ora wished there had been a facility like this when she and her siblings were growing up! Perhaps her life and many of theirs might have been so much less stressful. Ora was incredibly grateful that through her good fortune, her two younger sisters Elana and Simmi had had the good opportunity to attend college and secure well-paying jobs at AvaFay that allowed them to break free of the cycle of poverty they had grown up in.

Ora often wondered how it was that a person could be as extraordinary as Ava and realized that she would never know the answer, because no one, except other survivors of the *Shoah* [the Holocaust], could ever fully understand what the war had done to that generation and how it had changed them forever. But somehow Ora felt that Ava was destined for greatness, having nothing whatsoever to do with her life experience. It was her *neshama*, a soul that lived to connect to others. You could see it on her face and theirs when the children crowded around her. All the children, big and small, those diagnosed with emotional and/or intellectual disabilities, autism, Down Syndrome, generalized anxiety or oppositional defiant disorder, gravitated towards Ava, interacted with her, and literally presented as calmer and happier in her presence.

It wasn't only the children. Every staff member, administrator, volunteer, and benefactor of Judy's Place clamored to be in her presence, to simply talk to her or ask her opinion. Often, this put Ora in the awkward position of stepping in and tactfully ending these conversations, because even in their enthusiasm, respect and admiration for Ava, the interactions took a heavy toll on Ava's waning strength.

Ora understood Ava was aging rapidly and vividly recalled her great-grandmother in Yemen trying to cope with old age. She tactfully tried to encourage Ava to change her schedule. Although resistant at first, Ava eventually succumbed. She wanted to be well and full of vigor so that when her sisters eventually came to Israel, she could take care of them.

Ava was willing to concede that she needed help with her daily living, more so that her daughters, themselves middle-aged women, would not worry about her. She knew that Magda had a very hard time saying goodbye to her after their trip to Hungary. She understood her daughters though she herself had no mother for three quarters of her life. But she remembered as a girl, worrying about her own mother. Perhaps it was natural, perhaps not.

In any case, Ava decided that she would approach death as another chapter in her life. She would not indulge herself in useless tears to cause her daughters to mourn her excessively, not beyond that of their time honored cultural and religious traditions. When Ava went for a routine visit to her doctor, it did not surprise her that he found a tumor. She was not a fool and knew that she was going to die, and she accepted the fact. She also opted not to have chemotherapy or radiation. The good news was that the cancer was very slow growing and, in a region where it was excised entirely. Postsurgery, Ava's margins were clear. When Ava discussed her prognosis with Rose, she chuckled in agreement when Rose proclaimed that Ava indeed had as many lives as a cat.

"I am certain Ava," she said seriously, "that our wonderful God, while ready to greet you, knows you still have work to do here on earth."

She shocked Ava when she started to cry.

"Ava, you have made such a profound change in my life. All my education taught me next to nothing compared to what I learned from you," she said emotionally. "And it wasn't just the fashion, it was how to come to terms with what was best for the boys. I will never forget what you did for me, Ava."

"I did what any friend would do," replied Ava simply. "You knew all along what you had to do. I just listened."

"Not exactly," insisted Rose. "Who came with me to inspect six facilities until we found the right one, the right staff, the right mindset in giving the boys the best possible life? It was you Ava, and I'm guessing you never ever shared that with anyone."

"Why would I ever discuss something so profoundly personal with anyone?" asked Ava.

"Because I know how close you are to your sisters," said Rose.

"That is certainly true," said Ava, "but I learned in therapy that boundaries must be upheld, even in the face of closeness."

"You never cease to amaze me Ava," said Rose. "I cannot tell you enough how much our friendship enriches my life. I feel extremely fortunate that we met so many years ago. And I share in all the achievements your incredible daughters have made!"

56

"The worst enemy to creativity is self-doubt."
—Sylvia Plath

When Rabbi Shanzer got a call from Ora requesting that he visit Ava, he felt nervous and instinctively prepared himself for bad news. There was something about Ava Kertesz that tugged at his heart strings. He was not ashamed to admit that he simply adored her, admired her and always was happy when he was in her presence. He questioned often what it was that she represented to him and finally concluded that for him, Ava embodied the totality of resilience, exactly what the Jewish people possessed. Listening to Ava rhapsodize about the children at Judy's Place, her appreciation of Israeli wine, her love and endless generosity for her children and grandchildren and great-grandchildren simply pleased Rabbi Shanzer. He prayed daily for Ava, asking God to grant her good health until *Moshiach* [the Messiah] arrived. As he approached her home, he found himself tearing up. He knew this summons could only mean one thing, that Ava was dying. As he walked into her bedroom, Rabbi Shanzer's worst fears were confirmed. Ava was weak and frail, and without the benefit of makeup and being dressed in her beautiful outfits, looked every bit of her years. In true Ava style, in a matter of minutes, it was she who rallied and offered comfort to Rabbi Shanzer.

"Please my friend," she begged, "don't mourn me, not now, not ever. I have been extraordinarily lucky and have lived a wonderful life."

"I can't help it," cried Rabbi Shanzer, sounding to Ava, like a scared child. "I just need you to be ok, I know I don't sound rational or logical, but that's how I feel."

"Well," said Ava gently, "in that case, come and sit closer to me and let's talk until you feel better."

Ora, who had silently entered the bedroom, was astounded when she saw Rabbi Shanzer, a leading Rabbinical authority in all of Israel sitting on Ava's bed, his hand in Ava's without a word passing between the two of them. She wisely did not intrude on whatever it was that was happening, but instead tiptoed out of the room to arrange lunch for Ava's guest.

Eventually, Rabbi Shanzer took hold of himself and profusely apologized to Ava.

"Nonsense," said Ava. "If I had to choose a man to be the son I never gave birth to, it would be you. You and I both know we have a *kesher*, a connection that isn't easily defined. I knew it when I visited Fay and thereafter every single time, I met with you."

At that moment, Ava literally jumped out of her bed. "Baruch," she screamed. "I figured it out. Please, we must have a DNA test done today."

Baruch Shanzer looked at Ava and asked, "Why Ava? What are you trying to prove?"

"Something I have felt ever since I met you."

Ava could not be persuaded to say another word. Baruch left her bedroom and Ora arrived to help Ava dress. It seemed as if Ava gained strength she no longer thought she possessed. As soon as she was dressed, she made a few phone calls and within the hour both she and Rabbi Shanzer were on their way to meet with Israel's foremost geneticist.

Over the course of the next 30 days, both Ava and Baruch Shanzer were equally nervous. When the DNA sample came back, it conclusively confirmed what Ava already knew: Baruch Shanzer was her nephew. By a miracle, this child had survived. He was her beloved sister Surika's infant son who miraculously did not die in Auschwitz but was hidden for the duration of the war.

Baruch Shanzer was in total shock. He could not believe that his parents were not his biological parents and that he had never known he was adopted. Suddenly things that always puzzled him started to make sense. The gap in years between him and his siblings, his inability to effectively bond with his mother, his father's sad look whenever he tried to get close to him, his height and hair color, so different from his siblings and of course his overwhelming tie to Fay, Ava's granddaughter and ultimately to Ava herself. When NechaLiba Shanzer's daughters Bailu and Miriam, Ava's nieces, found out, they too were flabbergasted.

"How is this possible?" they asked Ava. "Didn't you tell us long ago, that you yourself witnessed your sister's children being murdered at Auschwitz? And how is it that our mother didn't know that our aunt adopted a child?"

"I can't explain anything," replied Ava slowly. "If I had to guess, I would say that your cousin Naftuli-Binyumin did not die that terrible day in Auschwitz and someone rescued him, hid him and even smuggled him out of Auschwitz. When no one claimed the baby after the war, your aunt and uncle decided to raise him as their own child. I remember your aunt telling me she was grateful to have a child, and it was many long years before she gave birth to the rest of you."

That her beloved sister Surika's son had survived the war enveloped Ava in an incomparable feeling of peace. It confirmed her belief and solidified her hope that not all was lost, that miracles indeed did happen.

At her next visit with her oncologist, Ava insisted she was well and her doctor, reluctant until he ran tests to confirm, admitted that she looked well. Though she was over 100 years old, Ava indeed possessed boundless energy. She was planning a trip to America with Baruch, who reclaimed his birth name, Naftuli-Binyumin, so that he could meet his aunts and their families. She simply did not have time or patience to deal with cancer. When Dr. Raanan personally arrived at her house Ava was not surprised. Though he was a pre-eminent doctor with many patients, he was a respectful young man who also admired Ava and wanted to deliver the test results to her in person. A rare individual. Ava entered her library where the doctor sat waiting to see her. She could see the pain on his face and spared him.

"Dr. Raanan," she said briskly, "I know why you are here. Please I beg of you, don't be sad. I have had so many extra years. I should have died in 1945, alongside my mother and sisters. Who am I to have *taanot* [complaints], after living such an incredible life?"

Dr. Raanan could not control himself and began to sob. "I wanted to bring you good news."

"Well," said Ava, "you actually did. You reminded me that I must make use of my remaining time and do what I need to do. So, thank you, because in my arrogance, I thought that perhaps I had cheated death once more."

Ava laughed and reiterated that she had no fear of death. But that night while talking to Zita and Kati on the phone, she stubbornly clung to her feeling that she wasn't about to die anytime soon. Both of her sisters were in fairly stable health and could not wait to see Ava and their nephew.

"Chavala," said Zita, lapsing into her sister's birth name, "if you want to live, you will. No one, not even God himself would start up with you!"

For one moment all three were transported back to Auschwitz, arriving as Chavala, Feygala and Malku, sisters who desperately wanted to escape the fear, shame, degradation, pain and loneliness of their new existence. Collectively they recalled how they beat death, desperately clinging to life, to honor their mother's last wishes that they survive and live happy lives.

"Hurry Avala," cried Zita. "I can't wait to see you and Naftuli-Binyumin."

As they hung up the phone, Ava felt a renewed sense of well-being she had not enjoyed since Imre died. She was not sick, regardless of her test results. If she survived Auschwitz, she could survive anything.

57

"Children are the living messages we send to a time we will not see."
—John F. Kennedy

Not only was Ava's entire family transformed by the sheer miracle of Rabbi Shanzer being a blood relative, but so too was all of Israel. Once again Ava found herself in front of television crews in her home. Everyone in Israel and eventually in America, Australia, and Europe, all clamored for details about the miraculous reunion of this family. Rabbi Shanzer was uncomfortable with the notoriety, but because it gave Ava such satisfaction, he willingly endured all the questions.

It seemed as if everyone in Israel had a connection to the *Shoah*. It was everyone's secret fantasy to be reunited with relatives whom no one could confirm died in the Holocaust or as in the case of baby Shanzer were whisked away by loving people who cared for a child who was not their own. It once again brought attention to the devastation of the Holocaust beyond the concentration camps, but rather in its aftermath. For Naftuli-Binyumin Shanzer, knowing he found his real family was life changing. He remembered well when his daughter introduced him to Fay Zweig. He remembered feeling responsible for her in a way he could not describe, when on the surface she was simply a Jewish teenager from America. When he met Ava, he again felt a connection he could not explain. Now it all made sense to him, and he was relieved. He was proud to be part of Ava's family and sat for hours in Ava's kitchen as she told him stories about his mother and father and baby sister. He cried tears of joy when Ava's face lit up as she told him about his mother, her piousness, her charity and kindnesses and her rare beauty. On that Ava was emphatic.

"Naftulika, *meyn kind*," she said, lapsing into Yiddish, calling her nephew by his true name, crooning to her 70-year-old nephew as if he were an infant, "you look exactly like your mother. She was known throughout all of Baia Mare for her beauty. Every boy wanted to marry her; every mother wanted her for a daughter in law."

Naftuli-Binyumin sat still, mesmerized by Ava's stories. All his children and grandchildren were in awe of what happened to him. It confirmed to all of them that life was simply unpredictable. Chava Sara decided that she needed to address this issue, so that other families, globally, might be inspired by their family story and begin the arduous task of doing research and corroborating details from a time when there were few if any records. Perhaps other families would be as fortunate as them and would find evidence that not all of their family were murdered but miraculously survived. ChavaSara arduously began the task of setting up a network of volunteers who would be available to help families locate their relatives. She reached out to Yad Vashem with their vast database and in a matter of months, set up a hotline to help anyone who needed assistance in starting a search for family members. Eventually, she collaborated on a book with her cousin Suzi, Fay's mother who was honored to help write a book to celebrate the homecoming of Naftuli-Binyumin Shanzer. The book was extremely well received. It seemed as if everyone near and far wanted to rejoice with their families. And no one was happier than Fay Natan.

"Ma," she said gleefully to her mother Suzi, "when I think back to my time in Yerushalayim, I never felt alone. I absolutely always felt like Rabbi Shanzer and ChavaSara were my family. Regardless of our differences, I felt a connection to them. There were days when I was so lonely, missing my life and my family and they understood me and carried me. This is such a huge miracle, and we are so lucky."

The day before Ava, Dani, Fay and Naftuli-Binyumin Shanzer were scheduled to fly to New York, Ava developed a dry cough. Out of a sense of extreme caution she went again to see her doctor. Relieved that Dr. Raanan cleared her for traveling, when she got a call in America a few days later from Dr. Raanan, she wasn't surprised. Once again, she preempted him.

"Doctor," she began jubilantly, "I know why you are calling, and I couldn't be happier."

"You know?" asked Doctor Raanan. "How? Did my assistant already call you? I am sitting here with my colleagues. We are absolutely amazed at your latest scans. In fact, we are going to publish your case in the medical journal of medicine. *Gveret* Kertesz. You are in remission; you are cancer free."

For the normally reserved doctor who himself was a descendant of Holocaust survivors who trained himself early on to never reveal his emotions, the much-needed release of tears was cathartic. He simply could not talk, sobbing for minutes, while Ava merely waited, seated on Magda's peach silk couch. Finally, Dr. Raanan composed himself long enough to speak.

"I wish you continued good health Ava. All of my patients will know from today on that they can never give up, that miracles in medicine do happen. I look forward to seeing you in three months. Shalom shalom," he concluded.

Ava smiled broadly and called Magda, asking her to arrange a celebratory dinner. Naftuli-Binyumin, on hearing the news merely held on tight to Ava, no longer bound by the laws of *negiah*, he considered his aunts Ava, Zita and Kati to be his mothers and often hugged and embraced them.

To see the four of them when they were reunited was a sight Judy,

Suzi and Magda and their cousins knew they would never forget. Not a sound could be heard as they embraced. For the three women it was an affirmation of faith, that their sister's son had survived, had brought many children into the world, all of them devout and God-fearing. It was an enormous moment in their lives. When ChavaSara's youngest daughter gave birth to a baby girl and named her Sara, after her grandmother, it all came full circle. A new Surika would take her place in the family and surely her namesake in heaven was rejoicing. The satisfaction Ava and her sisters felt was rejuvenating. None of their aches and pains or age-related frailties mattered. All they cared about was their nephew and his family. They were determined to make up for lost time and spent hours upon hours listening to him, looking at pictures and admiring the life their nephew led.

Naftuli-Binyumin Shanzer doted on this baby as if she were his first grandchild. He couldn't get enough of her, picking her up and bringing her daily to visit Ava. When Ava lovingly called the little baby by her namesake's name Surika, she instantly remembered her beloved older sister and shed tears, again and again. Life was so good to her. Even Kati and Zita bounced back to better health. They adored their nephew Naftuli-Binyumin Shanzer, remembered meeting him at Fay's wedding and making fun of Ava, who at that time kept insisting she felt connected to him.

"*Dragam*," said Zita, "we owe you an apology. You were right! How did we not see it?"

"I told you," shouted Ava, while laughing. "I just knew."

"Thank God," said Kati. "We have lived long enough to see this miracle. I am hoping Avala that your invitation is still open? I really want to meet all of our nephew's family."

"Are you kidding me, Katushka? It would be my honor; my privilege and it would mean everything to have you in my home."

The Reiss sisters, the matriarchs, began to plan for the trip back to Israel. In conjunction with their trip, Ava impulsively decided to hold a huge family reunion on Purim. Ora made the arrangements for the hall, ChavaSara, her sisters and her daughters, along with Fay and Dani planned the extensive menu and Zak made all the travel arrangements. All told there would be over 200 people in attendance; four generations of family who were profoundly grateful to be alive, to be the descendants of one Jewish family in Baia Mare, Hungary who miraculously continued to exist in spite of Hitler's maniacal plan to annihilate every Jew from the face of the earth.

At the celebration Rabbi Naftuli-Binyumin Shanzer, as he was now officially known, got up to speak. First, he talked at length about Queen Esther *Hamalka* and her uncle Mordechai; their mission to save the Jews of Paras and Madi, their determination to reverse the death decree issued by Haman, a high-ranking official in King Achasverishos' government. And then he spoke about Hitler.

"But we are gathered here today, my beloved family. We are a testament to the fact that Hitler did not succeed. I can't say enough about my beloved ImaAva," this being the new title he bestowed on Ava, calling her Ima. "Is there anyone here who doesn't know of her deeds, her generosity and love of humanity? She is the Queen Esther of our lifetime, saving countless lives every single day. What did I ever do in my life to deserve to be in her life, I ask someone to tell me?"

In a room with many babies, toddlers, children, teens and adults, there was not a sound. Every single person was riveted to their seats, spellbound by the passionate words of Rabhi Shanzer. "*Hodu LaHashem Ki Tov*, let us give thanks and praise to almighty God for all the good," he screamed at the top of his lungs. "Raise a glass with me and let's give thanks to Hashem for this *bracha*, this blessing that he has given us."

Every man, woman and child celebrated. It was a Purim feast like no other. Even the youngest children understood that something special was happening in their midst. Ava and her sisters were dressed in gowns with crowns on their heads and were toasted repeatedly. The children presented them with magnificent bouquets of flowers.

Ava smiled at her sisters. "Thank you for never abandoning me, for feeding me emotionally when I was starving. This is what God had in store for us. I hope Surika is resting better in heaven, knowing that Naftuli-Binyumin is exactly where he belongs."

In looking at her nephew, Ava saw a distinguished, pious man who was totally at peace with himself. A man who devoted himself to God, family and country, who struggled and overcame the vague notion that something was off kilter most of his life. His incredible journey had finally given him the answers he knew were waiting and indeed repaired his anguished soul.

58

"One word frees us of all the weight and pain in life. That word is Love."
—Socrates

Judy arrived at work the next day anxious to celebrate Purim with the children. Like her siblings, she was astounded at the turn of events in their family and felt incredibly happy for her mother, her aunts and especially for her cousin Naftuli-Binyumin Shanzer and his family. As she pulled into her parking space, ever observant, Judy saw an unfamiliar car in the small lot behind the residences. Thinking perhaps that a health official was visiting the facility, she walked in briskly.

"Shalom," she greeted the receptionist and in rapid fire Hebrew asked who was in the building, only to find that one of the children was being seen by an uncle who just arrived from Chicago.

Judy went to her office assuming her staff would eventually inform her of what had transpired during the visit. Although most of the children were Israeli born orphans or abandoned by parents who could not care for them, some did have relatives who reached out occasionally. The facility policy was to allow visitors in all the common areas and then to investigate further if permission was requested for off-site visits.

Four hours later when Judy was about to take her usual walk around the facility, she was startled to see Ava arriving. "Mamuka," she called out with joy in her voice, "I can't believe you came in today."

"Why?" said Ava laughing like a mischievous girl. "Is there some reason I shouldn't see the children today?"

"Maybe," said Judy, "because after last night's celebration you just might need 24 hours of uninterrupted rest? Is that so outrageous?"

"Well," sniffed Ava, "for your information, I did rest, all night and all morning. I did not garden or do yoga. I left both of my sisters snoring and I'm only staying for a short while. Does that meet with your approval?"

"Yes, Mamuka," conceded Judy. "I just wish for once, you would act your age! You know we love having you here, but you need to take it easy."

"Judyka," pleaded Ava, "it's enough when I look in the mirror. I know exactly how old I am, she joked. But coming here, having a purpose, to make these children happy, keeps me young."

"I couldn't agree with you more," said Judy softly. "So come, let's go to the kitchen and see what the older girls are creating for the *seudah;* it will no doubt be a magnificent delicious feast."

As mother and daughter made their way to the kitchen to inspect the meal preparation, they were approached in the corridor by a gentleman. Both looked at him quizzically.

"Ladies," he began in English, "pardon my intrusion. I know who you both are, but you don't know me. Allow me to introduce myself."

Judy was uncomfortable being accosted in the lobby and steered both her mother and the guest to the dayroom. "Follow me," she said.

As Ora settled Ava into a comfortable chair, Judy waited for the gentleman to speak.

"My name is Gil Goldman. I came to visit my nephew Yehuda and to discuss the possibility of getting custody of him."

"Well," said Judy amiably, "you certainly don't need my

permission. You would need to speak to his social worker and then petition the court to prove that you can provide a safe stable environment for Yehuda. If that is the case, we would be thrilled for Yehuda. *Halevi*, every child in our care had a family to return to."

Mr. Goldman looked at Judy and smiled.

"I wish I had been in a position to come for Yehuda sooner, but that was not possible. Now, I am fully able to commit and to care for my sister's child and I will stop at nothing, even if it means relocating to Israel. I have no wife or children of my own; Yehuda has no other family other than me—we belong together."

Judy listened, glanced at her exceptionally quiet mother and began to rise to signal that the conversation had ended. It was then that she noticed a glimmer in Ava's eyes.

"Excuse me," said Ava in nearly perfect English, "I am so happy to make your acquaintance, Mr. Goldman and I can totally relate. I was just reunited with my very own nephew, and I know exactly how you feel."

Judy laughed inwardly. Was her mother finally losing it? Comparing the reunion with Naftuli-Binyumin Shanzer to that of a four-year-old? Once again, she attempted to end the conversation only to find her mother and Mr. Goldman chatting like old friends. It was uncanny how Ava could still charm any man, at any age, of any background.

And now, Gil Goldman was divulging the details of his life as a photojournalist, his recovery from a very serious injury sustained while in Kabul on assignment, his best-selling book and tour across America and his desire to care for his nephew. Other than his social security number, Ava had determined, in 15 minutes, everything that she needed to know, primarily that Gil Goldman was a very eligible bachelor. Judy listened in abject horror when she heard the dreaded words. "Please Mr. Goldman, you must join me for dinner this evening."

Gil Goldman, having no idea what Ava was up to, graciously accepted. As soon as he left, Judy turned to her mother. "Exactly what are you thinking?" she asked Ava who by now was on the phone, instructing her kitchen staff to prepare an extra plate for their guest and to make sure that both her sisters were still not sleeping.

"Those two," she chuckled. "Such *shluffers*. Sleeping hours after the sun rises!"

"Mamuka," said Judy, interrupting her mother. "I know exactly what you are doing. It's not going to work, so spare yourself the disappointment. I am not interested in dating. I've told you so many times. I am fine the way I am."

"Yes," said Ava absentmindedly, distracted by the thought and image of Judy falling in love with this fine man. "I know what you said, and I know what I know. Is it too much to ask you to join us for dinner tonight?"

"Oh Mamuka," sighed Judy. "Of course I'll come because you won't stop badgering me until I agree. I just wonder if Dr. Levy would approve of this."

"Dr. Levy," said Ava breathless with excitement, "I adore her! She is a rare, kind, wonderful, compassionate and brilliant doctor and understands a lot about emotions and human nature, but... she is not your mother. Trust me Judyka, I know a little more than her when it comes to my own daughters."

Judy burst out laughing and hugged her mother. "You win, Mamuka. And don't you dare tell me what to wear or what color lipstick to put on!"

"Me?" asked Ava. "Tell you what to wear? As if you didn't know on your own that your pink wool suit would be perfect for dinner, with that gorgeous Ann Fontaine blouse."

Ava smiled broadly. Tonight would be a new chapter for Judy. If God let her live this long, then she was sure it was to make at least one more wedding in her beautiful garden.

On the way home Ava dozed off in the car. She had already put in a full morning and needed a moment to revitalize her rapidly waning energy. When she came into her house, she was relieved to see that her sisters were dressed and in good spirits. She still worried obsessively about them, now more than ever as they aged. She was thrilled to find them laughing while visiting with their own daughters and grandchildren, all of whom were staying an additional few days, and who simply wanted to relive the incredible family reunion that had just taken place. Ava was taken aback by the number of visitors, surprised that they all were congregated in her living room instead of in a local restaurant. She quickly explained the situation to her sisters in Hungarian and within the hour the house was cleared of everyone who stopped by. Ava laughed at how thrilled her sisters were to be in on the plan, their commitment to somehow pushing Judyka into getting married as urgent to them as it was to her. It felt like old times when they banded together for physical and emotional survival.

～

That night at dinner Gil Goldman graciously endured question after question by Ava's sisters. The two sisters were not nearly as subtle as Ava, and Judy was mortified; she looked like she wanted to disappear. In fact, she liked this man and was terrified that her mother and aunts would scare him off. She tried to steer the conversation to politics and the economy, anything to move beyond why Gil Goldman was not married, if he was a *Kohen* and how much he was worth. By the time dessert was served, the elderly ladies somehow elected to move to the verandah for a cup of tea and Judy was left alone with Gil Goldman.

"My apologies for the interrogation," she began hesitantly.

"Oh no please," laughed Gil. "They are amazing women. I have never in my life met or even read about Holocaust survivors, much less sisters, at this age, who are still going strong. Lucky you, the genes you carry are extraordinary."

Judy smiled in gratitude. Gil Goldman was a very nice man, even if he was nine years younger than her. Naturally when she called Suzi and Magda, they were excited for her and totally minimized the age difference.

"So what?" said Suzi blithely.

"Who cares?" said Magda. "You look 20 years younger than your age anyway. If in fact this goes somewhere, all you have to concern yourself with is how you feel when you are with him. Do you want to tell him about your day? Do you want to share your life with him, the struggles, and the challenges? Does he make you happy?"

Judy slowly nodded her head although her sisters couldn't see her doing so. She knew she really liked Gil, as ridiculous as that was, having met him just a mere few hours ago. But she was also smart enough to know that 10 dates would not change how she felt instinctively. And so, she dared to allow herself to speculate and fantasize about a new kind of existence. Could she even contemplate giving up her own personal space? Could she actually give up her independence? Finally, she asked herself, did she like him enough to give up the loneliness that had become her constant companion, a fixed habit that she had simply gotten used to? She knew the answer. She was not going to rush, she would continue spending time with Gil and hopefully would be ready to take a chance in the not so distant future. She would not let fear—her constant steady, reliable, loyal companion since childhood—prevent her any longer from taking a chance on having a partner that she was physically and intellectually attracted to, a man she respected, a man she admired and a man that she knew she was starting to like a great deal.

Watching her daughter, Ava was ecstatic. She simply couldn't hide her joy at seeing Judyka so happy. Far more so than when she was married previously. Ava remembered no one paying attention to her misgivings, trying desperately to steer her daughter to a far more appropriate match. This time it would be a man who was her equal; one who was worldly and knowledgeable, who had endured and overcome trauma and still retained his zest for life, without resentment, anger or hostility. He was a perfect gentleman, and naturally Ava took all the credit. Perhaps what pleased Ava the most was that he was not a descendant of Holocaust survivors. To Ava that meant Gil had less baggage, less trauma to navigate. She felt sorry for him for losing his only sister but was impressed that as a bachelor he was willing to completely change his life to take care of his sister's child. That was a sacrifice that Ava could identify with. Later she discussed Gil with Baruch Natan, Fay's husband and he too liked what he heard about him. Increasingly, Baruch found himself not only drawn to Ava and his great aunts, but also to his cousins by marriage, Judy, Magda, and Suzi, feeling as if he was their brother. They in turn felt very close to him and admired his commitment to Fay and the life he had with her.

59

"History will judge us by the difference we make in the everyday lives of children."
—Nelson Mandela

When Dani got undressed that night, she looked at her stomach and knew she was pregnant. In 24 hours, a blood test confirmed her hunch. At the age of 46 she was going to have a baby. At first Dani was terrified of the potential problems associated with her age, but when she visited her ob-gyn who referred her to a well-qualified high-risk pregnancy specialist who was extremely confident and reassuring, she felt much better. She was in superb physical health and the doctor saw no complications whatsoever. Eliyahu and the boys were ecstatic. They speculated daily on whether Dani was carrying a baby boy or girl.

Eight months later, Dani's daughter arrived. Magda was deliriously happy, arriving in Israel six weeks before Dani's due date and staying six weeks after. This was a special time in Dani's life and Magda was thrilled that Dani wanted her to be there. She also adored the boys, they were no less her grandchildren than her biological ones and she delighted in watching them approach their new baby sister. For Dani, life was now complete. On occasion, while at the park, when young mothers assumed she was the baby's *savtah* [grandmother], she felt bad and worried if she had been selfish to have a child at her age. She calculated that she would be 59 at her daughter's 12th year confirmation bat-mitzvah, well past menopause, and middle-aged. When she expressed her concerns to her cousin Fay, Fay reminded her of their very own mothers hitting their prime in their seventies and eighties and their grandmother and great-aunts at age 100 still fully cognitively functional. It was then and there that Dani realized she was worrying prematurely for nothing.

"Perhaps," she said slowly to Fay, "it's pessimistic thinking that I thought I successfully ridded myself of. All that I can remember from my childhood, besides my Aunt Judy hugging me too tightly, was my mother's aura of unhappiness. I felt so helpless. I desperately wanted to rescue her from her misery, but I didn't know how to help her! But I am not, I repeat, I am not going to ever make my princess feel uncomfortable and worry about me. I suppose I will have to rely on my *emunah*, faith and your brilliant ability to be logical to get me out of my own head."

Fay hugged her cousin, so very happy that Dani would have a child of her own, happy too that they were as close as sisters and could support each other. For Dani, watching her miracle baby grow and seeing her in her grandmother's arms made Dani happier than she could ever imagine. She was overjoyed that she and her mother had found a path to a loving relationship, which didn't include having arguments or disagreements, but also, more importantly, was not born of vicarious trauma symptoms embedded in their DNA.

Once again Ava was in the news. It seemed as if Israeli society was obsessed with her every move. She was invited to speak at every *Tzahal* national military graduation, every national *Yom Hashoah* Holocaust Remembrance Day celebration and at every school graduation from *gan* to high school. Naturally, she could no longer attend all of the events she was invited to, and coaxed Judy and occasionally Suzi and Magda to attend in her place.

"After all," she told her sisters emphatically, "I see the queen of England is doing the exact same thing. She's no spring chicken either. She won't let Charles assume the throne, but she sends him, her youngest son Edward and her daughter Anne everywhere on her behalf. I just can't figure out why they can't fix Anne's look, she is just so unattractive!"

Her sisters laughed at the idea of Ava comparing herself to the monarchy.

"That sounds about right, *dragam* Ava," said Kati. "Thanks for the laugh. Just remember your age and take it easy."

"*Igen* Katika," replied Ava, "how incredibly lucky are we, to have lived this long? I am ready anytime God wants me. I have no complaints. My one worry is who will I spend my time with: Lajos or Imre?"

"Maybe Chavala," said Zita sarcastically, "you can focus on Mamuka and Tatuka instead of your two husbands?"

"You know what? You are right, my darling sister. Do I need husband headaches in heaven?" said Ava. "No man comes without headaches. Good advice! I'll be solo and waiting for both of you. Then we can have a proper reunion with Mamuka and Tatuka."

Although the sisters were joking, there was much truth to their banter. They would all eventually die peacefully in their sleep, within 30 days of each other, buried side-by-side. At their funerals, as they requested, there was no wild sobbing or shrieking, just acceptance. It was what they wanted and repeatedly told their daughters. For Ava's daughters, a world without Ava in it was that much less light and joyful. They met and spoke often with Naftuli-Binyumin Shanzer whom Ava named in her will and left a substantial sum of money to provide for him, his wife and family. Ava was well aware of her own daughter's needs and actually discussed with them her plan to add her nephew to her will. As she expected, each of her daughters was on board. In fact, they were happy to share their mother's estate with their cousin, knowing how much Ava loved him, and that he was an extension of her beloved sister Surika.

It was Naftuli-Binyumin, along with each of her sons-in-law and grandsons who recited the mourner's kaddish three times a day for an entire year. Suzi, Magda and Judy faithfully upheld the traditional mourning rituals for the entire year, never once deviating from the cultural norms that dictated that they not listen to music, not buy new clothes or attend parties, weddings or concerts. It was a year in which they talked incessantly about their mother, her courage and convictions, her triumphs, and her long life. The three of them wanted to keep her memory alive and each did so in their own way. They each dedicated themselves to educating every descendant in the family so that even the youngest members of the family would remember Ava Kertesz, the matriarch of the family, who was determined to live another day and rise from the ashes of Auschwitz.

60

"The pain passes, but the beauty remains."
—Renoir

Naftuli-Binyumin was inconsolable when Ava died. He felt as if life had cheated him twice. He hid his pain, being there for his sister-cousins, advising them, and offering spiritual comfort. He was amazed at how rational and calm they were, while inwardly he was exactly the opposite, angry, belligerent, sad and unwilling to accept that Ava was gone. How ironic he mused, that he, the Rabbi who hundreds of people turned to in times of sorrow, was himself in desperate need of guidance and the only person he wanted was Ava herself. He tried hard to remind himself that she was at peace, and it was selfish of him to want her, but he simply found it difficult to quiet the child in him who longed for the woman he felt was the closest he would ever know as a mother, far more so than the woman who clothed and fed him, far more even than the woman who birthed him.

When Suzi, Judy and Magda were invited to meet with their mother's attorney to discuss Ava's considerable estate, it was Naftuli-Binyumin who came up with an idea that the women were drawn to almost immediately.

"Sisters," he began, in a voice laden with emotion. "This house where our beloved Ima spent so many happy years, should in my humble opinion be used to provide comfort to others, exactly as it did during her lifetime. I can remember every single occasion I and my family spent here. How would you all feel if we would transform her home into a small short-term residence for people recovering from trauma?"

Ava's daughters found themselves involved in a project that they knew would honor their mother's legacy. She had lived through trauma to ultimately find growth and this home would do the same. The house would be alive with the sound of men, women, and children, all of whom would have a safe haven, a place where they could regroup, free of charge, a place where therapists and social workers would be available as well. It was a plan that resonated with Ava's daughters. Ultimately what made all three of Ava's daughters the happiest was knowing that their heroic mother had changed the trajectory of their lives and now in this house others would have the same opportunity.

When the mayor of Jerusalem informed Judy that the local council had unanimously approved renaming the street Ava lived on to *Rchov Hamalka* Chava Kertesz, Judy cried. When she called her sisters to tell them that the street their mother lived on would be known as Queen Chava Kertesz street, they all cried together, overcome with emotion.

"It looks like we seriously underestimated Mamuka's reach," said Suzi. "I always had the feeling she was constantly doing small things for others, little gestures like a handwritten note, but it wasn't until I started getting calls and texts, emails and letters describing in detail how Mamuka fought for change, right here in *Yerushalayim* [Jerusalem]. I just never knew! Ora told me of how Mamuka literally changed the trajectory of her life and that of her two sisters and later two younger brothers; I had no idea of the extent. It seems like now, dozens more people are clamoring to let the world know that they too were impacted by our mother!"

Their beloved mother, beloved also to many others, would be

forever memorialized by being referred to as a queen on the very street in Jerusalem, where she walked daily.

It didn't stop there. At the residence, a year later, Judy officially named the kitchen and gardens Ava's Place, and in New York, Magda renamed the take-out counter at her store Ava's Place. Seeing Ava's name in various places simply felt right for those who knew her, adored her and missed her.

When Naftuli-Binyumin's youngest granddaughter gave birth to a baby girl, she named her Chava and that too felt like the most perfect way to assure that Ava would always be remembered. Baby Chava played with her aunt Surika who was a mere three years older than her but bossed her around as if she were a grown-up. Naftuli-Binyumin, formerly known as Shulem-Baruch, adored watching his granddaughter and great-granddaughter, both bearing the names of his mothers, one whom he could not remember but who gave birth to him and the other who found him and restored him to his roots. He thanked God daily and prayed for the souls of all three of his mothers, including the one who raised him, but never thought it necessary to inform him that he was adopted. He knew he had mixed emotions about his adopted mother, but finally came to make peace with himself, knowing this was exactly what Ava would have wanted.

61

"I would rather die of passion than of boredom."
—Vincent van Gogh

When Ava's house was fully renovated so that it could accommodate 15 guests, it was everything she and her three daughters could ever have imagined. Ava's daughters had taken their mother's trauma and extended its boundaries from the Holocaust to modern-day life with traumatic circumstances that impacted families. On opening day, Naftuli-Binyumin spoke on behalf of the family. "ImaAva was an extraordinary woman. Like her sisters and thousands of other survivors, she simply wanted to live another day. But she was unique. Perhaps the only person I ever knew who had the courage to address the transmission of trauma and do something about it. Besides making a commitment to herself and her daughters to understand how Auschwitz had indelibly changed her, she also wanted to help others. Daily, she gave charity, her time and her heart in helping others. If it was a hug someone needed, that was what she gave. It surely wasn't only about opening her purse strings, but rather her heart. And so my sisters and I have taken her beautiful home and created an oasis for survivors of trauma here in Israel. It is our hope that for anyone who chooses to come here, that this respite from pain and suffering will arrest the process of transmitting trauma generationally. I have no doubt that Ava is watching from above and is satisfied that her home and generosity most certainly will change the trajectory of lives for those who heal here. And now, if you will join us for a tour of the home, which was planned in its entirety by Ava's daughters, to reflect their mother, to offer peace and tranquility so that those who find themselves here, start the process of healing. May we all merit good health and continue to bring honor to Ava through our good deeds."

The group of reporters and dignitaries representing the Israeli government were in awe of this privately funded facility. The music room was outfitted with musical instruments and a baby grand piano for concerts. The reading room was filled with books of every genre, comfortable leather couches and recliners, along with a refrigerator stocked with beverages and bowls of fruit. There was a meditation room and a sunroom, an indoor pool created so that natural sunlight came through and illuminated the entire area. The outdoors was arranged so that one could rest and take in the view of the majestic flowers and trees and even see the rows of fruits and vegetables growing. Every bedroom was tastefully furnished in soothing colors, each a story unto itself.

One of ChavaSara's grandsons Mordechai and his wife Nechama, newly married, managed the home, from security to housekeeping and maintenance, and to purchasing food and supplies. Ora's sisters Kiki and Michal managed the guest rooms including towels and linens and fresh flowers for the bedrooms and common rooms. That at least 16 people would find meaningful full-time employment running the house, pleased Ava's daughters no end.

Overnight the house became a huge success and eventually, over the course of three years, similar houses sprung up in Tel Aviv, Haifa and Bnei-Brak, all government funded, strictly following the prototype of Ava's Place in Yerushalayim.

The media could not get enough coverage of Ava's Place. Doctors and nurses praised the home where individuals healed from catastrophic events. Dozens of testimonials were published where individuals and the children vividly recalled how the environment and support at Ava's Place allowed many to begin the painful process of healing from trauma. For women who suffered traumatic miscarriages, for those who lost sons in battle, for those who survived terrorist attacks or lost family members to illness or accidents, Ava's Place helped them find meaning once more. There was no charge for staying at Ava's Place, not for room or board, not for the holistic therapies available on premises, nor for the referrals to social workers, psychologists, or psychiatrists.

That Ava left a considerable estate astounded her daughters. Magda knew that Imre was a very wealthy man, but what she and her sisters were not privy to were the bonds and blue-chip stocks he bought 60 years ago, which Ava held onto and were worth a huge fortune at the time of her death. Ava's estate could easily finance running the home, without incurring any cost to Magda, Suzi or Judy or encroaching on the many gifts Ava left to each of her grandchildren and their children. That Ava spent much time with her attorney prior to her death was evident in her planning and directives. She left a charity fund that was available to any of her descendants if they ever needed an interest-free loan or an outright sum to further their education, start a business, plan a wedding, or purchase a home. She appointed Naftuli-Binyumin along with Baruch Natan as co-executors of her will and named each of her daughters as directors of the trusts she established for their families. It was overwhelming to take it all in and each daughter, in her own way, was overcome with mixed emotions, mostly of awe and reverence for their mother.

62

> "In my lifetime, I witnessed the worst of man's inhumanity, but I also experienced love and happiness."
> —Suri Rosenberg, Holocaust Survivor and mother to Alice, Ruthy and Esther

Ava's daughters were pragmatic and realistic. In some ways they resembled their mother, and in some ways they resembled their father Lajos. Therapy and life had taught them well. They didn't sugarcoat their memories of a childhood that often was difficult, unstable, and unhealthy. They remembered their struggles, their hard times and challenges but ultimately, they also remembered their mother's evolution over time, as a courageous human being, flawed but passionate, consumed with boundless energy and love for mankind. Perhaps what was most meaningful and certainly life changing for all three was their mother's capacity and willingness to change. That she was committed to baring her soul in therapy in front of her three daughters, to amend and correct actions and words that affected them in their most vulnerable stages of development simply said it all. It made each of her daughters love her that much more. It changed the trajectory not only of their lives, but of their own daughters and granddaughters.

Living without her infectious exuberance, her quotes, her delightful smile and her never failing encouraging words took some adjusting. Judy was grateful that Mamuka lived long enough to know that she was truly happy and was in a committed relationship with Gil, while both Magda and Suzi continued to find enormous joy, fulfillment and satisfaction in their careers, their relationships with their spouses and with their own daughters.

Magda was ecstatic when she was approached by a major kosher producer of frozen foods and in time, a great number of her bestselling food items became available in every major supermarket in the United States under the Ava's Place label. Customers who did not have access to the store could shop online or in various specialty supermarkets in Miami Beach, Boca Raton, Baltimore, Denver, Dallas, and Los Angeles and enjoy traditional chicken soup with matzo balls, stuffed cabbage, potato kugel and a whole host of scrumptious desserts, from miniature raspberry flavored *linzer* tart cookies to the decadent chocolate *dobos* torte, to side dishes, crepes and blintzes that were the hallmark of Hungarian kosher cuisine.

Suzi continued to hold workshops and speak when invited, both in Israel and all over America. The story of Ava's survival, endurance, faith, and story of triumph was one that not only her family would never forget. It became her legacy. As the years passed, Ava's daughters laughed at themselves growing older and more wrinkled, and they cried, especially when they toured Auschwitz with their own daughters on the first anniversary of their mother's death. As they walked on the hallowed ground, they uttered not a word and held onto each other for solace and comfort. It was right then and there, when they viewed the barracks that their mother and aunts had been forced to sleep in for nine excruciatingly long months, that the three sisters, Ava's daughters finally understood the depth of the bond their young, vulnerable mother had formed with her own sisters. It was a bond that saved Ava's life on two occasions and one that carried her and her sisters their whole lives, especially when memories of the past encroached on their ability to be happy.

In old age Magda, Suzi and Judy—just like their precious mother and her sisters—dealt with adversity and challenges and found that the invaluable lessons their mother taught them, stood the test of time. They gracefully accepted what was beyond their control and like their mother, they sought to find meaning in life by extending themselves to others. They gave charity far and wide and extended themselves to individuals in need. At the same time, they were grateful for all that they had, the love of family, the fulfillment of personal goals and precious memories of opportunities their parents and aunts and uncles who impacted their lives. The sisters thoroughly enjoyed every aspect of their lives, laughed often and most importantly, they lived to love another day, exactly as Ava, throughout her long life, had hoped and prayed they would.

ABOUT THE AUTHOR

Born in Brooklyn, New York, Elizabeth Rosenberg acquired a Masters and Doctoral degree researching the ramifications of the transmission of trauma from Holocaust survivor to their offspring.

The author considers herself fortunate to have been raised by Holocaust Survivor parents who—in spite of the horrific trauma they endured—role modeled empathy, compassion, faith and resilience. As such, the author derives enormous happiness amongst her beloved children and grandchildren and extended family of sisters, nieces and nephews and cousins, a commitment and dedication to clients, anticipates new experiences and challenges, and her career as an inspiring author.

Readers are encouraged to share their thoughts and comments with the author by contacting her at:

toliveanotherday1945@gmail.com.

The author is available to speak at forums holding discussions related to epigenetics and the transmission of trauma, post-traumatic growth and resilience, 2nd and 3rd generation survivors of the Holocaust and women's rights.

AMSTERDAM PUBLISHERS HOLOCAUST LIBRARY

The series **Holocaust Survivor Memoirs World War II** consists of the following autobiographies of survivors:

Outcry. Holocaust Memoirs, by Manny Steinberg

Hank Brodt Holocaust Memoirs. A Candle and a Promise, by Deborah Donnelly

The Dead Years. Holocaust Memoirs, by Joseph Schupack

Rescued from the Ashes. The Diary of Leokadia Schmidt, Survivor of the Warsaw Ghetto, by Leokadia Schmidt

My Lvov. Holocaust Memoir of a twelve-year-old Girl, by Janina Hescheles

Remembering Ravensbrück. From Holocaust to Healing, by Natalie Hess

Wolf. A Story of Hate, by Zeev Scheinwald with Ella Scheinwald

Save my Children. An Astonishing Tale of Survival and its Unlikely Hero, by Leon Kleiner with Edwin Stepp

Holocaust Memoirs of a Bergen-Belsen Survivor & Classmate of Anne Frank, by Nanette Blitz Konig

Defiant German - Defiant Jew. A Holocaust Memoir from inside the Third Reich, by Walter Leopold with Les Leopold

In a Land of Forest and Darkness. The Holocaust Story of two Jewish Partisans, by Sara Lustigman Omelinski

Holocaust Memories. Annihilation and Survival in Slovakia, by Paul Davidovits

From Auschwitz with Love. The Inspiring Memoir of Two Sisters' Survival, Devotion and Triumph Told by Manci Grunberger Beran & Ruth Grunberger Mermelstein, by Daniel Seymour

Remetz. Resistance Fighter and Survivor of the Warsaw Ghetto, by Jan Yohay Remetz

My March Through Hell. A Young Girl's Terrifying Journey to Survival, by Halina Kleiner with Edwin Stepp

Roman's Journey, by Roman Halter

Beyond Borders. Escaping the Holocaust and Fighting the Nazis. 1938-1948, by Rudi Haymann

The Engineers. A memoir of survival through World War II in Poland and Hungary, by Henry Reiss

Spark of Hope. An Autobiography, by Luba Wrobel Goldberg

Footnote to History. From Hungary to America. The Memoir of a Holocaust Survivor, by Andrew Laszlo

Farewell Atlantis. Recollections, by Valentīna Freimane

The Courtyard. A memoir, by Ben Parket and Alexa Morris

Beneath the Lightless Sky. Surviving the Holocaust in the Sewers of Lvov, by Ignacy Chiger

Run, Mendel Run, by Milton H. Schwartz

The series **Holocaust Survivor True Stories** consists of the following biographies:

Among the Reeds. The true story of how a family survived the Holocaust, by Tammy Bottner

A Holocaust Memoir of Love & Resilience. Mama's Survival from Lithuania to America, by Ettie Zilber

Living among the Dead. My Grandmother's Holocaust Survival Story of Love and Strength, by Adena Bernstein Astrowsky

Heart Songs. A Holocaust Memoir, by Barbara Gilford

Shoes of the Shoah. The Tomorrow of Yesterday, by Dorothy Pierce

Hidden in Berlin. A Holocaust Memoir, by Evelyn Joseph Grossman

Separated Together. The Incredible True WWII Story of Soulmates Stranded an Ocean Apart, by Kenneth P. Price, Ph.D.

The Man Across the River. The incredible story of one man's will to survive the Holocaust, by Zvi Wiesenfeld

If Anyone Calls, Tell Them I Died. A Memoir, by Emanuel (Manu) Rosen

The House on Thrömerstrasse. A Story of Rebirth and Renewal in the Wake of the Holocaust, by Ron Vincent

Dancing with my Father. His hidden past. Her quest for truth. How Nazi Vienna shaped a family's identity, by Jo Sorochinsky

The Story Keeper. Weaving the Threads of Time and Memory - A Memoir, by Fred Feldman

Krisia's Silence. The Girl who was not on Schindler's List, by Ronny Hein

Defying Death on the Danube. A Holocaust Survival Story, by Debbie J. Callahan with Henry Stern

A Doorway to Heroism. A decorated German-Jewish Soldier who became an American Hero, by W. Jack Romberg

The Shoemaker's Son. The Life of a Holocaust Resister, by Laura Beth Bakst

The Redhead of Auschwitz. A True Story, by Nechama Birnbaum

Land of Many Bridges. My Father's Story, by Bela Ruth Samuel Tenenholtz

Creating Beauty from the Abyss. The Amazing Story of Sam Herciger, Auschwitz Survivor and Artist, by Lesley Ann Richardson

On Sunny Days We Sang. A Holocaust Story of Survival and Resilience, by Jeannette Grunhaus de Gelman

Painful Joy. A Holocaust Family Memoir, by Max J. Friedman

I Give You My Heart. A True Story of Courage and Survival, by Wendy Holden

In the Time of Madmen, by Mark A. Prelas

Monsters and Miracles. Horror, Heroes and the Holocaust, by Ira Wesley Kitmacher

Flower of Vlora. Growing up Jewish in Communist Albania, by Anna Kohen

Aftermath: Coming of Age on Three Continents. A Memoir, by Annette Libeskind Berkovits

Not a real Enemy. The True Story of a Hungarian Jewish Man's Fight for Freedom, by Robert Wolf

Zaidy's War. Four Armies, Three Continents, Two Brothers. One Man's Impossible Story of Endurance, by Martin Bodek

The Glassmaker's Son. Looking for the World my Father left behind in Nazi Germany, by Peter Kupfer

The Apprentice of Buchenwald. The True Story of the Teenage Boy Who Sabotaged Hitler's War Machine, by Oren Schneider

Good for a Single Journey, by Helen Joyce

Burying the Ghosts. She escaped Nazi Germany only to have her life torn apart by the woman she saved from the camps: her mother, by Sonia Case

American Wolf. From Nazi Refugee to American Spy. A True Story, by Audrey Birnbaum

Bipolar Refugee. A Saga of Survival and Resilience, by Peter Wiesner

In the Wake of Madness. My Family's Escape from the Nazis, by Bettie Lennett Denny

Before the Beginning and After the End, by Hymie Anisman

I Will Give Them an Everlasting Name. Jacksonville's Stories of the Holocaust, by Samuel Cox

Hiding in Holland. A Resistance Memoir, by Shulamit Reinharz

The Ghosts on the Wall. A Grandson's Memoir of the Holocaust, by Kenneth D. Wald

Thirteen in Auschwitz. My grandmother's fight to stay human, by Lauren Meyerowitz Port

The series **Jewish Children in the Holocaust** consists of the following autobiographies of Jewish children hidden during WWII in the Netherlands:

Searching for Home. The Impact of WWII on a Hidden Child,
by Joseph Gosler

Sounds from Silence. Reflections of a Child Holocaust Survivor, Psychiatrist and Teacher, by Robert Krell

Sabine's Odyssey. A Hidden Child and her Dutch Rescuers,
by Agnes Schipper

The Journey of a Hidden Child, by Harry Pila and Robin Black

The series **New Jewish Fiction** consists of the following novels, written by Jewish authors. All novels are set in the time during or after the Holocaust.

The Corset Maker. A Novel, by Annette Libeskind Berkovits

Escaping the Whale. The Holocaust is over. But is it ever over for the next generation? by Ruth Rotkowitz

When the Music Stopped. Willy Rosen's Holocaust, by Casey Hayes

Hands of Gold. One Man's Quest to Find the Silver Lining in Misfortune, by Roni Robbins

The Girl Who Counted Numbers. A Novel, by Roslyn Bernstein

There was a garden in Nuremberg. A Novel, by Navina Michal Clemerson

The Butterfly and the Axe, by Omer Bartov

To Live Another Day. A Novel, by Elizabeth Rosenberg

The Right to Happiness. After all they went through. Stories, by Helen Schary Motro

Five Amber Beads, by Richard Aronowitz

To Love Another Day. A Novel, by Elizabeth Rosenberg

Cursing the Darkness. A Novel about Loss and Recovery, by Joanna Rosenthall

The series **Holocaust Heritage** consists of the following memoirs by 2G:

The Cello Still Sings. A Generational Story of the Holocaust and of the Transformative Power of Music, by Janet Horvath

The Fire and the Bonfire. A Journey into Memory, by Ardyn Halter

The Silk Factory: Finding Threads of My Family's True Holocaust Story, by Michael Hickins

Winter Light. The Memoir of a Child of Holocaust Survivors, by Grace Feuerverger

Out from the Shadows. Growing up with Holocaust Survivor Parents, by Willie Handler

Hidden in Plain Sight. A Family Memoir and the Untold Story of the Holocaust in Serbia, by Julie Brill

The Unspeakable. Breaking my family's silence surrounding the Holocaust, by Nicola Hanefeld

Eighteen for Life. Surviving the Holocaust, by Helen Schamroth

Austrian Again. Reclaiming a Lost Legacy, by Anne Hand

The series **Holocaust Books for Young Adults** consists of the following novels, based on true stories:

The Boy behind the Door. How Salomon Kool Escaped the Nazis. Inspired by a True Story, by David Tabatsky

Running for Shelter. A True Story, by Suzette Sheft

The Precious Few. An Inspirational Saga of Courage based on True Stories, by David Twain with Art Twain

Dark Shadows Hover, by Jordan Steven Sher

The Sun will Shine Again, by Cynthia Goldstein Monsour

The series **WWII Historical Fiction** consists of the following novels, some of which are based on true stories:

Mendelevski's Box. A Heartwarming and Heartbreaking Jewish Survivor's Story, by Roger Swindells

A Quiet Genocide. The Untold Holocaust of Disabled Children in WWII Germany, by Glenn Bryant

The Knife-Edge Path, by Patrick T. Leahy

Brave Face. The Inspiring WWII Memoir of a Dutch/German Child, by I. Caroline Crocker and Meta A. Evenbly

When We Had Wings. The Gripping Story of an Orphan in Janusz Korczak's Orphanage. A Historical Novel, by Tami Shem-Tov

Jacob's Courage. Romance and Survival amidst the Horrors of War, by Charles S. Weinblatt

A Semblance of Justice. Based on true Holocaust experiences, by Wolf Holles

Under the Pink Triangle. Where forbidden love meets unspeakable evil, by Katie Moore

Amsterdam Publishers Newsletter

Subscribe to our Newsletter by selecting the menu at the top (right) of **amsterdampublishers.com** or scan the QR-code below.

www.ingramcontent.com/pod-product-compliance
Lightning Source LLC
LaVergne TN
LVHW041911070526
838199LV00051BA/2580